Praise for
The Girl Who Could Breathe Under Water

"Emotions leap off the page in this deeply personal book from Bartels."

Library Journal

"Bartels explores troubled relationships, questions of truth and memory, and how stories are created and told."

Booklist

"Bartels continues to amaze, and this—at least until the next book—is her best."

Life Is Story

Praise for
All That We Carried

"This subdued tale of learning to forgive is Bartels's best yet."

Publishers Weekly

"*All That We Carried* is a deeply personal, thoughtful exploration of dealing with pain and grief. . . . Erin Bartels makes it shine."

Life Is Story

"Bartels proves herself a master wordsmith and storyteller."

Library Journal

"Erin Bartels has a gift for creating unforgettable characters who are their own worst enemy, and yet there's always a glimmer of hope that makes you believe in them."

Valerie Fraser Luesse, Christy Award–winning novelist of *Under the Bayou Moon*

"Simply stunning. A novel not to be missed!"

Heidi Chiavaroli, award-winning author of *Freedom's Ring* and *The Tea Chest*

Praise for
The Words between Us

"*The Words between Us* is a story of love found in the written word and love found because of the written word. It is also a novel of the consequences of those words that are left unsaid. Bartels's compelling sophomore novel will satisfy fans and new readers alike."

Booklist

"*The Words between Us* is a story to savor and share: a lyrical novel about the power of language and the search for salvation. I loved every sentence, every word."

Barbara Claypole White, bestselling author of *The Perfect Son* and *The Promise between Us*

"If you are the kind of person who finds meaning and life in the written word, then you'll find yourself hidden among these pages."

Shawn Smucker, author of *Light from Distant Stars*

Everything Is Just Beginning

Books by Erin Bartels

We Hope for Better Things
The Words between Us
All That We Carried
The Girl Who Could Breathe Under Water
Everything Is Just Beginning

Everything Is Just Beginning

A Novel

Erin Bartels

a division of Baker Publishing Group
Grand Rapids, Michigan

Published by Revell
a division of Baker Publishing Group
PO Box 6287, Grand Rapids, MI 49516-6287
www.revellbooks.com

Printed in the United States of America

Library of Congress Cataloging-in-Publication Data
Names: Bartels, Erin, 1980– author.
Title: Everything is just beginning / Erin Bartels.
Description: Grand Rapids, MI : Revell, a division of Baker Publishing Group, [2023]
Identifiers: LCCN 2022024333 | ISBN 9780800742676 (casebound) | ISBN 9780800741655 (paperback) | ISBN 9781493439720 (ebook)
Subjects: LCGFT: Novels.
Classification: LCC PS3602.A83854 E94 2023 | DDC 813/.6—dc23/eng/20220526
LC record available at https://lccn.loc.gov/2022024333

23 24 25 26 27 28 29   7 6 5 4 3 2 1

For Mom
who taught me that if you're going to sing,
you may as well *sing*

and for Dad
who showed me that nothing soothes the soul
like really loud music

Liner Notes

I never wanted to live at my Uncle Mike's. Partly because I swore I'd never have anything to do with my dad since he clearly wanted nothing to do with me. (Being my dad's twin brother, Uncle Mike is about as close to my actual dad as anyone could be). And partly because he's the type of guy whose entire life screams *failure*, and the more your path crosses with his, the more likely you are to become a failure yourself. Truthfully, I do a good enough job of that on my own.

But then, if Uncle Mike hadn't taken me in when Rodney and Slow kicked me out, I wouldn't be covered in mud and standing in this pit with Natalie Wheeler.

Yeah, that Natalie Wheeler. Daughter of reclusive guitarist-turned-producer Dusty Wheeler and onetime-flower-child-singer-songwriter Deb Wheeler, who also happened to be Mike's across-the-street neighbors and long-suffering landlords.

Mike's house was never meant to be a house. It was just the break trailer for the construction crew that built the Wheeler estate twenty years ago back in 1970. Mike was on the crew, and the Wheelers rented him the property cheap after their sprawling contemporary glass and stone house was finished. I guess because one of them liked him and one of them pitied him.

I'm not one hundred percent sure which impulse first inspired Natalie Wheeler to give me the time of day, but right at this moment, I don't really care. Right at this moment, I'm seeing more clearly than I ever have in my short and rather disappointing life that maybe I'm meant for something . . . better. It doesn't really matter to me how we got here.

That said, it probably matters to you—or if it doesn't yet, it will shortly—so maybe I should start earlier. Maybe the night I first made it through the door of the Wheeler house. The night I first saw Natalie. Even if she didn't see me.

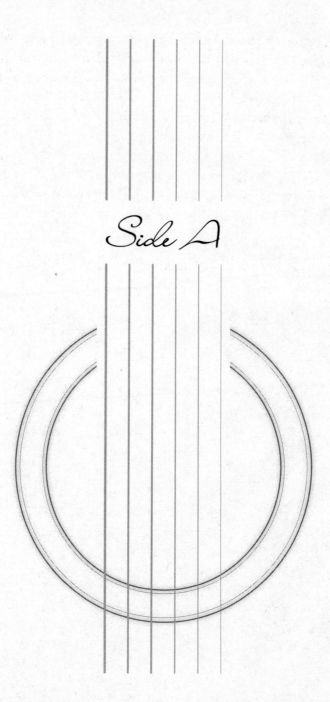

Side A

Track One

I wasn't invited.

I should probably make that clear right off the bat. Because I don't want you to get the wrong idea about me. I'm nobody special. I don't know anybody important, and nobody important knows me. I just happened to know somebody who knew somebody. Or rather, I happened to have the same name as somebody who knew somebody.

The invitation I pulled out of the rusty mailbox did say Michael Sullivan, but it wasn't for me and I knew it. It was for my uncle, who I happen to be named after. Not because my dad wanted to honor his brother, but because my mom preferred his brother to him and wanted to get back at him for missing my birth twenty-two years ago. Only I go by Michael, not Mike. The invitation said Michael. Probably because Mrs. Wheeler has class.

It arrived on Wednesday, December 27, 1989. I knew Mike wasn't going to be around for New Year's. I hadn't been living with him long, but it was long enough to notice a few patterns.

One: he smoked a pack of Camels every day.

Two: he never slept at home on weekends.

Three: he was bad with money.

Four: he listened almost exclusively to Lynyrd Skynyrd.

Five: he was wildly superstitious.

When it came to ringing in the new year in style at the Wheeler house, four out of five of those facts worked in my favor.

As I came back inside with the mail and knocked the snow off my boots, I heard Mike on the phone talking to his friend Carl. I knew it was Carl because of the voice Mike was using. He used one voice for work, another voice for girls, another voice for friends, and another voice for Carl, who was a friend but also someone who routinely loaned Mike money and rarely got any of it back.

I slipped the thick envelope (which had been sent through the post office even though I could see the iron gate at the end of the long Wheeler drive from the kitchen window—like I said, classy) into my pocket and listened as Mike convinced Carl to pay for gas for a road trip out to California, where Lynyrd Skynyrd was playing the Cow Palace on Sunday the 31st. Then they'd swing by Vegas on the way back to Michigan, where Mike was certain he'd win enough money to cover what he owed Carl as long as Skynyrd opened with "You Got That Right" and closed with "Sweet Home Alabama" (see also: superstitious). When he hung up the phone and started throwing some underwear and jeans into a duffle bag, I knew what I was going to be doing on New Year's Eve.

Mike left the next morning without so much as a "Stay out of my room"—which the lock rendered unnecessary anyway. You might think he could have invited me to go along with him. I liked Lynyrd Skynyrd okay. The guys and I occasionally threw in a cover of "Simple Man" when we played gigs, which wasn't as often as Rodney had wanted but proved to be more often than I managed to show up (see also: being kicked out).

A good uncle might have made an effort to bring his aspiring rock star nephew out to California to live it up a little at a big concert. And I was over twenty-one, so I wouldn't have been a drag on them in Vegas. But I knew he wouldn't ask me to come. I was bad luck.

The day I was born and my mom named me after him, Mike lost half of his squad in a firefight somewhere west of Quảng Ngãi. For the next couple decades, whenever something went wrong in Mike's life, which seemed like it was more often than in most other people's, there was some way in which I was to blame. He routinely cheated on his girlfriends, but they dumped him because it was my eighth birthday or I had talked to him earlier in the day or I was watching the same TV show at the same time. When he got injured on a construction job, it was because my baseball team got mercied, not because he had been up drinking the night before. The day I got my first guitar—a right-hander even though I'm left-handed—he was sentenced to one hundred hours of community service after his third drunk and disorderly offense. The night I first kissed a girl, he was stranded in Detroit with a dead car battery.

The only reason he let me come live at his place when I found myself homeless back in August was because I promised to pay him rent and he needed the money. He always needed money. Most of the time he tried to stay out of the house—which was just fine with me—and when we were there at the same time, he was always looking at me sidelong, like I was contagious or something.

So when he left without me on Thursday morning, I was nothing but relieved. I had three boring days of work at Rogers Hardware in downtown West Arbor Hills to get through, days when I'd be marking down Christmas lights and stocking gardening supplies that people would look at for the next three freezing, snowy, slushy months but no one would actually buy until after Easter. Then it would be New Year's Eve and I would finally see what was on the other side of that iron gate across the street.

When Sunday rolled around it was windy and warm, nearing forty degrees in the afternoon. I'd spent the morning sleeping late and eating three bowls of half-stale Cocoa Puffs because the milk was going to expire, then digging around in my drawers for something to wear to the party.

The invitation had been printed in gold on heavy paper, but it said "Come As You Are" at the bottom of it. "As I Was" usually meant ripped jeans, a concert T-shirt, and a denim jacket, though I'd been trying to save up for a leather one I'd seen at the mall. But that didn't seem right for a party announced in gold lettering. I had khaki slacks for work, but that wasn't really "As You Are" for me. That was just something I had to do to keep a roof over my head and gas up the car and pay for pedals and strings and maybepleaseGod a better amp someday.

However, Uncle Mike had a closet over on the other side of the thin wall, and for all his faults, he always looked cool. Actually, maybe that was the problem with him. What you saw was not exactly what you got. It fooled people into trusting him when he was only slightly more dependable than his brother—which was not at all.

He'd locked his bedroom door, as always, but it wasn't hard to pick the lock. I had plenty of experience doing just that to get into various houses or apartments when I either lost my keys or was accidentally-on-purpose locked out by the people I was crashing with.

16

Mike was a middle-aged contractor and I was a skinny wannabe rock star built more like Steven Tyler than Henry Rollins, so most of his clothes would be too big on me. Definitely I'd have to wear my own pants. But Mike was also secretly sentimental, so he never got rid of certain things, even if he couldn't stretch them over his growing gut. He had faded T-shirts from concerts I wish I'd been old enough to go to, a black motorcycle jacket I assume he must have worn during his glory days of roving across the country following bands and girls and pipe dreams, his old army junk from Vietnam.

I settled on a pair of my least ripped jeans, Mike's Goose Lake Music Festival tee—nothing said I'm a legit Detroit musician like a nod to the legendary 1970 concert—and the black leather jacket, which I knew would land me in either the hospital or, more preferably, the morgue if he ever found out I'd touched it and gotten my bad luck all over it. I tied my finally-shoulder-length hair at the back of my neck and pulled out a few strands around my face so it didn't look too polished or purposeful—cool wasn't cool if it wasn't effortless—and laced up my black motorcycle boots. No, I didn't own a motorcycle, though when I was little I apparently rode on the back of my dad's once. According to my mom, there's a picture of it somewhere.

I was ready to go. It was 4:59. The party didn't even start until 9:00.

I caught the tail end of a football game I didn't care about, half watched the news talking about Panama and Israel and some bomb threat on some airline, then turned up the volume when *Life Goes On* came on, but it was a rerun. I killed the TV and turned on the radio instead, but it was mostly year-end junk. Top songs of 1989, but not actually being played in full, and most of them were pop shlock—Paula Abdul and Debbie Gibson and Milli Vanilli.

I secretly did like some of that crap—it was just so catchy—but synthesizers and drum machines wouldn't get rid of the churning I'd started to feel in my stomach when I thought of walking through the door at a party I wasn't really invited to and where I wouldn't know anyone.

I turned the radio off and popped *Slippery When Wet* into the tape deck, following it up with *Hysteria* and then *Appetite for Destruction*, which I turned off after "Sweet Child O' Mine." Axl's pinched, perfect whine still rang in my ears as I crossed the dark street and approached the open gate of the Wheeler house. I thought of how Axl would walk into a party, shoved my hands into my jeans pockets, and put a friendly sneer on my face, the kind of expression I used to get through gigs without a panic attack.

The winding driveway was already lined with cars at 9:15. Nice cars. Some new, some classic, all perfectly shiny except for the spatter of salt water just behind the tires. Who washed a car in the winter? Rich people. What did "Come As You Are" mean to rich people? Ties and sport jackets? I didn't own a tie, and I'm not sure Uncle Mike did either. Well, maybe. For court dates.

I could feel my heart rate tick up and sweat gathering on my scalp and my palms. I almost turned around and called this what it was—a bad idea. But then the last thing Rodney had said to me when he and Slow gave me the boot from our crappy apartment in Plymouth (which he always told people was in Detroit) replaced Axl's aching E-flat in my brain. *"The minute you're not a drain on this band, the minute you actually have something to offer, that's when you can come back. Not one second sooner."*

Knowing Dusty Wheeler . . . that would be something to offer. That might make up for me missing the odd gig or five. That might make up for the fact that my equipment kind of sucked. That might make up for Slow's girlfriend hitting on me right in front of him, which, hey, wasn't my fault to begin with but also didn't bother me all that much because she's pretty cute and is one of the few people who makes me feel kind of good about myself in kind of a bad way.

If I could get a demo to Dusty, I'd be worth something to those guys. Maybe they'd even give a few of the songs I wrote the time of day. Maybe I could actually sing lead once in a while instead of Rodney, who was always a little flat and on the unintelligible side.

I picked up my pace and pushed through the panic. I wasn't going back to that trailer right now. That trailer was the past, evidence of a forgettable life in a disappointing family. My future was waiting for me at the end of this driveway.

Track Two

The house my uncle built was nothing like I'd been imagining every time I saw those iron gates. It was a plain, one-story stone rectangle broken up by other rectangles—front door, garage door, windows. If Robin Leach had taught me anything, rich people—to say nothing of the rich *and* famous—were supposed to live in over-the-top miniature palaces with columns and fountains and hedge mazes. I mean, wasn't the extravagant lifestyle half the reason for getting into the entertainment business?

Maybe I was dressed just fine.

I'd never have known a party was going on from the silence when I got to the door. I stood there a minute, listening hard, listening for voices, music, laughter—anything to indicate I hadn't gotten the date wrong or imagined the cars lining the driveway. Nothing. Should I ring the doorbell? Or just walk in? I didn't have time to make a choice. The door opened and the raucous party sounds spilled out, along with three black guys in crisp suits and a white guy in khakis carrying a basketball.

"Oh, sorry," the white guy said when he realized he'd practically shoved me off the wide stone porch.

"See if he wants to join us, Bill," one of the others said, holding his hands up for the ball. Bill tossed it his way.

"He can't join us," said another. "He's not part of the bet. Dennis, give me that ball."

Dennis palmed the ball and held it at least nine feet in the air. "Come and get it."

The shorter guy laughed, then started in on some fancy footwork despite the wing tips he was wearing, faking one way then another, then leaping up and knocking the ball from the taller man's hand.

Bill spoke up. "The bet doesn't matter. There's no way you can win anyway, even if you have three." He leaned way down to me. "You wanna play?"

I looked at the other three guys once more. They looked sort of familiar. The way your math teacher looks when you see him at a bar after you've graduated. Like you know you know him, but you aren't sure who he is out of his proper context.

"Come on, kid," the fourth guy said. "We'll sign the ball for you after and you can keep it."

Only then did it dawn on me who I was talking to. "Thanks," I said, waving a hand. I meant to say "I'm good" next. Like, I'm all set. But it came out "I'm no good." Which was true. But still.

A couple of the guys looked surprised to be turned down.

"Ah, forget it," Dennis said, slipping out of his suit coat. "Joe, you're with me. Isiah, you're with Bill." They all turned away and focused on the basketball hoop above the garage.

I swallowed down my embarrassment, opened the front door, and hoped that our paths wouldn't cross later in the night. It wasn't a strong start, I'll give you that.

The door shut behind me, and I was in a large foyer covered with shoes save for a path to a closet and four large blank spots left by the size seventeens now out on the driveway. I hated taking my shoes off in public. But worse than walking around in dingy socks at a fancy-stationery party was being the only guy whose big black boots were mashing down the carpet. I sat on a bench positioned against the far wall and started untying the laces.

To my left there was an open stairwell leading down to a lower level, and a burst of deep male laughter bounced up it and onto the main floor. But I could also hear the party somewhere behind me, on the other side of the wall at my back. Kitchen noises and voices and someone playing a piano—rather well, in fact.

I placed my boots in one of the empty spots on the floor and headed for the kitchen. Best to get a drink first. It was easier to walk into a roomful of people if you had something to do with your hands. Plus the kitchen was where moms hung out, and most moms could be counted on to offer you food and give you helpful information, like pointing out where the bathroom was or guiding you to the area where the people your age were hanging out. I mean, not my mom. But most moms.

The kitchen was large, but with as many people as there were in there, it could hardly be called spacious. I squeezed by a lady in a pink top wearing a silky scarf that nearly touched the floor and scanned the room. One of these women had to be Deb Wheeler. Should I introduce myself? Assume they had seen me once or twice over the past several months—though I had never managed to get a glimpse of them—and would know who I was? Or should I stay under the radar since I hadn't actually been invited?

A lady with short, bright red hair and too much makeup—meant, no doubt, to hide her advancing years—pushed an open bottle of Perrier into each of my hands.

"Take these out to Pinky and Stevie, would you?" At my look of confusion, she added, "At the piano."

I followed the sound of the piano through the dining room overflowing with food and into a sunken living room with wall-to-wall white carpeting. Beautiful people lolled on white leather couches in front of the large stone fireplace on the opposite wall or congregated in little pockets and corners of the vast room. Above the fireplace hung a large rug with American Indian designs woven into it in crisp white, black, yellow, and red. Overhead, an enormous chandelier made of deer antlers lit the vaulted ceiling and threw careless shadows across the room. To my immediate left, by yet more windows, was a shiny black baby grand piano at which a black man with long braids and a slight white woman with short brown hair swayed and played and sang a duet. Stevie and Pinky, presumably.

His voice was familiar. Hers was not. It was lower and bigger than you might expect for someone her size. Kind of soulful. Kind of sexy.

I edged around so I could see their faces. The man was wearing dark sunglasses. Of course. I don't know why I should have been surprised that Dusty Wheeler hung out with Stevie Wonder. But I was. I thought of the men playing two-on-two out front. Who else had been across the street in the past few months while I sat stupidly clicking through network television on my uncle's saggy couch? Who else might be here even now? Was this girl someone important? Some famous jazz singer I didn't know about? I couldn't think of any real person named Pinky.

The song ended, and the crowd clapped—and I would have if I hadn't had the two bottles of Perrier in my hands. I clinked them together a few times in lieu of applause, and Stevie turned my way. "You play?"

"Mike doesn't play piano," Pinky said without looking at me. "He can't even keep a beat."

Well, that was uncalled for. And not even true—the beat part, at least. How would she know anything anyway? How did she even know who I was?

"I brought you water," I said.

Stevie held his hand out, and I placed the bottle against his open palm.

Pinky frowned. "You're not Mike."

"Nope." I held the other water out. She made no move to take it.

"Why are you wearing his clothes?"

Crap. "Excuse me?"

"I can smell the Camels on them."

"Lots of people smoke Camels."

She looked at me skeptically, not quite meeting my eyes.

"He let me borrow his jacket," I lied. I didn't know how this girl knew Mike, but I sure couldn't have her ratting on me when he got home.

She slid off the bench, and Stevie slid to the middle and resumed playing. A thin strip of pale skin showed between her boxy black cropped sweater and the waistband of her silver stretch pants. Large silver hoop earrings glinted on either side of a face devoid of makeup but also not needing it.

"Do you want this water or not?"

"Are you his nephew?"

"Yeah."

"Ah."

What had Mike told her about me? Was she one of the girls he talked to on the phone sometimes? She seemed way too young for him.

She put her hip out of joint and held out her hand. "Are you ever going to give me that water?"

I waved the bottle in the air, but she didn't make a move for it. I set it down harder than I should have on top of the piano, and a little shot of water jumped out the open mouth.

"Relax, man," she said, snatching the bottle and putting it to her lips. "Not a great first impression you're making. An impression, no doubt. But not a great one."

"Yeah? Same to you."

I turned and headed back through the dining room, through the kitchen, and into the foyer, then down the steps I'd seen a few minutes earlier. The lower level was as packed with people as the living room. Blues played at high volume on the hi-fi, and on the television—smaller and older than I expected—hordes of reunited Germans smiled and popped champagne at the Brandenburg Gate in Berlin. Then the screams and whistles and fireworks half a world away were replaced by shots of revelers in Times Square. Add in the chatter and laughter and the room was uncomfortably loud. And that's saying something, coming from someone in a band.

If I could still consider myself in the band.

I could smell cigars, but no one was smoking. There must be another room. I went past a wall of overflowing bookshelves, through a door, and into a long hallway painted in high-gloss black and red. It had the feel of some kind of back entrance to a club you needed a secret password to get into. A man came through a nearby door and let a haze of smoke out with him, along with the clack of billiard balls. He nodded at me as we squeezed past each other in the narrow hall. I took a breath and stared at the green door that had closed behind him.

That was where Dusty Wheeler would be. Smoking cigars and playing pool. Stuff rich guys did with their rich buddies.

A place the little pixie with the sultry voice and the attitude probably wouldn't venture and therefore the best place to be. I opened the door with more confidence than I felt and more racket than I should have. Someone scratched at the billiard table and shot an accusing glance up at me in the doorway.

I stifled the urge to back out the door and headed into the room like I belonged there. There was a bar to my left, reminding me that I still hadn't gotten a drink, only delivered a couple. Behind it stood a short, rather portly, monumentally scruffy man with an unkempt salt-and-pepper beard and a mane of hair that looked like it hadn't been combed since the Carter administration. His rumpled white shirt was open at the neck to allow the little tufts of his gray chest hair to breathe. Hard to do in the smoky air. A cold draft swirled into the room from a cracked sliding glass door, but it wasn't enough ventilation with half a dozen guys smoking in there.

"What'll it be, son?" the man said without a smile.

"Uh . . ." I stalled. What were other people drinking? I scanned the room.

"We don't have that," the bartender quipped, still unsmiling.

"A beer?"

"We got that."

He turned to a small fridge that looked like a reject from the set of *The Honeymooners*. I dug in my pocket for some cash. A bottle of Miller Lite appeared in front of me.

"Gotta keep that lithe figure," the bartender said.

I couldn't tell if he was making fun of me, so I assumed he was. I lifted a crumpled five.

"Keep your money, buddy. This is a party." He picked up a fat cigar from below the counter and sucked it back to life, kind of a reverse CPR.

I turned my back to him and leaned on the brass bar rail.

There was no trace of Times Square or Berlin or the chatter of the last room, despite it being just next door. Here the only sounds were an occasional low voice, the clacking of the balls on the pool table, and the low sounds of an upright bass, a high hat, and a muted trumpet squeezing out a laid-back tune from the reel-to-reel in the corner. The walls must be soundproof.

"You just gonna stand here all night?" the bartender said.

I shrugged. "Maybe."

He came around to the other side of the bar and nodded at the pool table. "You play?"

"Sometimes."

"Meet me back here at two and we'll play."

"Two o'clock? In the morning? People will still be here then?"

"No, that's why I'm telling you to meet me at two. Geez, you kids today are idiots." He wiped his hands on his wrinkled pants and looked to me for an answer.

"Sure," I said, knowing full well I would not be staying up to shoot pool with this crazy old man at 2:00 a.m.

He gave me a nod and left the room.

I tugged on the beer and watched the guys play pool. They took their shots without rushing, without posturing, without even putting much muscle behind any of them. They floated around the table, one way then another, like they were following some kind of choreography, like the shots were all there and didn't need to be looked for or planned, just made. Like life was all laid out for them.

Ten minutes later I stood up straight and felt swimmy. Buzzed on one beer. I hadn't eaten anything since the three bowls of Cocoa Puffs nearly twelve hours ago. I'd have to risk running into either the Pistons or Pinky to go get some food.

I left the room as quietly as possible. Across the hall a bright red sign above another green door flashed RECORDING. Was Dusty in there?

Back through the loud room with the blues and the Berliners and up the stairs to the main floor and the foyer full of shoes. Through another wall of floor-to-ceiling windows in the front hall, I could see across a dark courtyard to the sunken living room with the piano and the white couches. Which meant anyone in the living room could see me. I examined the faces in the crowd. Dusty Wheeler would be, what? Mid to late fifties by now? Maybe sixty? I'd only ever seen one picture of him, backing up Jimi Hendrix at Woodstock. He was way in the background, grainy, out of focus, a collection of black dots on white newsprint. Really it could have been anyone, but the caption listing the people in the picture had included his name.

I saw Pinky walking past the window, the fingers of her right hand just grazing the glass, the crowd parting ahead of her. I poked my head around a corner in time to see her open and close a door at the end of a long hallway. Coast clear, I headed for the dining room and piled a small plate with shrimp, cheese, olives, and any number of fancy little morsels I didn't have names for, then sat in a chair in the corner and commenced inhaling.

People drifted in and out. Some glanced my way, some offered me a smile, some bothered to say "Happy New Year" and raise their glass. But no one actually introduced themselves. No one asked my name. No one wanted to know my story. No one knew me coming into this night, and no one would know me going out of it.

Eventually I wandered into the now-empty kitchen and checked the clock on the wall. 11:47. It would be midnight soon. A new year. A new decade. A bright new future, if newspapers and magazines were to be trusted. *Time* and *Newsweek*, which traded on fear and disaster all year long, were suddenly awash with optimism about the coming decade. The toppling of autocratic regimes. The waving of flags. The tearing down of walls. The dawn of a new era of democracy and peace. "Come Together" and "Kum Ba Yah" and "We Are the World" all piling up like an accident on I-94. It was big. Big enough that you kind of felt the energy of it as a buzzing electrical field all around you.

Why was everyone so hopeful?

I turned to leave, to head back down the long driveway lined with beautiful cars, back to Mike's trailer, back to my actual life—how was this my actual life?—then realized I was not alone. A woman was standing in the kitchen doorway, looking at me. Salt-and-pepper hair fell in waves down her back. A long white and gold floral dress hung on her gaunt shoulders like it was still on the hanger. Her large hazel eyes shone with a light that was flickering but not quite out.

"You must be Mike's nephew," she said, extending a thin hand.

I shook it gently. "Yes, I'm Michael."

She smiled at me, and I felt a little prick of golden joy in my chest.

So this was Deb Wheeler. Or what was left of her. While there was only one picture of Dusty Wheeler, I'd seen several of his gorgeous wife in her younger years. Doe-eyed with long wavy brown hair and a set of pipes that every girl I knew tried to pretend she had but never did. Deb had put out three records in the late 1960s. Then she never recorded another song.

I tried to reconcile the woman before me with the one from the album cover I saw on the top of my mom's stack anytime my dad reappeared for a few days then disappeared again. She listened to lots of different kinds of music and had managed to pass on her rather eclectic taste to me, but *Homeward* had been her go-to soundtrack when it came to that sacred mixture of righteous anger and heart-searing loneliness a forsaken woman felt. That Deb was vibrant and attractive and a little bit dangerous. That Deb looked like trouble—the good kind. This Deb was shrunken and fragile.

She kept smiling, but her eyes looked suddenly sad. "I'm so sorry. I haven't been a very good hostess tonight. I was just resting in the bedroom."

She opened the fridge, and the light from inside it traveled through the fibers of her dress, the way sunlight used to shine through the girls' dresses at church the few times we went. But there was nothing alluring about this. Deb Wheeler looked like she'd just stopped by on her way to the grave.

She shut the fridge without getting anything out of it.

"Do you want me to get you something?" I asked. "The dining room's still full of food."

"Oh, no, I'm not hungry. I just opened the fridge out of habit."

She padded across the room, fuzzy red house slippers poking out from under the long skirt of her dress. She pulled out a stool at the counter, sat down, and motioned at me to do the same. I obliged, grateful to finally have someone to talk to.

"Mike said you're in a band?"

"Yeah." I wanted to ask her when she interacted with Mike, but she kept talking.

"And what is it called?"

"The Pleasure Centers. I didn't pick the name."

"Mm, and what do you play?"

"Guitar."

"Genre?"

"Oh, you know, just rock music. Like sort of metal but not real hard-core stuff usually. Good melodies. Some harmony. We have a couple ballads the girls like. Kind of like Guns N' Roses meets Bon Jovi meets Scorpions."

"Arena rock."

My heart rate ticked up a notch at the thought of having to play in front of tens of thousands of people. It was what I wanted, but it also kind of made me feel like throwing up. "Well, we haven't played any of those yet."

"Hair band?"

I cringed at the term I'd always hated and looked at my hands. "Not exactly."

"Spandex or leather?" she said, a mischievous twist to her mouth.

I laughed. "I just wear jeans mostly. Rodney did try the span-dex thing once. His sister's aerobics pants. Ripped the seam in the back and she beat the—" I caught myself. "Oh, sorry."

"Michael, my entire life has been lived with musicians, art-ists, and writers. There's absolutely nothing you could say that would shock me and very little that would offend."

I glanced at the clock. "Almost time. Don't you want to join the party?"

She put a bony hand on mine. "You're good enough com-pany for me. Anyway, if we stay here I know I'll have a hand-some young man to kiss at midnight."

"What about your husband?" Where was Dusty Wheeler anyway? This night was kind of a waste if I didn't meet him.

"Oh, he's in the recording studio tonight. They're laying down a few tracks for some project while they've got everyone in town. They've been at it off and on most of the day. 'The New Year Sessions' or something is what they're calling it." She pointed at the clock. "One minute."

Who was *they*? Who else was in that room? "He wouldn't take a break to ring in the new year with you?"

"I wouldn't want him to. That's why we've stayed together so long when practically every other musician's marriage has fallen apart. I've always been one hundred percent behind his work and he's always been one hundred percent behind mine. Every opportunity is met with an enthusiastic yes. No jealousy, no nagging, no resentment, no compromise." She looked at the clock again. "Thirty seconds. Too bad you'll be stuck kissing this old lady."

I smiled. "You're not so old."

"No, I'm not." She smiled back. "And I do believe you're old at heart."

I wasn't sure what she meant by that. But somehow coming from her, I assumed it was good.

The countdown started in the living room.

Ten.

"Here we go," she said.

Nine.

She watched the clock.

Eight.

I examined the side of her face.

Seven.

She looked in my eyes.

Six.

"Mom?" came a voice from the dining room.

Five.

"In here, Natalie."

Four.

I turned on the stool for my first glimpse of Natalie Wheeler.

Three.

I was looking at the piano player.

Two.

Pinky.

One.

Screams and shouts from the living room. Two thin hands grasped my face, two lips pressed against mine, and then that killer smile again as Deb turned to the young woman in the doorway. "Natalie, this is Mike's nephew, Michael. Michael, this is my daughter, Natalie."

"We've met."

Track Three

Natalie or Pinky or whatever her name was approached her mother. "Do you want to say hi to anyone before you go to bed?"

Deb put her hand on her daughter's face. "I think perhaps I will install myself in the living room and let people come to me. How's that sound?"

"I'll help you." Natalie touched Deb's upper arm, running the sleeve of the white and gold dress between her fingers. "I knew you'd choose this one."

Deb shrugged her thin shoulders. "What can I say? It's my favorite, and I won't have many more chances to wear it."

All at once I felt quite clearly that I didn't belong here, in this room, in this moment. I stood. "It was nice meeting you both. But I guess I better be on my way."

"So soon?" Deb said. "Natalie, don't let him leave yet. I'll get situated in the living room myself. I don't need any more help to walk around my own house than you do."

She slipped out of Natalie's grasp and floated out through the dining room, leaving the two of us standing there like kids told by their parents to go play with each other. I searched for something to say, but I was coming up empty.

Natalie broke the silence. "So where's Mike anyway? He's almost always here for New Year's."

He was? "California. Then Vegas."

She sat on one of the open stools and tucked her hands between her thighs. "That rat."

"How do you know Mike?"

"I mean, he lives across the street."

I leaned back against the kitchen counter and almost knocked a glass over. "So do I. You didn't know me."

"You haven't lived there long enough. Anyway, I knew *of* you."

"Well, I didn't know *of* you. Why didn't Mike tell me about you when he told me who lived in this house? If you spend so much time together."

"I never said we spend a lot of time together."

"You know what brand of cigarettes he smokes."

"Touché. When I was a kid, he was always working on something over here. I've been at school. I was hoping he'd be here tonight. We invited him for Christmas, but he said he was spending it with family. I guess that meant you."

Ah, yes. Christmas. I had gone—briefly—to see my mom at her new boyfriend's house and never got past the entryway. Mike had been with some girl. There had been no tree, no presents. I spent most of the day driving and listening to music with the vague thought that nothing was really stopping me from leaving the state and starting over somewhere else, somewhere a little more hospitable. Somewhere with less snow and more sun and a bunch of people who didn't know that they should have low expectations of me.

"All right, so what did Mike tell you about me?"

She smiled unexpectedly, and that same little prick of joy popped deep in my chest as it had when Deb smiled.

"He said you were in a band. The Pleasure Centers, was it?"

"I didn't pick the name."

She let out a little laugh. "I wouldn't own up to that one either."

"Seriously, I wanted to call us Molly Ringworm."

She wrinkled her nose. "That's not much better."

I shifted my weight and remembered I didn't have my boots on. I walked across the kitchen so I was on the other side of the counter from Natalie, hiding my grayish socks.

"He also said you were kind of a screwup and your bandmates kicked you out of the apartment, and that's why you were living with him."

She paused as if to give me room for rebuttal. But what could I say? It was true.

"Anything else?"

"Yeah. He said you were bad luck."

"Of course he did." I leaned down, trying to meet her eyes. "What do you think?"

"I think you make your own luck. Luck is nothing more than a reflection of how hard and how long you've been working at something combined with what you consider the marks of success."

"What do you mean by that?"

"You don't know what hard work is?" She smirked.

"No, the last part."

"Oh. Like if your definition of success in music is being in the Top 40 and playing to sold-out arenas and having a new hit single every month, odds are you're going to be disappointed. Very few people make it to that point, and talent often has little to do with it."

I thought of the top songs of 1989 I'd heard earlier that night and silently agreed.

"But if success to you is continually getting better at your instrument and performance and writing songs that move people and mean something no matter how many people hear them, that's all within your control. There's no luck involved."

"So you don't think I'm bad luck?"

She laughed. "Mike makes a lot of dumb decisions. If there's any bad luck in his life, he invited it in himself." She finally looked in my eyes—or nearly so. "I haven't made my mind up about you yet."

I gave her the practiced smile I always gave girls at gigs, the one that usually elicited a smile and a blush in return, but before I could gauge its full effect on Natalie, a small group of people came in through the dining room on their way out the door. She turned to play hostess, and I took the opportunity to look around.

I grabbed the closest champagne flute, lipstick stained though it was, and emptied the dregs from three nearby bottles into it, filling it nearly halfway. I pulled myself out of the flow of people beginning to say their goodbyes and headed the opposite direction of the sea of footwear in the foyer. I found the door to the laundry room. Then one to the garage, where a giant silver Cadillac slumbered next to a vintage red Mustang convertible with a creamy white canvas top.

Across the hall, a door was cracked but no light spilled out. I eased it open, expecting to find a couple making out like in the movies, but it was empty. I flicked on the light and shut the door. Double bed, nightstand, dresser, closet, Western art on three walls. The fourth was another wall of windows. The room looked unused, the southwestern print blanket perfectly smooth, the deep-pile carpet plush with no real wear pattern. I peeked into a few drawers, but they were empty. Closet, empty except for a vacuum.

I picked up a slim red book from the nightstand and flipped through the pages. A guest book. Some names were unfamiliar to me, but many I knew. Not because I knew *them*, but because everybody did. Deb had said she'd spent her life with musicians, artists, and writers. Apparently she didn't even have to leave the house to do it.

Though there were a few entries that were nothing more than names and dates, most guests had left notes of thanks, some of them running on for multiple pages. They thanked Deb and Dusty and even Natalie for their hospitality, counsel, and patience as they went through a divorce or worked to beat a drug habit—there were a lot of those—or grieved the falling of their star. Clearly Mike had spent a lot of time in this house. Had he crossed paths with any of these guests? Did he have a voice he used just with them?

I put the book down even though what I really wanted to do was bring it to a record store and see how much all of these signatures—not to mention very personal information—were worth. I'd never sell something like this, even if it was mine to sell. I just wanted to know.

I unlocked a sliding glass door and found myself on a dark flagstone patio outside. The crescent moon shone through bare treetops. Beyond the patio, the ground sloped down, and I could just make out a stepping-stone path emerging from the melting snow. I shut the door, fished the Zippo out of my pocket—I didn't smoke, but I did like to be able to light cigarettes for pretty girls—and made my way slowly down the path by its weak light, my socks soaking up little puddles of freezing water.

As I descended the hill, the house rose up on my right. To my left was only darkness, one of the things West Arbor Hills was known for. Apparently, when the area was being developed as a bedroom community between Detroit and Ann Arbor in the sixties and seventies, they'd made a big deal about keeping things natural, which meant cutting down as few trees and bringing in as few streetlights as possible. Most houses couldn't be seen from the road or even from other houses. Mike's trailer being so close to the road probably drove them all nuts. But I guess people like the Wheelers could do what they wanted.

The path curved around the back of the house, where an even larger stone patio was half covered by a wooden deck one story above and dimly illuminated by the lights from one of those walls of windows. I closed the Zippo and walked to the windows, which, as it turned out, looked into the room with the pool table. The sliding door was still cracked, but there were no men smoking cigars or lining up shots. The room was empty.

I eased myself inside and shut the door against the cold, which I was now feeling quite keenly through the rips in my jeans and the dampness in my socks. The pool cues were all lined up in the rack on the wall, the balls all in the bowels of the table. Empty glasses and beer bottles rested on coasters around the room and all along the bar. The ashtrays were filled with the butts and bands of spent cigars. The reel-to-reel was still and silent.

I thought of the kitchen strewn with dishes and glasses. About the thin woman who would probably be washing up tomorrow with the help of her daughter—I'd seen no professional help other than the bartender all night. I switched the reels, threaded the tape, and hit Play. Then I got to work.

To the sounds of a laid-back four-piece jazz ensemble— piano, bass, trumpet, drum kit—I dumped the ashtrays, collected the empties, and washed the glasses in the sink behind the bar, including the lipstick-stained champagne flute I'd finished off. I wiped down the bar top and ran a carpet sweeper I found in a corner over the short burgundy carpet. I felt like I was fourteen, cleaning up after Mom had her heart broken again. I was turning all the liquor bottles so the labels faced out when I realized that the dumpy guy from behind the bar earlier was standing just inside the door, watching.

"You're early," he said, looking at a gold watch on his wrist. "But I see you made good use of your time down here."

"I wasn't drinking anything."

"Why not?"

"I just mean—"

"Relax, kid." He made his way behind the bar. "What'll it be?"

"Nothing. I'm fine."

"You're cleaning up after a party you weren't invited to. Clearly you need to relax."

"How'd you know I wasn't invited?"

"Because I don't know you, and I know everyone at my parties."

For just a second, I felt like you do when a deer jumps out in front of your car and you manage a dozen distinct thoughts, punctuated by curse words, in the space of about half a second. You've got to decide what to do—brake? swerve? hit the dang thing?—but at the same time you're trying to remember if you left a burner going on the stove and wondering if roadkill deer is okay to eat.

"You're Dusty," I finally managed.

"I am."

"Oh, man. I thought you were a bartender."

"I know." He put two of the clean rocks glasses on the bar, picked a bottle off the shelf, and poured a finger of Scotch into each one.

"Why didn't you introduce yourself?" I asked.

He looked at me from under wiry eyebrows and picked up

his glass. "Where's the fun in that?" He clinked the tumbler against the one still on the bar in front of me and took a sip. "So who are you?"

"I'm Michael Sullivan. Mike's nephew."

"I figured as much." He looked at the leather jacket. "You look like him."

"He and my dad are twins."

He nodded. "Well, there you go. You ready to play, Michael?"

"Sure thing." I took a sip of the Scotch, trying not to wince.

"You know that won't burn if you let it sit on your tongue a moment before you swallow it."

I struggled to recover my voice. "Noted."

Dusty shook his head and ambled over to the pool table. He placed the triangle on the felt and began filling it with the numbered balls. "Here," he said, rolling the cue ball down to the other end. I stopped it with my hand and placed my drink on the edge of the pool table.

"Not there," Dusty said, holding his glass with four fingers and pointing with the other. "Over there. Use a coaster."

"Sorry." I quickly relocated the drink to a small side table and busied myself with choosing a cue.

Dusty tightened the cluster of balls with his knuckles, then pulled the triangle off and inserted it into its slot in the table. "Guests break."

I hadn't played much pool in my life, but I did know that I wasn't great at breaking. I didn't want to look like I didn't know what I was doing. Not in front of Dusty Wheeler. "No, that's okay. You go ahead."

"House rule." He chalked his cue and made no move toward the table, much as his daughter had made no move toward me when I offered her the bottle of mineral water.

"All right." I lined up the shot, told myself not to scratch, and popped the end of the cue into the ivory ball like a pinball machine. It smacked into the first ball dead center and sent the others rolling around the table. Not great. Nothing actually went into a pocket, but several hit the bumpers. So not as bad as it could have been.

Dusty emitted a sound that had the tenor of tepid approval, lined up his first shot, and pointed with his cue. "Seven, side pocket." He sank it and looked for his next move.

"We're calling shots?"

He looked up at me. "You don't want to call the shots?"

"I'm just not that great at pool is all."

"Six, corner pocket." He sank it. "Would it be easier for you if I got all these solids out of your way first? Five, corner pocket." He sank another.

Was he going in numerical order? "Looks like maybe that's exactly what will happen."

He sipped his Scotch. "Life is easier when there are no obstacles." He leaned over the table. "Four, side pocket." He sent the cue ball into the nine ball, one of mine, which knocked the four right into the side pocket. "But sometimes what looks like an obstacle is actually useful to you. Three, corner pocket."

I laughed. "Why did you ask me to play if you're just going to win in one turn?"

He sank the shot. "Why do you think I make my guests break? I want to give them an opportunity to get the first ball in so they'll have a chance. Two *and* one, side pocket." *Smack.* Both balls disappeared.

"Is this why you weren't playing when I was down here earlier?" I said. "Does no one ever want to play you?"

Dusty smiled cheekily. "You're not as dumb as you look."

"Thanks?"

"Eight ball, corner pocket." He sent the ball careening into the pocket, then stood up straight. "Want to go again?"

"No thanks." I put my cue on the rack and sat in a leather chair. "I've had enough embarrassment for the night."

Dusty started sending the striped balls into the pockets. "So tell me about yourself, Michael."

I took another sip of the Scotch, letting it sit on my tongue a few seconds before swallowing. He was right. Less burn. "Did my uncle tell you anything about me?"

"Mike and I don't talk much. Deb and Natalie have more patience for him than I do. Deb told me he had a nephew living with him who was a musician."

"I play guitar in a band with a couple buddies of mine from high school."

"Three-piece?"

"Four. I play rhythm guitar, Rodney plays lead, Slow's on the bass, and we're constantly chasing down drummers. Hard to hold on to them for some reason."

"Mercurial devils, aren't they?"

I said yes even though I didn't know what that meant.

He sank the last striped ball, sent the cue ball after it, and hung up his stick. "Want to play me something?"

I choked on a mouthful of Scotch. "Excuse me?"

He walked to the door and beckoned with his hand. "Leave the drink there."

I followed him across the red and black hall and into the room that had had the RECORDING sign lit up earlier in the night. Through a window in the next door, I could see the control room with the zillions of knobs and slides spreading out along the sound board. Another door led to the live room, which was lined with acoustic panels and peppered with instruments and microphone stands.

Dusty ushered me into the live room and made a sweeping gesture with his hand. "What'll it be?"

The room was chock-full of options. A drum kit filled one corner, a baby grand piano another. A quilted black blanket half covered a number of instrument cases. And an impressive array of expensive guitars stood at attention on stands. Though I was left-handed, I'd always played right-handed because coming across used left-handed guitars that I could afford was rare. It made it a heck of a lot easier to maneuver when it came to borrowing other people's instruments. Plus I could take advantage of a moment like this, which would likely never come around again. I picked up a white Fender Stratocaster that looked just like the one Jimi Hendrix had played at Woodstock and plugged it into a wah-wah pedal.

"Good choice," Dusty said, as though there were any bad choices in the room, then he left, shutting the door behind him and appearing a couple seconds later in the control room. He pushed a button, and his voice came over a speaker. "Play me something."

I pulled the strap over my head then lengthened it, settling the guitar at my crotch. A glance through the window revealed Dusty shaking his head the same way he had when he'd called my generation "idiots" earlier in the night. I shortened the strap a bit and wished I hadn't let a whole week go by without playing much of anything. I wasn't ready for this. I was going to blow it.

I pulled a pick from my pocket—I never left home without one—took a slow breath, curled my fingers around the neck of the guitar, and pressed the strings. I picked out the first two measures of the last song I'd listened to before entering the Wheeler house, realizing almost immediately that it was the worst song I could have picked. I could play the opening riff, the chords, and a fill or two of "Sweet Child O' Mine," but I wasn't nearly good enough to play Slash's incredible solo.

Dusty's irritated voice rang out over the PA. "No, no. I meant play me something of yours. You're not in a cover band, are you?"

"Sorry." Thank God.

Having dodged that bullet, I riffled through The Pleasure Centers' set list in my mind, rejecting every song until I was out of options. It had not occurred to me until that moment that I didn't really like my own band's music. Rodney's songs were predictable and limited mostly to power chords, fuzz pedals obscuring his lack of talent. Slow's were, well, slow, and the guy couldn't write a hook to save his life.

But Dusty was waiting, so I started into the song we always opened with and looked anywhere but through the window into the control room. I sang Rodney's words, approximating his voice—hopefully minus being out of tune—and barreled through the song as fast as I could. In just a few minutes it was over, the last note fading until I stopped it altogether with a hand on the strings. I took a breath and looked into the control room. Natalie was standing next to her father, her mouth moving. Then Dusty walked out of the room.

Natalie pressed a button, and her voice came over the speaker. "It's derivative."

I stood there with the Stratocaster hanging from my shoulders, waiting for more, expecting Dusty to come into the live room, maybe give me a pep talk or some pointers. But the door never opened. He was gone.

"Did you write that?" came Natalie's voice again.

"Uh, no. My friend Rodney did."

She nodded. "He shouldn't be writing the songs for your band."

This was true, but irrelevant at the moment. I'd just blown my chance with Dusty Wheeler. My chance to get back into the band. My chance to be something more than just a guy who worked at a hardware store and lived with his loser uncle.

"Do you write any of your own songs?" Natalie said.

"Yeah."

She sat down in the chair her father had vacated. "Play me one of those."

"Uh, I don't—I don't write much for electric."

"So grab an acoustic."

My eyes searched the room, landing on a Martin acoustic with a sunburst finish. I placed the Stratocaster on its stand.

"Unplug the Strat," Natalie commanded.

"Oh, sorry." I turned off the amp and pulled the instrument cord out of the Stratocaster, then settled the strap of the Martin around my back, wondering who else had played this particular instrument. The people in the red guest book upstairs flashed through my mind. Maybe John Denver or Johnny Cash or Bob Seger. It should have been inspiring. Instead, it just amplified how much of an amateur I was.

I stood at the microphone, paralyzed. I'd never played any of my songs for someone else after Rodney rejected them. I never even played them for myself if Mike was in the house. It wasn't that I didn't think they were good. But clearly others didn't think they were. Natalie wouldn't think they were.

I stood there for so long that Natalie's voice came over the speaker again. "Michael?"

"Yeah, sorry." I played a G chord, then a C. Then nothing.

"You don't have to play one of yours if you don't want," Natalie said into the silence. "Just do something you love to play."

Something I love to play.

Without thinking at all, I started plucking the first notes of "Don't Think Twice" by Bob Dylan. Natalie smiled, and I knew I'd chosen well. I held a number of the notes longer than Dylan did and changed up the melody a bit to accommodate my lower voice. And I guess I sang it sadder than he did too. I knew it was supposed to be the kind of thing a freewheeling cad with nothing tying him down might say as he happily left town, off on another adventure. But I liked it better if the singer sounded like deep down he wished he wasn't that way. Like he knew he should stick around and work his problems out rather than just hightailing it out of town when things got tough. Like he didn't believe himself when he said it was all right.

When I sang a song like that, a song with a story, I always closed my eyes so I could lose myself in it, so I could see the movie in my mind. The taillights of his car disappearing over the horizon. The bereft woman in an empty room. The way the morning sun touched the underside of the clouds, offering a taste of beauty amid the darkness. With my eyes closed, I could almost leave my body, leave my life, and land there in that other reality that existed only because my fingers and my voice were making it exist right then, at that moment, and the moment I stopped playing, it would be gone.

As the last note died out, I opened my eyes. Natalie wasn't in the control room. Another listener who thought I wasn't worth their time.

"Not bad," she said from where she now stood in the open door of the live room.

I smiled too big, then caught myself and bit the inside of my cheek.

"Much better than the first thing I heard."

"Yeah, well, Rodney's no Bob Dylan," I said, following it up quickly with, "and neither am I," deflecting even the smallest possibility that she might be offering me a compliment. Though, if I was honest with myself, I was half-starved for even the slightest bit of encouragement. Where other people might have ambition or courage or tenacity welling up inside of them, all I had was a deep dark pit that got a golden coin of support dropped in every once in a while but otherwise remained empty, hungry.

"Do you play any other instruments?" she said.

"I'm passable at the bass and I can pluck out a melody line on the piano, but that's about it. You? I mean besides piano."

"Guitar. Banjo. Mandolin. Ukulele. Violin. Anything with strings, really."

"Dang. Overachiever."

She offered a shrug. "Everyone's good at something."

"Play me something. Something you love to play."

She pressed her lips into a thin smile. "Okay."

She started walking toward the piano, tripped on an errant trumpet case, and went down hard on one knee. I rushed over to give her a hand up, but she stood without assistance.

"Are you okay?"

She cursed and rubbed her knee. "I hate it when new people come in here. There's a system for a reason."

"Whoa, calm down. I thought you saw it or I would have warned you. I mean, it's right in the middle of the floor."

Her brow wrinkled as she turned my way. "You know I'm blind, right?"

"Clearly," I said, joking. Only then I realized that she wasn't. "Wait. You're blind?"

She let out a half laugh, half scoff. "Wow. You are a very unobservant person."

I flipped back through my interactions with Natalie that night. How she didn't take the water from my hand. How she'd thought I was Mike because I smelled like Camel cigarettes.

How her fingers lingered on walls and furniture and people's arms. How she never really met my eyes. How my perfectly charming half smile elicited no response from her.

"Yeah, I mean, I guess I knew there was something different about you," I stammered, "but I thought you just didn't like me for some reason."

"The jury's still out on that," she said.

I picked up the trumpet case and tucked it among the other cases beneath the quilted blanket. "Anyway, I did notice you kept your hands up in the air when you fell just now so you wouldn't injure them. Your hands are more important to you than your knees. I observed that."

"Hand me the phone. I'll alert the media."

She walked the rest of the way to the piano with no other trouble. I hovered nearby, my hand extended, as though I were back in gym class spotting someone at the weight bench during my least favorite PE unit. Even as I did it, I knew it was unnecessary. If something hadn't been out of its proper place, she wouldn't have had any problem navigating her own house.

Instead of sitting down at the keyboard to play, Natalie pulled the bench out a little and sat facing the center of the room. "Hand me that Martin, will you?"

I pulled the guitar strap back over my head and guided the neck into her open hand. She settled it on her thigh, secured the capo at the third fret, and began picking out "Landslide" by Fleetwood Mac. I sat on a bass amp nearby and watched her closely, my gaze moving from her left hand to her right to her face. She looked at nothing even as she sang about seeing her reflection in snow-covered hills.

It's funny how often you hear a song and don't think about what it means because it doesn't really mean anything to you. But as I listened closely to the lyrics and to Natalie's voice, which had a sad kind of beauty to it, I thought of the thin woman in the white and gold dress upstairs. I didn't even know this family, but I knew that changes were coming for them. I was observant enough to know that Deb Wheeler was in the process of disappearing.

The song ended. Natalie blinked rapidly for a second, her eyelashes like hummingbird wings, then she started into a song I'd never heard, picking out the notes with a precision I envied. After a minute or so, the notes trailed off, and she strummed a few chords and then stopped.

"That was cool. Does it have any words?"

"Not yet. Music first. Words later, if I'm lucky."

"The words always come first with me."

She yawned.

"I should go," I said.

"You *are* the only one still here. That's what I came to tell my dad. That everyone was gone and Mom was ready to go to bed."

"So he didn't leave the room just because I sucked so bad?"

"Well . . . maybe not *just* that." She held out the guitar to me. "I mean, I don't want to put words into his mouth."

I placed the Martin carefully back on its stand. "So was the word 'derivative' one of yours or one of his?"

"I'm not sure I should say." She grinned and stood up. "I'll walk you out."

I let Natalie lead me out of the studio, through the now-silent family room, and up the stairs into the foyer, where my big black boots sat alone on the stone floor. She stood with her hand on the doorknob as I pulled them on and tied the laces.

"You have to work tomorrow?" she said.

"You mean today?"

"Yeah."

"No."

"Why don't you come over later. Sometime in the afternoon."

I allowed myself to smile, knowing she couldn't see it. "Sure."

She opened the door and took a step back to allow me through. "Get some sleep," she said and closed the door.

But as I walked down the pitch-black driveway, now empty of the cars that had lined it earlier in the night, I knew that sleep wasn't in my immediate future.

Who could sleep after meeting a girl like that?

Track Four

The minute I got back to the trailer, I took off Mike's jacket and his shirt and carefully reinserted them in their proper places. I gave the room a once-over, determined that everything looked exactly as it had when I first entered it, and locked the door. In my own room I pulled out my neglected Oscar Schmidt and wished it was the Martin I'd played less than twenty minutes ago. I tuned the old stretched-out strings, reminded myself—again—that I needed to get new ones, and hugged the cool wood against my bare stomach. Then I started to pick out what I could remember from Natalie's melody.

Over and over, my fingers searched out the tune, like trying to find a light switch in the dark. I was missing something, but I couldn't figure out what.

I fished my notebook from the floor beside the bed and scribbled a couple lines.

> the truest feeling is an ache
> a vague, insistent pulse of pain

I put the notebook down and placed the words upon the web of the melody I couldn't quite grasp. I tossed in a minor chord. Better.

I picked up the notebook again.

>a part of you refuses rest
>don't matter if you're cursed or blessed

I almost crossed out that last part. The rhyme was too obvious. But nothing better was coming to mind, so I let it lie for the moment.

Rodney's criticism of the last song I'd shared with him rolled over to the front of my mind.

"Can't you write something about girls or parties or something? That crap's depressing."

But even when I tried to write about girls and parties, my songs still ended up on the melancholy side. As I had just proven to myself (if there was any doubt), I wasn't that good at parties. And girls made me self-conscious. Other than the fake smile I'd worked on, I had no idea how to interact with them.

>it hurts inside to know you failed
>admit your will could not prevail
>to finally know without a doubt
>your cowardice has found you out

That was the beauty of being in a band—while I was silently trying to figure out what to say, girls just assumed I was thinking super deep, angsty thoughts that could only be expressed in a song. And maybe I was, but mostly it was just some iteration of "Stop screwing up, moron."

>nowhere left to run and hide
>can't escape the place inside
>where all your failures ~~coaless~~ coalesce (?)
>into a ball of emptiness

I put down the pen, picked up the guitar, plucked out the notes. My voice was ragged from the smoke and the late hour. It *was* depressing. I crossed out everything after the first two lines. Those I kept. Those were real. Those were true. Maybe the only thing I really knew to be true. An ache was an ache. It was painful, whether it came from sadness or desire, regret or yearning. Deb Wheeler's golden smile. Dusty Wheeler's disappointment. Natalie Wheeler's performance of "Landslide." Each one like a drop of acid eating away a part of my gut.

You couldn't fake an ache like you could fake a smile.

I put the guitar back in its case and dropped the notebook on the floor. Ran over those two lines again and again as I took a shower, trying to get that melody right, the soap getting smaller in my hands. The water turned cold. I got out and dried off and brushed my teeth while droplets of water from my hair slid down my chest and back and evaporated somewhere before they could reach the yellowed linoleum floor.

I sleepwalked to my room, flicked off the light, and fell into bed.

> the truest feeling is an ache
> a vague, insistent pulse of pain

That was what I'd always kind of felt was missing from The Pleasure Centers. Real feeling. It had been missing from almost everything, actually, for a while now. Music, sitcoms, even those shows like *Donahue* that supposedly featured real people with real problems—it all felt manufactured, all smacked of insincerity. Like everyone on stage was wearing a hidden earpiece and the director was off in the wings, hissing instructions. "Okay, start crying . . . *now*!" They'd get you all stirred up, but by the time the credits rolled, everyone would be hugging and apologizing and promising to do better. Every problem solved in half an hour, minus the commercials.

Life wasn't like that. Life was a mom you saw maybe once a month and a dad you'd seen fewer than ten times in your entire existence. Life was a talented blind girl whose mother was dying. Life was all the stuff you wanted to happen that didn't and all the stuff you didn't want to happen that did.

I looked out the window and wondered if the light I saw was the dawn.

It was two o'clock in the afternoon when I finally woke up. The milk had turned overnight, and the few pieces of bread left in the bag were spotted with green mold. A single egg sat in the carton. I fried it up, covered it in ketchup, and ate it from the pan, then chased it with a handful of dry Frosted Flakes.

I chose my clothes carefully, even though Natalie wouldn't see them. I wanted to look good in case Dusty or Deb was around. Black jeans with the tears all down the front of the thighs, my Metallica "Ride the Lightning" tour shirt from when they played in Royal Oak when I was seventeen, my faded denim jacket.

Across the street the gate was still open. I hurried up the driveway—the weather had turned cold again—but slowed when the house came into view. A van from a cleaning service was in front. The garage door was open and the Cadillac was missing. I rang the bell and waited. Rang again. Nothing.

I went into the garage and knocked on the door to the house. When still no one answered, I opened the door a crack. "Natalie?" Then louder. "Natalie?"

A woman poked her head around the kitchen doorway. "She's not home."

"Is Deb here?"

The woman pulled yellow rubber gloves from her hands and approached me. "They're not home. You'll have to come back later."

I backed into the garage. "Do you know when you expect them back?"

The woman put her hand on the open door and began closing it, slowly. "You'll have to come back later."

The door latched, and I heard the deadbolt turn.

I stood stupidly in the garage, looking at the closed door. Why'd she tell me to come over if she wasn't going to be here?

I started down the driveway, slower now. Back in the trailer I turned on the TV. Every channel was a soap opera. I left it on for the noise while I stared out the kitchen window, looking for that big ol' Cadillac.

Daytime turned to prime time. I ordered a pizza and ate most of it while flipping between *Designing Women* and football I didn't care about.

I was about to call it a night and go to bed when headlights swept across the kitchen. They were back. But it was too late to go over, and tomorrow I had to work. I chucked the pizza box with its three remaining slices—tomorrow's breakfast—into the fridge and headed for my room.

Then the phone rang.

I was close enough to pick it up before the second ring, but I let it ring three times. "Hello?"

"Michael, it's Natalie."

"What happened today?" I didn't even try to keep the edge out of my voice. "I thought you told me to come over, and then you were gone all day."

"We had to take my mom to the hospital."

"Oh." Michael, you selfish jerk. "Is she okay?"

"Well, no. But she's home."

"Why didn't you call me?"

"Yeah, that was my first priority."

I didn't know what to say.

"Listen," she continued, "I know it's late, but do you still want to come over?"

I tried not to sound too eager. "You sure that'd be okay?"

"Yeah. Just don't ring the bell. Come around the back of the house and I'll let you in the pool room. You know where that is?"

"Yeah."

"Okay. See you in a minute."

She hung up the phone. I quickly checked my reflection in the bathroom mirror. Nothing between my teeth. No telltale signs that I'd been watching *Designing Women* while waiting glumly for her to get home. Then I remembered. It didn't matter.

I walked through the open gate, up the drive, and around the back of the house, down the same path I'd taken the night before. She was waiting at the sliding glass door in gray sweatpants and a plain black T-shirt. She opened it before I had a chance to knock.

"How'd you know I was here?"

"Heard the footsteps, how else?" She slid the door closed.

"Last night it seemed like these rooms must be soundproof."

"The walls are, not the windows."

"I couldn't hear the party through the windows upstairs when I got here last night. Only when the door opened."

"Well, you're not blind. And odds are, you've done some damage to your hearing being in a band called The Pleasure Centers."

"I didn't pick the name."

"So you said."

I put my hands in my pockets and rocked back on my heels. Now what?

"Want to listen to some music?" she said.

"Sure."

"This way."

"Should I take my boots off?"

"We won't be going in the living room."

I followed her out of the room, down the dark hall, and past the family room to a door I hadn't noticed the night before. Like the others, it was painted green. Unlike the others, it had a little dial above the doorknob that said VACANT.

"This is the listening room." Natalie opened the door and turned a dimmer knob. "Enough light?"

I turned it down a little, my fingers on top of hers. "There."

If she felt the little shock of electricity I did when I touched her hand, she made no indication as she coolly crossed the room. My eyes followed her sliding between two large black leather chairs and up to a wall of the highest-end stereo equipment I'd ever seen. Tall speakers faced the chairs at a slight angle. The turntable was flanked by battalions of record albums on floor-to-ceiling shelves. Dusty had to have a copy of every record ever pressed.

"Whoa."

"So what'll it be?" she said, echoing her dad offering me a drink.

I crossed the room in four large strides and ran my eyes across the thin spines of the albums with their tiny titles and artist names.

"Just tell me what you like," Natalie said. "They're not in any logical order."

"How do you know what's what?"

She pointed to little black labels beneath each slot. "They're numbered." She grabbed a clipboard that hung on the side of the shelf and flipped through the sheets on it. "And here's the list."

I ran my fingers over the labels, feeling the little bumps of Braille. The list was typed on a typewriter. Beneath each line, more Braille.

"When we get a new record, it just goes in the next slot and gets added to the bottom of the list. So I know that number 314 is always going to be *American Pie*, 327 is always going to be *Piano Man*, 445 is always going to be *Thriller*, 501 is always going to be *Graceland*, 514 is always going to be *The Joshua Tree*."

"You guys are still buying vinyl?"

"Dad says cassettes are for people who have no sense and that compact discs have no soul. He hasn't even bought a CD player yet, and I doubt he will. He has a tape deck for demos, but that's all he uses it for." She hung the clipboard up. "So what do you want to listen to? Clapton? Bowie? Petty?"

"Surprise me."

A sly smile crossed her lips. "Have a seat."

Natalie turned to run her finger across the numbers on the second shelf, and I settled myself into one of the leather chairs. To my left was a black side table supporting a stack of well-thumbed-through back issues of *Stereophile* magazine. A similar table was to the right of the other chair. Both tables came equipped with an ashtray and a drink coaster. The wall to the right was adorned with three framed record albums—Deb's albums—while the wall to the left sported framed covers of half a dozen issues of *Rolling Stone*.

I was trying to make sense of why these particular issues

had been displayed—favorite artists? important dates?—when Natalie pulled a record from the shelves and said, "Here we go." I couldn't tell in the dim light whose face was on the album cover. In a matter of seconds, she had the glass lid on the turntable raised, the record on, and the dust removed with an expertly placed brush. She lifted the needle and set it down perfectly in the first groove. A couple seconds later, a deep drum roll and a screaming trumpet heralded the oddly-Muppet-like-but-still-somehow-sexy voice of Billie Holiday singing "Lady Sings the Blues." Backed by a lazy piano, a low saxophone, a snare played with brushes, and an occasional clarinet and dirty-sounding trumpet, Billie seemed like she knew exactly what I was trying to write earlier. Like she knew all about that ache.

Sitting side by side in those big black leather chairs, Natalie and I listened to the whole first side of the album at high volume. Then she flipped it and we listened to the B-side. No talking. Just listening. Eyes closed. Mind wholly focused on the soundwaves emanating from those gorgeous speakers with their mellow East Coast tone until the last melancholy notes of "I Thought about You" were replaced by the rhythmic scratching of the end of the record.

Natalie made no move to stop it. I opened my eyes, half expecting her to have disappeared once more. But she was still there in the chair. Asleep. I stood quietly, lifted the needle from the record, and stopped the turntable. I slid Billie Holiday back into the paper sleeve, back into the jacket, back into slot 53, and covered the turntable.

"Hey," I whispered, lightly tapping Natalie on the shoulder. She stirred but did not open her eyes. "Yeah?"

"You fell asleep."

She sat up. It seemed to take her a second to remember where she was, who I was. Then her expression cleared. "What'd you think?"

"Beautiful." I let the word hang there for a minute. "I haven't heard much blues lately."

"I'm listening to a lot of it these days." She sighed. "Just feels right, you know? Just like . . ."

She trailed off, lost in a futile attempt to put words to a feeling she was still in the middle of. That was the hardest time to write—before you'd gotten through it, when you were most desperate to put it into words. Music was healing, but so often it was more healing for the listener, who got the fully formed song at the moment of their deepest pain, than it was for the songwriter still muddling through and hating how inadequate they were to the task. At least, that's how it was for me.

"I put the record away for you," I said. "And I should go. It's late. I have to work tomorrow."

She stood. "Sorry."

"No, it's fine." I started for the door. "Should I go out the back?"

She ran a hand through her short hair. "Um, yeah. No, that's fine. We can use the front door. I'm sure everyone's asleep by now." She turned off the light. "Where do you work?"

"Rogers Hardware. Downtown."

We headed up the stairs.

"Well," she said at the door, "we should do this again. Maybe not so late."

"Yeah." I hesitated. "Can I have your phone number, or . . . ?"

"Oh, yeah. Sure." She disappeared into the kitchen for a moment and then emerged with a little piece of paper with some numbers scrawled across it. "Can you read it?"

I recited what I thought I saw.

"That's right," she said. "But you know I'll just keep the

gate open and you can come over whenever. I should be here. Maybe we can play together."

I knew she was talking about playing instruments, but for a moment I imagined us sitting in a sandbox with buckets and plastic bulldozers, and I almost wished that was what she meant.

"Maybe you can play me something you wrote," she continued.

"Maybe."

I could tell from the look on her face that she didn't actually want me to leave. It occurred to me that she couldn't do that. Couldn't tell that sometimes someone's face betrayed them. Maybe she didn't know hers was doing it right at that moment. She looked like a completely different person from the one I'd met twenty-four hours earlier. At the party she'd been cool, confident, catty even. Now she looked deeply lonely and just a little bit lost. I knew that look. I saw it in the mirror every day.

"I'll call you when I'm off work," I said. "Around seven?"

She brightened. "Sure."

"Okay. I'll see you."

As I headed down the driveway once more, I couldn't get the image of her sleeping face out of my head, and I knew I would do almost anything to see it again.

Track Five

How about 492."

"Ugh."

I looked up from the clipboard in my lap. "You don't like The Replacements?"

"So sloppy."

"So?"

"I don't like sloppy. I don't like listening to the musical equivalent of the sound a bag of broken glass makes when it's thrown in a back-alley dumpster."

"Like you've ever been in a back alley." I flipped through the pages on the clipboard again. "The Clash?"

"They're better than The Replacements." She slid a record out of a sleeve she already had in her hand. "But I like this sort of stuff better."

We'd spent the past two hours of the evening sipping glass-bottle Cokes in a bizarre folk-funk-jazz cyclone of Joni Mitchell, Miles Davis, Dire Straits, and Marvin Gaye. In the Wheeler listening room, it was like the artists were right there, at arm's length, doing a private concert. Now two women I'd never heard before walked in with their acoustic guitars and complex harmonies. It wasn't really my style, but I could tell they had talent.

"Who is that?" I said after the first side finished.

"They're called the Indigo Girls. Like it?"

"It's okay. You know folk isn't really my style, right?"

"You played Dylan."

"Yeah, well, I'm probably one of the few people who likes him better on electric."

"But you write for acoustic."

I offered up no argument. I wasn't exactly sure why I wrote on an acoustic. It just felt right. "Do you mostly listen to folk and jazz?"

She took the record off the turntable. "Yeah. And blues."

"No rock?"

Natalie shrugged. "Folk and jazz and blues are all sort of melancholy. They're what speak to me." She was in another black shirt, tight, long-sleeved, with baggy jeans that hid her feet so only her unpainted toes were visible and only some of the time.

"Why not rock?"

"I dunno." She slid the record back into place on the shelf. "Rock's more for if you're happy or angry."

"Punk?"

"Punk's for, I don't know, when you wish you had the guts to be an anarchist but really you're too weaselly to get up the nerve to do more than just give someone the finger." She put a hand on her hip. "So you just listen to rock and punk?"

"Mostly."

"So are you happy or angry?"

"Or weaselly?"

She laughed. "You don't seem weaselly."

"Do I seem angry?"

"I guess not." She picked up her empty Coke bottle. "But you're not happy either."

"Why do you say that?"

"Well, I know you don't like living with your uncle."

"How do you know?"

"Who would? Mike's a disaster."

"I thought you liked him."

"I do—I've always liked him—but I wouldn't want to live with him." She paused. "And anyway, you just have kind of a morose vibe about you."

I could take issue with that, but she was right. I did have a morose vibe. I didn't quite know why, but I always kind of felt like someone had it in for me. Like maybe God was as disappointed in me as I was in myself. I just couldn't shake it.

"I still don't get your relationship with my uncle," I said. "He's your handyman but your family invites him to Christmas and New Year's?"

"My mom invites him. My dad's not a big fan."

"Why?"

"Couldn't say, exactly. I think it has something to do with the year they built the house." Natalie screwed up her face in thought. "And maybe he thinks Mike is a little too friendly with Mom." She started walking out of the room, and I hustled to keep up. "I mean, I can kind of see where he's coming from on that. But all guys flirt with my mom." She reached the bottom of the stairs and spun around. "That's all it is, though. She's never been disloyal or anything."

I stopped short of running into her, but only barely. My face was just inches from hers. She seemed to sense it, took a step back, and headed up the stairs.

"Come on," she said. "I'll show you what Mike does for me."

Her baggy pants made swishing sounds all the way up the

stairs and down a hall to an open door. When she passed right by the light switch, I flicked it on, revealing what could only be her bedroom. It was neat and tidy, and the bed was made. The same southwestern theme that ran through the living, dining, and guest room was present here, with bedspread and framed watercolor paintings on the walls. Well, not all the walls. One was covered almost entirely with a giant bulletin board, which was in turn covered with an intricate collage of pictures cut out of books, magazines, and newspapers.

Natalie spread her arms out toward the collage. "This."

"I don't know what you're showing me here."

"This," she said again, putting an edge on it. "Ever since I was a little girl, every time Mike comes over he brings me something to add to it."

"My uncle brought you all this?"

"Yes."

I hesitated. "Does *he* know you're blind?"

"Of course." She pulled me farther into the room and sat down on her bed. "Every time he'd come over, he'd bring me a picture—animals, flowers, people, buildings—and he would explain what it was. Like, really explain it. Sometimes he'd make up a story about it. And then he'd ask where I wanted it and he'd pin it up there right where I said. Pick anything on there and I'll tell you what's all around it."

"Okay. The car."

"You have to be more specific. There are eleven cars up there."

I looked closer. "It's a red car with black racing stripes from the seventies. Maybe a Chevelle?"

"To the left is a yellow tea rose, to the right is an Italian family on a boat, above it are the Grand Tetons, and below it are a jellyfish and a skateboard."

"Wow. Exactly right." I sat down at the other end of the bed. "So Mike comes over to fix a sink or clean out the gutters, and he brings you a picture and tells you a story. Meanwhile, his own place is falling apart and he's never given me anything. Great."

"Oh, I hear it now," Natalie said.

"What?"

"Anger."

"Pfft. That's nothing."

She turned toward me, pulling her left foot up beneath her. "So why do you play the kind of music you played on New Year's Eve?"

"What do you mean?"

"That song your friend wrote. Are all your band's songs like that one?"

"I mean, they're similar. You need a core sound."

"But that wasn't angry."

"I don't think we sound angry in general. We sound . . . what was your word again? Oh yeah, 'derivative.' We sound 'derivative.'"

She smiled. "Hey, man, don't get mad at me. I was helping you out."

I clapped my hands on my knees. "So it was you. Not your dad."

She laughed lightly. "Yes, but he wouldn't have been able to hear what I heard. He knew it wasn't good. But he didn't know it was derivative."

I turned toward her, leaning in a little closer. "Derivative of what, exactly?"

"Your friend—Rodney, is it?"

I nodded, then caught myself. "Yes."

"Right. Does Rodney watch a lot of TV?"

I shrugged. "Sure, I guess so. Doesn't everyone?"

"Well, my dad doesn't. Which is why he didn't know that hook was lifted straight from *Charles in Charge*."

I was glad at that moment that Natalie couldn't see my face, because I could feel how stupid I must have looked as my mind quickly switched gears between vehement denial, sudden realization, utter disbelief, and complete embarrassment. Did Rodney know? Did he do it on purpose? Or was it just an accident of the subconscious sitcom swill we were all wallowing in every day?

"You didn't know either, did you?" Natalie said into the silence. "Don't sweat it. It happens. I'm sure the rest of your set list is more original."

Was it? I suddenly had that terrible feeling I'd always get before going onstage for a gig. The feeling that everyone was looking at me, waiting for me to screw up, waiting for me to fail.

"Listen, I gotta go," I said, getting to my feet. "Work tomorrow."

"Oh, okay." Natalie stood. "I didn't mean to be a jerk about it."

"No, I know," I said, shoving my hands in my pockets.

"Just figured you'd want to know before—"

"Yeah, no. I'm glad you said something."

We stood there awkwardly for a moment.

"Okay, well . . . shoot," she finally said. "We never played anything together."

"Next time." I walked through the bedroom door and down the hall to the foyer, Natalie's "Okay, bye" drifting away behind me, unanswered.

Back at the trailer I beelined to my room and started playing through the rest of the set list, my stomach sinking lower in my body with every song.

"Axe 2 Grind." *Who's the Boss?*

"Over You." *Growing Pains*.

"Shut Your Mouth." *Family Ties*.

"Maybe Tonight." *Perfect Strangers*.

"A Little Dirty." *ALF*.

Rodney had sped them up, slowed them down, turned major chords to minor, added a little, taken away. But they were all rip-offs. Every. Single. Song. Except "The Love Lottery," the one song of Slow's that Rodney allowed on the set list because the girls lapped up the nonsensical lyrics for some inexplicable reason.

Who else had noticed? Were people laughing at us behind our backs? I was suddenly happy about the depressingly small crowds at most of our gigs, suddenly full of rage that Rodney had dismissed my songs—my songs that weren't just a souped-up version of *Silver Spoons*.

I picked up the phone, started dialing Rodney's number—my old number—then hung up. I couldn't see the look on his face over the phone. I picked up the receiver again and dialed the number on the little sheet of paper Natalie had given me. She answered on the first ring.

"Want to go somewhere with me on Saturday?"

"Sure. Where are we going?"

"I want you to meet my band."

Track Six

I kept my head down the rest of the week, working at the hardware store during the day and working on my music at night. I heard Mike come in late Thursday night, bash around the kitchen a bit, then struggle with the lock on his bedroom door. The next morning I found him asleep on the couch, apparently defeated by his own security measures. He was gone again when I got home from work Friday night. The pine trim around his door had been pried off and the door forced open, the crowbar and hammer he'd used left on the floor atop a pile of splintered wood. If I'd gone to Vegas with him, I'd have bet on him losing big, and clearly I would have won.

Saturday I pulled up to the front door of the Wheeler house in my old silver Citation. I'd bought it a year ago from an acquaintance of Mike's for $500 plus a pretty decent Fender Squire I told the guy was a Strat. I kind of regretted getting rid of the guitar—it was certainly more reliable than the car had proved to be—but it couldn't get me to work.

I left the engine running so I wouldn't have to risk the embarrassment of it not starting on the first try with Natalie in the passenger seat. She answered the door in a black turtleneck sweater, hot pink pants, a black and white checked wool coat, and dark sunglasses.

"Do you have any shirts that aren't black?" I asked.

"Not since junior high," she said. "This way I never have to figure out which tops will go with which bottoms. Saves me the trouble of having to remember a color organization system in my closet."

"Makes sense."

"Arm," Natalie said, sticking out hers.

"Oh, sorry." I took her elbow and opened the car door. "You don't use one of those canes?"

She sat down and buckled her seat belt. "That's what you're for."

"Ever thought of getting a dog?"

She smiled up at me. "Again, that's what you're for."

She leaned away, and I swung the door closed and walked around to the driver's side.

"Actually," she said as I shut my door, "it's always been me and my mom. We go everywhere together. Except school. Friends help out there."

I put the car in reverse and cranked the wheel to turn around. "When do you go back to school?"

"I'm not going back."

"You already graduated?"

"No, I'm dropping out."

"Why?"

"My mom, why do you think? I'm not going to waste the time I have left with her away at school."

I pulled out, heading east. "What's wrong with her, if you don't mind me asking?"

"Cancer. She's had it before, a couple times. They took every-thing out not long after she had me—full hysterectomy—then when I was eleven she had a double mastectomy. Probably didn't need to, but she was playing it safe." She was quiet for a moment. "And now it's back again. In her lungs. Apparently the radiation therapy after a mastectomy has something to do with it. She never smoked—bad for the voice. Of course, she's been around smoke her whole life. You heard the stuff about secondhand smoke?"

"Yeah."

"Crazy, huh?"

"Crazy," I agreed. We drove in silence for a few minutes. "So what are they doing for her?"

"Nothing. She said this last time at the hospital was the last time she ever wanted to be in a hospital or a doctor's office or anywhere like that."

"So then, what happens?"

"What do you think?"

The light ahead turned yellow, and I slowed to a stop. "So that's it?"

Her lips tightened, parted. "That's it." She took a deep breath. "So where do these guys live?"

"Plymouth."

"And you lived with them?"

"Yeah. I moved out in August."

A half smile broke out on her face. "You mean you were kicked out."

The light turned green. "Moved out, kicked out. What difference does it make? I lived there, now I don't."

"It makes a difference because I'm going there with you right now. I'm trying to prepare myself for how awkward this might get."

I glanced at her then back to the road. "Why would it be awkward?"

"Do they know you're coming?"

"No."

"How do you know they'll even be there?"

I laughed. "Saturday afternoon? Where else would they be?"

"They don't work?"

"Slow's a janitor at a school, which is on Christmas break, and Rodney's still being supported by his parents. They're up late every Friday night at a party or a gig. They'll be there."

"Mm. How are they doing gigs without you? Did they get a replacement?"

The thought hadn't even occurred to me. We were always looking for a drummer to replace the last one who'd started a new job or moved out of town or otherwise completely disappeared. Had they been looking for a new rhythm guitarist? Had they found one?

"Maybe they have someone filling in for me for a while. I don't know. But that doesn't really matter for our purposes today."

She turned a little in her seat. "What are our purposes today? I said I'd come because I haven't been out of the house much lately, and frankly I'm getting a little stir-crazy. But now that you mention it, I'd love to know what you're up to and why you invited me to come along."

I took a deep breath. "You know that song I played, the one that is basically just *Charles in Charge*?"

"*Charles in Charge* with an edge—like, he's *really* in charge—but yeah."

"After you said that, I went home and played all of our songs."

"Whose songs?"

"My band."

"Oh yeah, what are you guys called again?"

"Very funny."

Natalie smirked.

"So I played through the whole set list, and they're *all* rip-offs of sitcom themes."

She laughed out loud.

"No, seriously," I said. "*Perfect Strangers*, *Family Ties*, *ALF*."

"*ALF*!"

"Yes."

"Oh my gosh, that's simultaneously the worst and best thing I have ever heard."

I could feel my ire rising. "Well, I didn't find it so funny."

"Why not? It's objectively hysterical."

"To you, maybe. But I was up there on stage playing the theme song to a show about a sarcastic alien who eats cats. It's a puppet, Natalie. A puppet!"

She was covering her mouth, but I could see her shoulders shaking as she tried to suppress the laughter.

"It's not funny," I said. "And anytime I've played something for the guys, Rodney's said no. He only wanted to do his own songs. And they're not even his songs!"

"I guess the lyrics are," she said. "Unless he poached them from somewhere else."

"No, the lyrics are his, I'm sure. They're stupid. Obvious rhymes, repetitive, and half the time they don't even make sense."

"So we're going over there to confront him about ripping off sitcom themes?"

"For starters."

"And you need me there, why?"

"As a witness. You're the one who pointed it out. So someone else hears it, not just me. I'm not just some angry, disenfranchised songwriter who's mad his band won't play his songs."

She crossed her arms. "But you are that, aren't you?"

I tightened my grip on the wheel. "Yeah, sure. Of course. But I'm not *just* that."

"Why do you care?"

"Huh?"

"Why do you care about this at all? You're not in the band anymore. So Rodney's an insecure hack with a set list he pulled out of *TV Guide*. What does that matter to you? Forget him. Do something else. Start your own band. Or be a solo act."

"That's not the point." I clenched my jaw. "You don't get it. That's not the point."

"What's the point then?"

How did she not get this? "The point is I had a bunch of great songs that I wrote—I made up from my brain, not copied—and he never even gave them the time of day. Meanwhile he's not even writing anything original at all."

"Okay. So what?"

"So he's making a fool out of me—and Slow—and he needs to know that I know what's going on here."

The smirk was back. "Until I said something, you didn't know what was going on."

"Yeah. I had to have you tell me I was playing TV themes. Do you even watch TV?"

"I have it on sometimes for the stories, such as they are. They're all pretty dumb, though."

"Yeah, they are."

"I just have an ear for music. Whatever I hear, it just gets stuck in here"—she tapped her head—"and I can't forget it. Besides, those theme songs are designed to be catchy."

"Exactly. What if we'd played a bigger show and they'd covered it in the paper, and some music critic noticed and told everyone to just stay home next time and watch ABC's Friday lineup?"

She laughed. "Yeah, but that didn't happen."

"And it isn't going to. Because we're not doing Rodney's songs anymore. We're going to do my songs."

Natalie pursed her lips. "Oo-kay." Then, "Got a radio in here?"

I punched Play on the tape deck and sped down Highway 14 backed by Van Halen's *1984*. I took the Beck Road exit too fast, then followed North Territorial Road into downtown Plymouth. A few miles and a few turns later, I stopped in front of my old apartment and killed the engine.

In the sudden silence, I saw this whole thing going very badly. I twisted in my seat to face Natalie. "Okay, what would you do?"

"Are we here?"

"Yeah."

"I wouldn't be here, for starters. But since we made the drive, and since I'm morbidly curious about your dysfunctional world, I say we go in. Maybe you introduce me like I'm this girl you're hanging out with who also plays music, and we just see where the night takes us."

"You mean just . . . hang out?"

"Yeah, why not?"

"I didn't come here to hang out. I came here to *have* it out."

"Just see what happens. Maybe it comes up, maybe it doesn't. Maybe you realize you don't really care and you're doing just fine and you don't actually need these guys to make music. Or maybe you all have a big laugh about it and you move back in and you get some gigs lined up and get discovered and you become a zillionaire."

I didn't think either scenario seemed likely. But I'd rather argue with Rodney than Natalie.

"Okay, I'll play it cool. For now."

Her hand found mine on the shifter. "Just do me a favor."

"Yeah?"

"Don't use my last name."

I couldn't take my eyes off her hand on mine, but I managed to respond. "Why?"

"Just don't. Okay?"

I looked up at her serious expression. "Should I call you Pinky?"

"No," she said flatly, pulling her hand back and unbuckling her seat belt.

I followed suit. "What's with that name anyway?"

"What's with it is that you can't call me that."

"Okay, geez."

We got out of the car, and I guided her to the door then up the stairwell, which, if possible, had gotten even more dirty and depressing in the past five months.

"Must be nice to be blind sometimes," I said. "You can't see how awful stuff looks."

"Oh, yeah," Natalie said, laying the sarcasm on thick. "I love it. I keep telling my friends to try it, but I think they just have trouble seeing the upside."

"Sorry. That was dumb of me."

"Yeah, it was."

At the door to 3C, I dropped Natalie's elbow and she slipped behind me as I knocked loudly three times. I heard the television being turned down, then footsteps, then a pause as either Rodney or Slow looked through the peephole. But when the door opened, it was Slow's girlfriend.

"Well, look who's here," she said, a sly smile twisting her mouth. She was wearing one of Slow's T-shirts, and if she had anything on the bottom it had to be something small, because all I could see poking out beneath the hem of the shirt were her bare legs ending in toes painted pink to match her lips.

"Hey, Brittney." I stepped inside, bringing Natalie along with me. "The boys home?"

Brittney backed up a step and looked Natalie up and down. "Who's this?"

"This is Natalie. Natalie, Brittney. She goes with Slow."

Just then, Slow came around the corner into the living room. "Is that Mikey I hear?" He was wearing nothing but a pair of too-tight acid-washed jeans.

"Times must be tough," I said. "You two have to share one outfit now?"

"You think I should give him his shirt back?" Brittney said, gripping the bottom of the tee like she was going to pull it over her head.

"Knock it off, Britt," Slow said. "Go wake up Rodney."

Brittney walked off with a coy glance back at me, which I pretended not to notice.

"Who's the movie star?" Slow said.

"Movie star?"

"The sunglasses," Slow said. Then to Natalie, "You need those in here?"

"I don't need them at all," she said, making no move to remove them.

I guided Natalie to the couch and sat down beside her. Brittney came back in, followed by Rodney. He, at least, was fully clothed.

"Well, well, well. If it isn't Michael Sullivan, back from the dead—I mean the suburbs. And look, Slow, he brought a girl. I think. Hard to tell with that short hair."

Play it cool. "This is Natalie."

He perched on the arm of a ratty chair I knew he'd stolen from a motel. "Where'd you get her?"

"We met at a party."

"Where, at Bayside High?"

"I'm twenty," Natalie said.

"So?"

"I'm not in high school."

"He means the way you're dressed," Brittney supplied from where she leaned on the wall near the hallway. "Like you're on *Saved by the Bell.*"

"What's *Saved by the Bell?*" I said.

"You know," she said. "Zack, Kelly, Screech, Mr. Belding? It's a new show."

"Sorry, Britt. I guess I must have missed it while I've been working a real job. Not everyone has as much time to watch TV as you and Rodney." I held Rodney's gaze a moment, but there was no flicker of understanding. Natalie nudged me in the ribs with an elbow. "Anyway, it's been a while, so I thought I'd stop by. See how things were going. Got any gigs on the horizon?"

"As a matter of fact—" Slow started, but Rodney cut him off.

"I told you how it was going to be, Michael."

"What?"

"You're out until you convince me you got the goods. I'm not going to be stuck on stage again with no one backing me up."

"I'm not saying I want in, Rod."

He looked at me kind of like Uncle Mike did. The way you'd look at an unwanted stray cat you could tell was angling for a handout and maybe a new home.

"Michael's too busy for The Pleasure Centers," Natalie piped up.

I was?

"Oh?" Rodney said. "Big music scene there at your uncle's crappy trailer in the suburbs?"

"You know Plymouth is a suburb, right?" I said.

"Whatcha got going on out there that's keeping you so busy?"

I waited for Natalie to tell Rodney. To tell me.

"Well?"

"He's starting a new band," Natalie said.

"What are you, his manager?" Rodney said.

"I'm his partner. Simon to his Garfunkel, Sonny to his Cher."

Rodney laughed and turned to Slow. "Michael is Cher."

"It's a duo," she continued, as though she hadn't noticed Rodney's interruption. "He writes the lyrics. I write the music."

"What do you play?" Slow asked.

"She can play anything," I said. "Piano, guitar, mandolin, banjo—anything with strings."

"Mandolin and banjo?" Rodney roared. "What are you singing, folk music?"

"It's got a folk influence," Natalie said. She was driving this train now. "And rock. And blues. And whatever else we feel like. It doesn't fit in your MTV/VH1/Billboard boxes."

Rodney sniffed. "I'll believe it when I see it. And you"—he pointed at Natalie—"you do the same. Michael's not the most reliable person you'll ever meet. Sometimes he plays like he's never heard the song before even though you've been playing it together for three years. Sometimes he just doesn't show up. Your duo is probably just going to end up a solo act sooner rather than later, so if I was you, I'd make sure I always sang lead."

"So what do you all have going on tonight?" Natalie said before I could respond. "You playing somewhere?"

"Not tonight," Slow said. "Brittney wants to go to Lips."

"I told her there's no way we're getting in there," Rodney said.

"I wish we could just go to the Music Institute," Slow said. "Can't believe it closed."

"That was all just black kids and queens anyway," Rodney said.

"But it was free."

"That's probably why it closed," I said.

"I can get you into Lips," Natalie said. "I don't know why you'd want to get in—techno sucks—but I can get you in."

"Britt likes to dance," Slow said.

"She just wants to be able to say she's been there," Rodney said. "I don't know why we can't just go to The Shelter."

Brittney looked at Natalie. "Didn't you say you're only twenty?"

"So?" she said.

"So it's a twenty-one-and-older club," Rodney said.

"If I can get you into Lips, will you all come to our first gig?" Natalie said.

Rodney rolled his eyes. "Sure. Where's it going to be? Someone's living room?"

"Saint Andrew's Hall."

I nearly choked on my own tongue. Rodney laughed out loud. Slow looked momentarily impressed, then followed Rodney's lead. Brittney was too focused on the prospect of clubbing to even react. "You're not wearing that to Lips, though, right?" she said in Natalie's direction.

"You're not wearing *that*, right?" Natalie said, not even knowing what Brittney was wearing.

I think I love this girl.

"We'll go back home and change," I jumped in. "And we'll meet you guys there at, what? Ten?"

Rodney was still laughing.

"Perfect." Natalie stood up. "Ready, Michael?"

I remembered to take her elbow, and together we started for the door.

"If you don't show—" Brittney started.

But we were already out the door and headed down the stairs.

"Saint Andrew's Hall?" I said. "Are you out of your mind? That's where people like Iggy Pop and The Pogues and Red Hot Chili Peppers play. Soundgarden played there a couple months ago. You can't even get on the lineup to be an opening act unless 89X plays your stuff or you kill it at open mic night at Paycheck's Lounge."

"So?"

"So there's no way—"

"Where there's a Wheeler, there's a way."

She said it with such unbridled confidence that I almost believed her. I wondered briefly what it felt like to be that sure of yourself, to know what you were capable of, to know your name meant something. That people just automatically wanted to help you up rather than keep you down.

Back in the car I said, "You *can* get us into that club, right?"

Natalie smiled at me. "Of course." She buckled her seat belt. "But seriously, techno is so awful."

"So why are we going?"

"You're looking for some sort of reckoning, right? Can't have a reckoning without the right moment. And there in the apartment? That wasn't it. Better kick the can down the road a bit."

The car started on the second try. "Why did you tell him we were a band?"

"Because we are."

I shifted to drive. "Oh."

Track Seven

ren't you coming in?" Natalie stood in her open doorway.

I stopped halfway down the porch steps. "I was going to go change."

"We have hours before we have to leave. Have dinner with us first."

The prospect of a meal that didn't come out of the microwave was enticing. I took a step back up. "You sure?"

"Of course. Why else would I ask?"

"I don't want to be any trouble. What if there's not enough?"

She found my hand and tugged me toward the door. "There's always enough."

Inside, she slipped out of her shoes and yelled, "Mom, Michael's coming to dinner."

A wrinkled face under a shock of bright red hair appeared around the corner. "Your mother is sleeping, Pinky."

Natalie covered her mouth. "Oops. Aunt Ruthie, this is Michael."

She came all the way into the foyer, hand extended, a question in her eyes. It was the woman at the party who'd given me the waters to take to Stevie and Pinky. Stevie and Natalie. So Pinky was just what her family called her.

"We met New Year's Eve," I said, shaking her hand. "Sort of."

"Right." She turned to Natalie. "Where'd you get off to? Your mother didn't know."

"I told her I was going out with Michael."

"Well, she didn't remember. You need to start writing things like that down or at the very least tell your father."

They both put a hand on the other's arm and laughed at some joke that didn't include me.

"Anyway," Ruth said, "dinner will be ready in twenty minutes, so go wash up and then come help me get it on the table." She turned to me. "You. Follow me."

Leaving my boots in the foyer, I followed Natalie's aunt into the kitchen, where the scent of fresh bread mingled with the smell of something rich and savory.

She lifted the top from a large pot on the stove and gently stirred its contents. "Wash your hands and finish making the salad for me."

A large wooden bowl on the counter cradled a variety of green leaves that looked like the stuff you'd pull up out of a crack in the sidewalk. On the cutting board beside it was a half-chopped green pepper. A parade of other vegetables waited in a line for their turn under the knife. I washed my hands, then sliced through the green pepper once, twice.

"How much of each thing do you put in?"

Ruth looked at me. "However much you want." Then, "Have you never made a salad before?"

"No."

She pressed her lips together and then smiled thinly. "Do you want me to do it?"

"I can do it."

"Okay, good." She wiped her hands on her apron, took it off, and tossed it over the back of one of the barstools. "Because I have to get Deb up." Then she was gone.

I started dismembering the vegetables. The last time I'd had a salad it was from the Wendy's SuperBar, and it consisted of ham cubes, hard-boiled eggs, cheese, croutons, and ranch dressing. And maybe one plastic tongful of nearly white iceberg lettuce. I only ate half of it because the other half got mixed up with the giant glob of chocolate pudding I'd gotten for dessert.

"What are you up to?" Natalie said from behind me.

"Your aunt told me to make the salad."

"Did she put kale in it this time?"

"What the heck is kale?"

"The really tough, curly leaves."

I checked the bowl. "Looks like it."

Natalie sighed.

"Want me to fish it out?"

"No, it's fine. She thinks stuff like that will keep Mom around longer."

I didn't know what to say about that, so I didn't say anything. I kept chopping, looking up every so often to watch Natalie set the table. She made several loops around, first with plates, then napkins, then forks, knives, and spoons. She filled glasses at the sink and set one down at each place setting. It was like watching the men play pool at the party. Deliberate, unhurried, sure.

"Michael," came Deb's lilting voice. She stood in the doorway to the dining room, wearing a baggy red sweater over a long denim skirt. Her hair hung over her shoulders in two long braids. "What a nice surprise."

"Hi, Mrs. Wheeler."

"Deb, please," she said. "I hope you came hungry. Ruth

always makes too much. And I see she put you to work." Deb came closer, looked into the salad bowl, and smiled broadly. "This looks perfect." She picked up the salad tongs, tossed the contents of the bowl, then took it to the table.

Ruth nudged me aside. "Go sit down. I'll finish up from here."

Natalie pulled a chair out for her mother, then one for me. Bowls of vegetable-laden soup appeared at each place setting. Bread was passed, and the giant salad bowl made the rounds. Ruth sat at the foot of the table, nearest the kitchen. Then Dusty came in, acknowledged my presence with a nod, and sat down at the head just as the women were putting napkins on their laps. He held out his hands, and they all followed suit. Natalie's aunt looked at me expectantly. I placed my right hand in hers and my left in Natalie's. Ruth had to stretch to reach Deb's thin hand, and I leaned over to make it easier.

"Heavenly Father," Dusty began. "We humbly thank you for the bounty of this table, the company of family and friends, the ability to share what you've given us, and the opportunity to nourish our bodies and souls together. Amen."

"Amen," Natalie, Deb, and Ruth said in unison.

I tried to say it too, but it didn't get past my closed throat. I'd seen lots of families eat together on TV, often while I was eating my own dinner off a TV tray while my mom was at work or on a date. But I'd never actually been part of the meal. Even on Thanksgiving, we ate in front of the TV so we could watch the Lions lose.

Dusty clicked a button on a remote control, and a second later music filtered in from the living room. Natalie and her aunt released my hands, and everyone set in to their food.

Across from me, Deb scooped up a spoonful of broth and blew across it. "It's so nice to see you again, Michael. We didn't have much time to talk at the party. Why don't you tell us a little more about yourself?"

"What on earth is this?" Dusty said, holding up a fork. There was something white and studded with seeds at the end of it.

Ruth squinted. "Looks like the middle of a green pepper."

He sighed. "Is this another one of those superfood things you read about in your magazines?"

"She must have been distracted while she was making the salad," Deb said, winking at me.

Dusty popped the offending piece of green pepper guts off his fork and wrapped it in a napkin. Ruth rolled her head around to look at me. Natalie squeezed my knee under the table and seemed to be stifling a laugh.

"So, you told me about your band," Deb continued, "but what else? Where'd you grow up? Where'd you go to school? What are you working on right now?"

"West side, mostly. Went to Redford High."

"That's where Dusty went to high school," Ruth interjected. "And George C. Scott."

"And that's where you started your band?" Deb asked.

"Yeah."

"His old band," Natalie said.

"Oh?" Deb prodded. "Are The Pleasure Centers no more?"

"No," I said. "It's in . . . flux."

"Michael and I are going to start something together," Natalie said.

Dusty's head popped up, a look of shock on his face. "Are you going to Juilliard too?"

"No," Natalie supplied. "Michael works downtown."

Dusty spoke to his daughter but kept looking at me. "How are you going to start something with him when you're in New York and he's downtown?"

I wanted to crawl under the table. This was just like the setup for a sitcom. The *TV Guide* description would read, "A pleasant evening goes off the rails when the rebellious daughter of a wealthy family declares she is quitting college to start a band with a local loser."

"I'm not going back to school next week," Natalie said matter-of-factly, just as her sitcom character would have.

Only, Dusty didn't follow the Incensed Dad script by blowing up. He simply said, "Oh?"

"I'm staying home with Mom, and while I'm here Michael and I are going to work on writing some songs and finding a sound and getting our first gig."

I watched Dusty for some sort of reaction. Sending me dagger eyes or sharing a desperate look with his wife. But he just dipped a hunk of bread into his soup and said, "Let me know if you need anything."

Natalie smiled at him. "Thanks."

I looked across the table to Deb, who was looking from her daughter to her husband, a wide grin on her angular face. "That sounds wonderful."

I allowed myself to relax the muscles I had involuntarily clenched in anticipation of a fight and took a bite of the salad I'd made. It was bitter and crunchy and took a lot of concentrated effort to chew. The soup was far better. But all around the table the Wheelers were munching like contented rabbits on their bowls of raw vegetables, Natalie somehow successfully avoiding most of the kale.

"How is your uncle these days?" Deb asked. "We don't see him much in the wintertime."

"I don't either," I said.

"Is he working?"

I shrugged. "I don't really know what he does. I rarely see

him. I'm at work before he gets up, and he's gone when I get home."

Deb shared a look with Ruth, who raised a penciled-in eyebrow.

"Next time you see him, tell him to call me, would you?" Deb said.

"Sure."

"Just leave the guy alone," Dusty said. "You can't fix everyone, Deb."

There was an awkward silence. I waited for more information, but it seemed that no one wanted to let me in on what we were talking about. Not that I couldn't make an educated guess. Mike had a list of vices as long as my arm. But which ones did the Wheelers know about? Which ones was Deb working on?

"Why don't you have him dig the koi pond this spring?" Natalie said.

"Oh, we're not putting in a koi pond," Deb said.

"But you said you wanted one."

Deb was shaking her head. "That was just a lark."

"You've always wanted a pond," Ruth said. "Ever since we were little."

Natalie turned to me. "She's afraid I'd fall in it and drown." To her mother, "I know how to swim, Mom."

"It's silly," Deb said. "There's no reason to go through the expense or the trouble of putting in a pond when I won't be around to enjoy it."

Again, I waited for the expected dialogue: "Don't say that! You're going to beat this thing!"

"All the more reason to do it now," Natalie said instead. "If he starts work when the ground thaws, there could be fish in it by Mother's Day." She took a sip of water. "That's it. That's

89

my Mother's Day present for you. So no more naysaying. It's happening."

Deb was shaking her head again, but she said nothing.

The conversation turned to other things, but I had trouble staying dialed in. I couldn't stop thinking about how nice these people were to each other. How nice they were to me and to my no-good uncle. How nice it was to be eating fresh-baked bread, homemade soup, and a salad that was strangely sort of growing on me. Was this what life was like for other people?

When our plates and bowls were empty, Natalie's aunt whisked them away and replaced them with plates of warm apple pie with scoops of vanilla ice cream melting on top. She poured coffee into mugs, which were passed around the table. Dusty changed the record on the living room turntable—how many stereos did this guy have?—and we stuffed ourselves with pie to the smooth sounds of Duke Ellington.

"Seems like you listen to a lot of jazz," I said to Dusty. "I'd always thought of you as more the rock 'n' roll type."

"No reason you can't be both," he said.

"Dusty's always had a pretty wide taste in music," Deb offered. "We actually met at an MC5 show."

"You're kidding."

"Oh, yes," Deb said. "Ruth and I were deep into the psychedelic scene for a while."

Ruth smiled. "We were out at shows every weekend. The Village, the Grande, the Früt Palace, Meadow Brook. We saw all the local acts back then."

"The Stooges, The Amboy Dukes, The Frost, Mitch Ryder and the Detroit Wheels, SRC," Deb said.

"They called us The Mystery Sisters," Ruth said.

"What was the mystery?" I asked.

"We used different names," Deb said.

"Every night we were out," Ruth said.

"Just to keep 'em guessing."

"We didn't really want anyone to actually know who we were."

"We didn't want it getting back to our parents we were part of that scene."

"So much drug use."

"And violence."

"But not by us."

"We kept our noses clean."

"Literally and figuratively."

"Oh, Ruth, no one was doing coke yet."

"True."

"At that point it was mainly marijuana."

"And acid."

"But we never did any of that junk."

My eyes bounced back and forth between them like the little square in Pong.

"You kept seeing the same people at different shows," Deb said. "Dusty wasn't typically one of them. He came one night with a friend."

"An acquaintance," Dusty corrected.

"He was the first person I gave my real name to."

"I thought we were done for then," Ruth said. "I was sure it would get back to our parents and we'd never be allowed to leave the house again."

Deb leaned over and touched Dusty's arm. "He was worth the risk."

"Did your parents ever find out?" I said.

"To this day they don't know," Ruth said.

"Nor will they," Deb warned.

"So where did you tell them you'd met?"

"At the symphony," Dusty said.

"It's still a concert," Deb said in her defense.

Dusty rolled his eyes. "She told them I played second violin. Then every time they saw me, they asked me to bring my violin next time so I could play them something. I had to buy a violin and learn to play it—well enough that I sounded like I played in the symphony."

"At least I didn't tell them you were first violin," Natalie said in unison with her mother, and I wondered how many times she'd heard this story.

Natalie stood up. "This has been lovely, but Michael and I need to get ready to go dance to terrible music with people he doesn't really like."

"Oh, where are you going?" Ruth said.

"Lips."

"Oh, Pinky," Dusty said.

"You hate techno," Deb said.

"I'm doing it for a friend."

"Michael, you like techno?" Deb said it like she'd just found out I was a Communist sympathizer. But all I could think of was that Natalie had just called me her friend.

"He certainly does not," Natalie said. "We're just setting up some dominoes, that's all."

"Well, drive safely, Michael," Deb said.

"And wear earplugs," Dusty added.

I made an attempt to help clear the table, but Natalie's aunt took my arm and steered me out of the kitchen, saying, "You need to go home and get changed." As I tied the laces of my boots, she leaned close to my ear. "You seem nice enough, but since you're Mike's nephew I will say this. That girl is not a toy and she's not a tool. When you're out with her, you can bet that whatever you do will make its way back to Dusty, and he is not as forgiving as Deb. And neither am I. Understand?"

"Y-yes," I mumbled. "Yes, ma'am."

She gave me a curt nod and went back into the kitchen.

I left my car in the Wheeler driveway and trotted across the street to the trailer, checking my motives all the way. I wasn't hanging out with Natalie because I thought she could get me anything. Was I? I'd wanted to meet Dusty for that reason, but I didn't even know Natalie had existed a week ago. She was the one who said she could get us into that club. And it was her idea to start a band, not mine. No, I wasn't using her. And I wasn't toying with her.

Had Mike? Why else would Ruth invoke his name? Had he brought Natalie all those pictures to curry favor? Had he tried to get to Dusty through Natalie? Or to Deb? Just how had he gotten his life so entwined with this family to begin with?

Mike wasn't home—not surprising on a Saturday night—so I couldn't get any information out of him at the moment. I stared into my dresser drawers, trying to figure out what people wore to techno clubs. Big jeans and baggy jackets and backwards ball caps? I didn't have any of that stuff, and neither did Mike. I wished I was just spending the night flipping vinyl with Natalie in the listening room. I hated the club scene. Too many people too close and too sweaty. The insistent, unchanging beats from a drum machine. The melodies that went nowhere. The repetitive lyrics that only talked about dancing—telling you to dance, then telling you to dance harder.

In the end, I changed my shirt to a plain white tee and pulled my hair back into a ponytail so it wouldn't get in my eyes. I wouldn't fit in, but hopefully I wouldn't stick out too much either.

Back at the Wheelers', Deb let me in and pointed me to Natalie's room, not knowing I'd already been there. I knocked on the half-closed door and pushed it the rest of the way open.

Natalie and her aunt sat facing each other on the bed. Ruth was applying lipstick to Natalie's open mouth, the finishing touch of what looked to have been a big project. Natalie smacked her lips, and Ruth placed a tissue between them.

"Blot," she said.

A moment later Natalie turned to me. "What do you think?"

"I think you don't need makeup," I said. "But you look very nice." Actually, she looked like a younger version of her overdone aunt, but I thought it better to be diplomatic with the artist still in the room. Especially after the warning I'd gotten earlier.

"Thanks, Ruthie," she said. Then to me, "Ready?"

"As I'll ever be."

Natalie stood up. She was wearing the exact same thing she had on earlier.

"I thought you were going to change."

"Why should I? Did you change?"

"Just my shirt. But I have no idea if this is the right thing to wear to a techno club."

"Who cares?"

"Most people."

Ruth zipped up her makeup bag. "Not Natalie. She never has." She gave Natalie an audible air kiss and threw a pointed look at me on her way out of the room.

The minute we were in the car, Natalie said, "I know the makeup is terrible, but she loves fussing over me. She doesn't have any kids of her own."

"What? It looks nice."

"Don't lie to me. I can hear the smile in your voice."

I bit the inside of my cheek. "I'm not smiling."

"Blech. It feels like my face is caked in mud and a snail left a trail of slime on my lips. You have to help me take it off before we get there. I have tissues and cold cream in my purse."

"I thought you didn't care what you looked like."

"No, what I said was that I don't care if what I'm wearing is the *right* thing to wear. I care what I look like. I just don't care what others think about it. I don't want the makeup on because it's not me. Why should I be anybody but me?"

I pulled out onto the dark road and headed for Detroit. It was a nice thought: always being yourself. The only question was, how do you know who that is?

Track Eight

I parked the car two streets down from the club, the only spot I could find. "You're sure you don't want me to drop you off first?"

"Yes. Now help me get this crap off my face." Natalie pulled a travel pack of tissues and a small plastic container from her purse and handed them to me.

"I don't know what I'm doing here," I admitted.

"Just rub the cream all over my face, then wipe it off with the tissues."

She closed her eyes and stuck out her face. It was what a girl might do just before you kissed her, and it was good Ruth had done such a number on her, otherwise I might have done something stupid.

I unscrewed the lid and dipped two fingers into what looked like coconut pudding and smelled like my mom after a failed date (see also: every date). I started on her blushed cheeks, swiped a finger over her nose, another over her forehead.

She pulled back. "Not in my hair."

"Sorry. Close your mouth." My fingers touched her lips, lingered. I pulled them back and took a silent, slow breath.

Get a grip, man. A dot on each eyelid. I screwed on the lid and wiped one cheek with a tissue.

"Harder," she said. "You'll never get it off that way." She grabbed my hand to show me how much pressure to use.

Tissue after tissue, I pulled the makeup off her cheeks, her eyes, her lips, until the package was empty and her face was pink and clean. "I think I got it all."

She rubbed her hands over her face. "Better." Then she shrugged out of her coat. "Let's go."

The line outside of Lips stretched for nearly half a city block despite the freezing temps and light snow. We located Slow and Brittney about two-thirds back and pulled them out of line.

"Where's Rodney?" I asked.

"He bailed," Slow said. "He didn't think you'd show up, number one. And he didn't think she could get us in, number two."

"His loss," Natalie said. "I mean, I guess."

At the front of the line, Natalie didn't even introduce herself.

"Hey, girl! It's Esto!" the enormous bouncer said, pulling her into a hug. "You look amazing. Where you been?"

"School. I thought you worked at City."

"I got this gig now."

"Sweet. You like it?"

"You know."

"Esto, these are my friends, Michael, Slow, and Brittney."

"Well, come on in, guys." Esto waved us in. "Tell your mama I said hi."

"Will do," Natalie threw back out the door.

"How did she do that?" Slow shouted into my ear over the pulsing beat inside.

I smiled and shrugged and kept walking. Brittney didn't even bother acknowledging that anyone had done her a favor in getting her into the *it* club. She yanked Slow onto the dance floor and quickly established herself as the worst dancer in the place. I was glad Natalie couldn't see what she'd inflicted on the other clubgoers with her underground celebrity.

"Do you want to dance?" she shouted.

"Not especially," I shouted back. "You want a drink?"

"Club soda."

"Stay here."

I squeezed my way through the writhing crowd in search of the bar. It felt like an hour before the bartender acknowledged me, but it was probably only five minutes. The thudding beat was jacking with my ability to gauge time. Finally, club soda in one hand and a beer in the other, I scanned the room, looking for Natalie, trying to determine the route I'd taken to get where I was in the first place. When I couldn't find her, I started weaving my way through the edges of the crowd. I'd nearly made it full circle back to the bar when I spotted her.

She was in the center of the room, dancing in a circle of light, ringed by people cheering her on. I didn't know anything about dancing, but even I could tell there was something odd about the way she moved. It wasn't bad, I didn't think. It wasn't awkward or jerky. And no one was laughing at her. It was more like something bordering on oblivion, a complete unawareness of what her movements looked like to others. Or maybe an unconcern. She didn't care what all those other people thought because she couldn't see them watching her. She may have heard a critical thing or two in her life, especially if she went to Juilliard, but she'd never felt a critical gaze. She floated above that basic level of human communication on some other plane. Untouchable.

The music changed and morphed, and she left the circle to the whoops and claps of the other dancers, who flowed into the enchanted space she had vacated. I met her in the crowd.

"Natalie," I shouted. "I've got your club soda."

"Let's get out of this melee," she said, hooking her fingers in my belt loop.

We made our way to the outer wall.

"Here," I said, trying to guide the club soda toward her free hand.

"Hang on." She pulled the turtleneck sweater off and fanned herself with one hand. Her bare white shoulders in her black spaghetti-strap tank top glowed blue then purple in time to the beat. She held out the sweater. "Trade you."

I put the club soda into her hand and took the sweater. She drank half the bottle in a series of long gulps. "Whew! It's so hot in here. Wanna go outside?"

"Sure."

"There's a back door."

"How do you know that?"

"There's always a back door. Plus I used to come here with friends when it was a concert place called Lights Out. Coffee, cool beatnik vibe. This"—she motioned all around—"is a travesty. Let's go."

Her hands found my stomach, then my waist, then my belt loop again. I led the way past the DJ to the back. He smiled and waved as we passed.

"Do you know the DJ?"

"Possibly."

"He just waved."

"Where?"

I turned her in the right direction and she returned the wave, which clearly delighted the little man behind the turntables. A moment later I found the back door. It was guarded by a guy even bigger than Esto out front.

"We're just going out for some air," I explained.

"Not this way you're not," he said. Then he saw Natalie and his whole demeanor changed. "Natalie? It's Ronald."

Natalie went in for a hug, and the big man lifted her off her feet. "Ronnie! I haven't heard your voice since my high school graduation. How are you?"

He put her down. "Not bad, not bad. I was in jail for eighteen months, knocked down from thirty-six. Good behavior."

"Nice! I'm glad you're out. You staying honest?"

He shook his head. "Trying. You know I'm trying."

"Good to hear it. Listen, it's hotter than Hades in here, Ronnie."

"Oh, yeah, sorry, Nat." He opened the door. "I'll leave it cracked for you."

"Perfect, thanks a million."

I tipped my head in gratitude to Ronnie as we escaped the aural hell he remained stuck in and emerged into a trash-strewn back alley in the bracing January air.

"You want your sweater?" I said.

"Ugh. Not yet. But I can take it if you don't want to hold it."

"I'll hold it for you. Just didn't want you to get cold."

"No chance of that anytime soon." She sipped her club soda.

"Hey, how do you know the bouncers here?"

"Esto I know from when he roadied for Alice Cooper, and Ronnie I know from rehab."

"Rehab? You were in rehab?"

"I wasn't *in* rehab. I used to visit rehab centers with my mom when I was a kid. We'd play guitar and do some singing and tell them about Jesus and stuff."

"Jesus?"

"Yeah, you know. The Son of God. The Prince of Peace. That Jesus."

"Oh, *that* Jesus."

"Har, har. Anyway, I'd say I know someone almost everywhere I go. It's nice. Someone's always happy to see me."

I took a sip of my beer. "That does sound nice. I don't know anyone who's happy to see me."

"That's not true."

"Even my friends weren't happy to see me. Rodney didn't even bother coming tonight."

"Rodney's clearly an idiot. I was happy to see you today, and I can't see anything."

I snickered. "I guess."

"No, I really was. I didn't care for you when I first met you, but you're starting to grow on me."

"I didn't care for you either," I said.

"But now . . . ?"

"I dunno. You're all right, I guess." I chucked her in the arm.

"Thanks." She chucked me back.

"How do you do that?"

"What?"

"How do you know where I am? How do you not swing and miss?"

"I don't know. How do you allow yourself to get hit by a blind girl?"

I let out a little laugh. "I like it. It's the only way I get human touch. That and weaving around through crowds of sweaty dancers."

"Oh, so you're hanging around me because I need to touch you to get around, is that it?" She was smiling, but I still felt the need to correct her. To correct Ruth's assumptions about me.

"I'm hanging around you because I like you—r company."

She finished off her drink. "I like you too. Now give me that sweater. It's freezing out here." She pulled the sweater back over her head and took a measured breath, as though preparing herself for some odious but necessary task. "Are we going back in there?"

"Do you want to?"

"Not especially."

"Really? For not liking techno, you sure were dancing like you did."

"I do not like techno. I do like dancing."

"So where do you want to go?"

She pursed her bare lips a moment. "I know a place you might like."

♥

"This is *not* a good neighborhood," I said, circling the block. "Are you sure about this?"

"Of course. You'll love it."

"And I suppose you know all these guys too? Told them about gentle Jesus, meek and mild?"

Natalie shrugged. "I might know someone."

"Look, I know you said you don't care if you look like you fit in, but seriously, you really don't look like you belong here. I don't even look like I belong here."

"You should have borrowed the leather jacket again."

"Yeah, so I could get pounded by Mike instead of the skinheads."

"They can't all be skinheads."

"Down here? They're mostly skinheads."

"If you're worried, we can just go back home. Or stop at a drugstore and get you a razor. What is your hair like anyway?"

"My hair?"

"Yeah, is it short, long, light, dark, straight, wavy?"

"It's longer. A little wavy. You can touch it. If you want."

Her hands remained on her lap. "What color?"

"Brown. Hey, were you blind at birth or did you lose your sight?"

"Birth."

"Then how can you even conceive of color? No offense."

"I put things in categories in my mind. Like with like. So, brown, for instance. Tree trunks are brown, rabbits are brown. Deer, chocolate, coffee, some cows, hardwood floors, my dad's slippers, dirt. I have an idea in my head of what brown means to me."

"What does it mean?"

Her lips turned up a bit at the corners. "Warm. Solid. Safe. My mom's hair was brown before it started turning gray, and I always loved running my fingers through it, so I have a lot of good feelings toward brown." She finally reached out to touch the side of my head. "I guess if you have wavy brown hair, we probably shouldn't shave it off just to hang out with a bunch of skinheads."

Her fingers in my hair were so distracting, I almost jumped the curb as I parked the car. "They can't all be skinheads," I said.

"Right. And hopefully whatever they're playing in there will dislodge the techno earworm that has burrowed into my brain."

We got out of the car and started picking our way along an unshoveled sidewalk toward the underground punk rock club I'd never heard of but Natalie knew exactly where to find. The city had clearly given up on this neighborhood, which was either a result of the anarchist element moving in or the impetus for it. Most of the streetlights were broken or burned out. Most of the windows were boarded up and painted over with uninspired graffiti. I was surprised there was even enough electricity still flowing into the neighborhood to power a single amp, but clearly there was. The syncopated buzz and thud of the band reverberated in the air, drawing us in the way a tornado picks up cars and trash and cows. Brown cows.

We handed over ten bucks apiece and squeezed into the packed room. I steered us away from the mosh pit up front by the raised platform that served as a stage, where three guys in ripped jeans, tank tops, and studded leather jackets battered their instruments and screamed into the mics. The guitarist had a blond spike and the drummer a lime-green mohawk. Only the bassist had no hair at all. Their eyes were ringed with black liner, their necks with dog collars.

It was too loud to talk, even by shouting, and since Natalie couldn't read lips or see any hand signals, I stuck close to her and scanned the crowd, which did tend toward the skinhead side of the punk spectrum. Most were dressed similar to the band and too busy slamming into each other to notice we were there. The music was raw, bracing, real. Night-and-day from the noise at Lips. It had a ragged edge I loved. But it was so out of the mainstream I couldn't imagine any of it getting radio play or getting on MTV, which was one of the reasons when The Pleasure Centers started that we'd decided on rock 'n' roll. We wanted airtime and throngs of female fans and interviews in *Rolling Stone*. Rock was the best way to get it.

After fifteen or twenty minutes, the band finished its set and loped off the side of the stage.

"What do you think?" I asked Natalie.

"Doesn't matter what I think. What do you think?"

"I like it."

Natalie smiled. "Good."

Another threesome took the stage, looking rather like the three who had just left. Except the drummer. He was older than his bandmates by at least twenty years and looked suspiciously like my Uncle Mike.

Only Mike didn't play drums.

"You gotta be kidding me," I said.

"What?"

"The drummer."

"You know him?"

"Not really," I said. "It's my dad."

Track Nine

Natalie's mouth opened in a smile. "You didn't say your dad was a musician."

"He's not. He's a drummer. Apparently."

She frowned. "You didn't know he was a drummer?"

"No. But I guess it makes sense."

"Why?"

"Because they disappear on you. Holding on to a drummer is like holding on to a note you can't quite reach."

My dad clicked his drumsticks together four frantic times, and the guitars came in when he hit the drumheads.

I grabbed Natalie's arm. "Let's get out of here."

"Don't you want to hear them?" she shouted over the music.

"No."

"Don't you want to talk to him after their set?"

I tugged her toward the door without answering. What were the chances that he would be here the same night I was? Unless he was here all the time. Esto, Ronnie, the DJ. Natalie knew people.

I stopped in the dirty snow just outside the heavy metal door. "Did you know he'd be here? Do you know my dad?"

"Of course not. I know almost nothing about you."

"How did you know about this place? This isn't your scene."

"Mike brought me last year. I took a chance it was still here."

She went out to clubs with Mike? I started guiding her back to the car, knowing I was walking too fast but not caring enough to slow down. She slipped, but my hand on her arm kept her upright.

She yanked her arm away. "Why are you so mad? I didn't know your dad would be here. I just thought you'd like the music, that's all."

I stopped walking. "I'm not mad at you. I'm mad at him." I touched her arm and we started walking again. Slower. "And at Mike."

I didn't cross paths with my uncle until I got home from work on Wednesday night. He was sitting on the couch, beer in one hand, cigarette in the other, *Unsolved Mysteries* on the TV.

I tossed my keys on the side table, giving them a high arc so they'd come down hard and loud. "Why didn't you tell me your brother was playing drums down at the Thrash Factory?"

Mike glanced at my keys and shrugged. "I didn't know you were interested."

"Well, I am. I'm very interested."

"Okay. Well, now you know."

I swung a kitchen chair around and straddled it. "I didn't even know he played the drums."

Mike motioned to the TV. "Michael, please."

I reached over and clicked it off. It sizzled a moment and went silent. "There." I smiled. "Now you can hear me better."

Mike sighed. "Steve's got his own life, man."

"What does that mean?"

"What, you think he should check in with you before he joins a band? Kid, you're an adult. He's an adult. You want to talk to him? Go ahead." He leaned across the coffee table and turned the TV back on.

I clicked it off again. "What's your relationship with Natalie Wheeler?"

He held up his hands. "What, am I on trial here?"

"I want to know. You're practically the live-in handyman at their house."

"If I was the live-in handyman, I wouldn't be here in this dump. And neither would you."

"And she said you took her to the Thrash Factory last year. And why'd you give her all those pictures?"

Mike smiled. "Ah, I see. You like her."

"So?"

"So you want to know if we ever . . . ?"

"Gross, no. You're old enough to be her father."

His smile vanished. "Yes, I am."

For one sickening second, I let the thought cross my mind.

"Old enough," Mike clarified. "She's not my daughter, idiot."

My lungs squeezed out a breath of relief.

"She was just their cute little girl always hanging around when I was working, so I brought her stuff. I felt a little sorry for her—being blind. Her world was so small."

Oh, sure. Poor thing. Growing up with rich parents who entertained famous people all the time and sent her to Juilliard.

"Why do you go over to their house for holidays?" I said.

"Where else am I going to go? They've got the best of everything over there. Great food, great cigars, great bar. I play a little pool."

"With Dusty?"

"Eh, sometimes. But he's not real fun to play with. There's always other people there. Relatives, friends. You know. It's not like I'm invited to a family dinner or anything. They're parties. Half of Metro Detroit gets an invitation. I'm nothing special." Mike raised the remote. "Are we done here now?"

I nodded. "Yeah. I guess."

He flicked on the TV. The *Unsolved Mysteries* credits were rolling. "Dang it, Michael! Now I'm never going to know if all the handprints on the back of that bus were really the ghosts of dead children pushing it off the railroad tracks."

He drained his beer, then stalked off to his room, leaving the TV on. I turned it off a third time and shouted after him, "Deb Wheeler wants you to call her."

I went to my own room and shut the door, then pulled out my notebook. I wrote a bit, crossed it out, started over.

> ~~small world, big dreams~~
> ~~a small world closing in~~
>
> a world that's contracting
> a part that you're acting
> a price you're exacting
> a smile that's distracting me
> from my world caving in
> you're saving me again
> slowly . . . slowly . . .

Felt like a chorus of something. Not the kind of stuff Rodney wrote, the kind of stuff I'd been singing harmony on. More like a big, crazy ballad. Like Aerosmith? What kind of music did Natalie think we were going to make together anyway?

I put down the pen, went into the kitchen, and dialed her number.

"Hello?"

"When are we going to start working on some songs?"

"Now?"

Natalie's fingers slid across the opalescent surface of the keyboard the way the penguins slid into the water at the zoo. Soft. Fluid. Completely in their element. She had been at the piano in the living room, mid-song, when Deb led me back through the kitchen and the dining room with a hand on my arm, which I suspected was more to steady her than to guide me. We stood quietly in the doorway, but Natalie had to know we were there. She would have heard the doorbell and my ungraceful footsteps on the stone floor of the foyer. Would have assumed that whoever got the door would bring me along a moment later.

It was odd to me that she hadn't stopped playing to let me in herself. Or maybe not so odd. Maybe she was ignoring me. I hadn't seen her since I dropped her off after the Thrash Factory. I'd been working, but not at night. I could have called her up anytime. Could have apologized for the sudden end to the evening and the dark, silent drive home. But the longer I waited to admit I'd been kind of a jerk, the more I hoped she'd just pretend nothing had happened. Like my mom with guys who treated her like trash but kept showing up on her doorstep.

I kind of thought Natalie's invitation to write some songs *now* was her doing just that. But maybe I was wrong. Maybe that *now* wasn't an invitation so much as it was her being surprised I'd have the gall to even suggest such a thing. I mean, yeah, I could have called her. But she could have called me too. And she hadn't.

Natalie's song came to an end.

"Lovely," Deb said. "Chopin?"

"Liszt."

"Lovely," she said again. "Michael is here."

"Yeah." She pushed back the bench. "Dad's using the studio right now, so we'll have to work up here. You have your guitar?"

I held the case up in the air like she'd see it somehow. "Sure. Though I was hoping to use one of yours again. My strings are really old. Not staying in tune for a whole song even."

"You can use mine," Deb offered. "It's in the bedroom. I'll just go get it." She walked through the living room and disappeared into the dark hallway.

I set my guitar on the floor against the wall and tapped my notebook against my thigh, maybe hoping some words would be knocked loose and I'd know what to say. "So," I started, but before I could get anything else past my teeth, Deb was back. She handed me her guitar as though presenting an award. I'd seen it before—on the album art in the listening room. It was a Gibson J-45, the kind played by Buddy Holly, Woody Guthrie, Bob Dylan, James Taylor. Probably cost less than fifty bucks new in the 1940s. Worth thousands now.

I took it from her with two hands and thanked her with a nod. She produced a set of new strings from behind her back and placed them on my guitar case. "For later," she said, then she went into the kitchen.

Natalie picked up a Taylor from a stand in the corner of the living room and settled into the embrace of one of the white leather couches. I sat down on the edge of the couch across from her and tried to read her mood on her face.

"So, what have you got?" she said.

"Me?"

"Yeah, you suggested we write. I figured you had something you were working on."

I looked at the notebook in my hands. "I've got a lot of stuff I've been working on."

"Okay, let's hear something."

I flipped through a few pages, rejecting song after song. She'd think this was trite. She'd think this was boring. She'd think this was about her (because it was, maybe, I don't know). I finally landed on the page where everything was scratched out except those two lines.

> the truest feeling is an ache
> a vague, insistent pulse of pain

I wished I could just hand her the notebook to read rather than saying it out loud.

"I've got a couple lines I like that I want to build on. But I'm not sure exactly what I want to say just yet or how I think it should sound."

"Hit me."

I cleared my throat. "The truest feeling is an ache," I said in a monotone. "A vague, insistent pulse of pain."

She repeated the words and nodded. "What's the melody?"

"I don't know. I liked that thing you were playing New Year's Eve. The thing without words yet. I thought maybe something along those lines."

She hemmed and hawed a moment. "That's kind of my song, though."

"Oh, no problem. I just liked it is all."

She bit her lip. "What about something like this?" She put her fingers to the strings and pulled a melody out of them.

I parroted it, singing the words out loud.

"Or maybe more like this," she said, changing it up slightly. "Eh?"

I sang it again. "I like that."

"Yeah," she said, and then she sang the words. "I like that. The assonance of *ache* and *vague* and *pain*. And the alliteration of *pulse* and *pain*. Very nice. What's next?"

"That's it," I said. "That's all I've got. I wrote some other stuff at first, but I didn't like it."

She plucked out the notes again on the guitar, followed it up with the next musical phrase that came to her.

"I like that," I said.

She played the two phrases again. I watched her fingers closely, fumbled through as quietly as possible on Deb's guitar, wished I'd had professional lessons and some more natural talent. In a guy-girl duo, it was the guy who was supposed to be the guitar player and the girl who was supposed to be the singer. This would never work.

"So what were you thinking when you wrote it?" she said. "What was the ache?"

"Oh, I don't know. Just kind of a . . . emptiness, I guess? Like a hole where something else should be."

"Like what? What should be there?"

A puff of air escaped between my lips. "I don't know, like family or hope or a sense of something to work for, like a calling maybe?"

"Something lost?"

"Maybe."

"Or something you never had?"

I nodded. "Sure."

"Or something you're anticipating losing?"

I gave her a long, hard look. "Yeah. All that."

She was quiet a moment. "Well, it can't be all that, because they're all really different things. It should be about one thing. And that thing can stand in for the other things. Whatever hole the listener has inside."

"Okay. What should it be about then?"

"If you want it to be something people listen to and sing in the shower and stuff, it should be about a girl. Either unrequited love or a breakup or something like that."

I could see the sense in that. But part of me resisted. Was that the feeling I'd had when I wrote those words? This was bigger than a breakup song. And anyway, if we did any song that was about a girl, wouldn't everyone assume it was about Natalie? Would she assume that?

"That's what the little Dusty on my left shoulder says to me anyway," Natalie continued. "But the little Deb on my right shoulder says maybe you need to get to the heart of this feeling and figure out what it's really about. Not knowing the words yet doesn't stop us from working on the song itself."

"In this scenario, is your dad the devil and your mom the angel?"

She laughed. "No, it's just how I think of the two perspectives that are always at war within my mind. The pragmatist and the artist. You know how part of you just wants to create something beautiful and not worry about what to do with it, but the other part of you kind of wants to make sure what you're making is something others would want to hear?"

"Sometimes I feel like that's the only thing I know." That, and the fact that everything this girl said made me like her more.

"Okay," she said. "So let's just focus on what little Deb would have us do right now. We can worry about little Dusty later."

For the next thirty minutes, Natalie fiddled with chords and melodies and countermelodies. I scribbled notes and followed along and strummed the chords she told me to while her fingers walked and skipped along the strings. And it sounded good. Better than anything I could have come up with on my own. And the unnamed ache became the feeling that I wouldn't be able to write words that would do the music justice.

"Are you staying for dinner, Michael?" came Deb's voice during a lull. "Ruth's not here, so it'll be more of a meat and potatoes night."

That was what I had been smelling all this time. And the ache became easily identifiable as plain old physical hunger. I looked at Natalie to see if she appeared pleased by the invitation. "Uh, yeah, that'd be nice, thanks."

We put down the guitars and picked up utensils and napkins and plates. I offered to mash the potatoes—surely I could do that without making a fool of myself—while Natalie set the table and Deb sliced meatloaf and ladled gravy into a boat. Deb inspected my work and declared it good. We were just sitting down when Dusty walked in with my notebook in his hand and a frown poking out between his mustache and his beard.

"Some decent stuff," he said, setting the notebook on the table and sitting down. "A lot of B-sides in there, but some potential A's as well."

"Where?" Natalie asked.

"His notebook."

"No fair," she said. "I didn't get to hear anything more than two lines."

"I'd imagine that's because Michael here didn't want to show you anything still half-baked."

I slid the notebook off the table and tucked it under my leg. I wanted to say, *Dude, I'm right here. At least wait to talk about me until I'm gone.* But I didn't say anything.

"You shouldn't have looked in that notebook," Deb said. "That's an invasion of his privacy."

Dusty waved her comment away. "It was sitting there open on the couch. And if he wants to be a real musician and record songs and perform, he's got to work with other people on it. Got to show those songs to someone eventually."

He held out his hands to say grace, and this time I was sitting directly to his left. I wiped the sweat from my palm on my pant leg and put my hand in his with about as much enthusiasm as I'd have putting it into the open mouth of a bear. I couldn't tell you what he actually said—whether it was the same as the prayer the last time or if he came up with something different to say to God each time they ate a meal—because I was so consumed with embarrassment and indignation and yeah, a little bit of anger. I wasn't able to wallow in it as long as I wanted to, though. Someone had asked me a question.

"I'm sorry, what?" I said into the expectant silence.

"Natalie was telling me the other day that she ran into some old friends of ours when you two were out," Deb said. "And she said your dad was playing at the Trash Factory?"

"Thrash Factory," Natalie said.

Deb acknowledged the correction with a shrug. "I was just wondering if you got your love of music from him."

I reached for the gravy. "Uh, no, Mrs. Wheeler."

"Deb," she said.

"Right. Deb. I don't actually know my dad. I mean, I recognize him because he's my uncle's twin and I've seen him here and there over the years. But he left before I was born."

"Oh, I'm sorry," she said. She paused, and I knew she was waiting for more information. But I didn't have much to give her. Finally she said, "Maybe it's just in your blood, then. I mean, Mike plays."

He does? "Plays what?"

"Guitar."

"Deb, just because you started teaching him guitar doesn't mean he plays it," Dusty said around a mouthful of meatloaf.

"He seemed to be catching on before I got sick."

"And then what?" Dusty said. "Have you heard him play anything since?" He turned to me. "Does he play the guitar?"

"I've never seen him play guitar," I admitted. "He doesn't even have a guitar."

Deb frowned. "I gave him one. A rather nice Ovation."

I gave her a pained smile. "Maybe he let someone borrow it?"

"He probably sold it," Dusty said. "Or lost it in a poker game."

"Or that," I said.

Deb deflated. "Glen Campbell gave me that guitar."

Dusty gave her a look that said she should have known better than to entrust it to Mike Sullivan. "When did you start playing, Michael?"

"Junior year of high school. Rodney wanted to start a band. I'm sure it was just about getting chicks. I didn't know how to play anything. He sold me his first guitar for fifty bucks and taught me a few chords so we could get started, and the rest I've just kind of figured out on my own. Or tried to. I wish I knew more. More of the technical stuff. Why one chord progression works and another one doesn't. It might take some of the guesswork out of it for me. I'm not very good. Nothing like all of you."

"You never took lessons?" Deb said.

I shook my head. "Never had the money for it."

"Natalie could teach you some things."

"Mom, please."

"I'm just saying."

"He didn't ask for lessons."

As comfortable as the first dinner I'd had at this table was, that

117

was how unbearable this one was turning out to be. I hated being talked about as though I wasn't in the room. It was something my mom did with her boyfriends, something Mike did on the phone.

"So, what about this band you're starting," Dusty said. "Got a name?"

"We haven't discussed that yet," Natalie said.

"A sound?"

"Working on it."

"Is it just going to be the two of you with guitars, or were you thinking of adding other musicians?"

"Just the two of us so far," she said, "but we'll see. We might write something that requires more people."

"Couldn't you just play the other parts?" I asked.

"On a recording, sure. But not live. Oh, that reminds me, Dad. We need a slot at Saint Andrew's sometime in the early summer."

"I really don't think—" I started.

"Better make it later in the year," Dusty said. "Give yourself time to play a few other places first. Maybe get some airtime on 89X. Jumping right into Saint Andrew's will be a hard sell. I mean, I can get you a slot, but you want to prime the audience a bit."

"No, it has to be Saint Andrew's, and I was thinking earlier would be better," Natalie said. "Like June."

He shook his head. "You won't be ready then. Wouldn't at least August be better?"

"I think we'd get a bigger audience in June," she said.

The implication was clear, and I avoided looking at Deb.

Dusty placed his hand on hers. "You'll be a better band in August."

She pulled her hand away. "Make it June. We'll do a short set. Open for someone else."

Dusty shook his head and reached for the salt. "You need a sound and sample songs so they can put you with the right headliner. And really, at least one song for the radio will help you out a lot."

"Of course," Natalie said. "We'll get you a demo by March."

"You realize that's only six weeks away?" I said.

"No problem." She popped a forkful of mashed potatoes into her mouth. "What else do we have to do?"

"Did you forget I have a job?"

"But your nights are free, right?"

"I guess."

"Okay, then work during the day, come over for dinner afterward, and then we'll write and practice."

The prospect of spending that much time with Natalie—to say nothing of real, home-cooked meals every night of the week—was tempting. But I couldn't shake the feeling that this entire enterprise was doomed to fail. It wasn't enough time. Our taste in music was too different. Saint Andrew's Hall was too big. It held a thousand people. I'd never played for more than about a hundred. It seemed like everything that had potential to be bigger than that, I ended up missing. Because my mom needed help or work called me in or I overslept.

Though, if I was honest, those were just the excuses I came up with to justify my absence. It wasn't really about other obligations or even laziness. It was because sometimes I just couldn't make myself get up on stage. I hated myself for it. Rodney had every right to be mad at me for missing our gigs. It was a rotten thing to do. But then, so was stealing the melodies of other people's songs and passing them off as your own.

That was what I had to remember. I was doing this to show Rodney that I was a good songwriter, a good singer. That I could write us better songs, get us better gigs. I knew people now. I had something to offer. This thing with Natalie was just temporary. A step on the road back to The Pleasure Centers, back to rock 'n' roll.

"Well?" Natalie said.

I took a sip of water and swallowed down my lingering uncertainties. "Let's do it."

Track Ten

If this were a movie, this is where the montage would go. The crane kicks on the beach, the dancing in the warehouse, the pounding sides of beef. There'd be shots of pens leaving trails of ink, fingers on strings, furrowed brows, meaningful glances, crumpled pages of rejected efforts. And behind it all a song that grew in intensity, implying that success was imminent. Then everything would fall apart. Nothing would go as planned. There'd be some sort of misunderstanding and friends would turn on each other, and it would look like all was lost. Twenty or thirty minutes later, everything would be patched up, all would be forgiven, victory would be secured. Freeze frame on the triumphant hero.

That was the pattern of every story. You could set your watch by it. They glossed over the trudging daily effort to get you to the moment of high drama. It made a movie better, I guess, but it made real life harder somehow. Because real life? It's the trudging daily effort. That's pretty much all it is. It's a slog. Especially if you're trying to create something worth sharing. But the movies make that part look easy, compressing weeks or months of effort into a three-minute song that'll be the B-side of the cassingle.

People call my generation lazy. But maybe we aren't lazy. Maybe we're just waiting for "Eye of the Tiger" to start.

Rocky Balboa ended the Cold War with a boxing match. We finished writing the first song for the demo tape the same day the first McDonald's opened in Moscow. It had taken three weeks to write one song and get it tight enough for an audience. At this rate, we wouldn't have enough songs to fill even a half-hour set until July.

It wasn't the one we'd started working on, the one about the ache I still couldn't quite name. We set that one aside in favor of something less esoteric—a song about war. Because even though the bloodless war we'd grown up with was ending, there were rumblings and grumblings during the evening news that all was not well in volatile little pockets of the world.

War was easy to write about. Down with tyranny. Defend the helpless. We have to leave the world better for our children. Rah-rah-America. Make the chorus something people can sing along to with gusto and you've got yourself a hit.

Natalie pulled the melody out of her guitar on the first try, and the lyrics came together in a matter of hours. It was figuring out all the other parts—Natalie added practically a whole orchestra's worth—and laying down the recording that took so long. That, and the argument.

When I brought up the fact that we wouldn't be able to play the song at the gig because we didn't have people to play all the parts live, Natalie said she'd already contacted a number of musicians who'd jumped at the chance.

"Who?" I asked.

"Classmates."

"From Juilliard?"

"Of course. The semester will be over by then, and this gives everyone an excuse to come visit. I can send them the parts to work on, and they'll arrive ready to perform."

"So it's going to be you with a bunch of your friends, who

can all play way better than I can, and me just standing up there like a chump who doesn't know what he's doing? I'll look like a fool."

Natalie waved my words away like they were a cloud of cigarette smoke. "I don't know what you're so worried about. You play fine. No one's going to be judging you. Anyway, lots of rock stars aren't actually all that good. They just have a strong stage presence and great backup."

"So you agree," I said. "I'm not that good."

She sighed heavily. "That's not what I said."

"But it's what you meant."

Natalie held up a hand. "Don't tell me what I meant. I meant what I meant. You've got nothing to be ashamed of. It's not a competition. They'll be there backing *you* up. They'll be at the back of the stage, nothing but sounds, no faces even. You're the one in the spotlight. You're the personality. Heck, we can even name the band after you if you want. Mike on the Mic or something."

She laughed at her silly little turn of phrase, trying to change the subject. But I wasn't ready to let this drop yet. "That's not what I'm talking about. I'm not talking about who gets the spotlight. I don't want the spotlight. I'm already going to be the talentless hack when it's just you and me up there. How much worse will I look when I'm the worst of half a dozen?"

"Of course you want the spotlight," she said. "That's why you're so mad at Rodney."

"That's about stealing material."

"Okay, but it was also because he didn't give your songs a chance, right? You wanted to do your songs before you even knew about the sitcom themes, and I bet you wanted to be the one singing them too. And now you can. You'll be the front man."

She wasn't wrong, and it was annoying. "You should have asked," I said. "You should have asked me before you offered parts to a bunch of people I don't know. And you should have asked me if I even wanted to start a band with you instead of declaring it in front of my real band."

She laughed. "That's not your band. That's Rodney's band. Clearly." She got serious. "But you're right. I should have asked you. I thought I was doing you a favor, but I should have asked."

She was quiet a moment, waiting for me to say something, but I didn't know what to say. She couldn't undo any of it. I wasn't going to tell her to un-ask her friends.

"So," she said, a penitent expression fixed on her face, "do you want to start a band with me? I promise if you say yes, you won't regret it."

I bit the inside of my cheek to keep from smiling. "Do you also promise, from this day forward, to run big things by me before you commit to them? Like when and where our first gig is going to be and who else is in the band?"

She put her hand over her heart. "I promise. They're not even really in the band. They're the touring musicians, the studio musicians, you know? I'll even let you name us as penance for my previous sins."

I laughed. "I'm holding you to that."

"But not Molly Ringworm, because then everyone will think my name is Molly. And also ringworms are gross."

"Actually, I have given it a little thought already."

"Yeah? Let's hear some ideas."

I picked up my notebook from the music stand, flipped a few pages, and scanned the list I'd begun the week before. Names that had seemed clever when I wrote them down now seemed juvenile. There was a whole string of bad almost-puns. Tuna Meltdown. Rock Collective. TaxiDermatologist. There were some that were a little better. The Inscrutables. The Eclectics. I finally landed on one that was totally vanilla but didn't seem like something that would get me laughed out of the room.

"How about M&N? Like, for Michael and Natalie?"

She frowned. "Sounds too much like M&Ms. Who would name their act after candy?"

"Oh, yeah. I hadn't thought of that. I don't think I said it out loud."

"What else you got?"

I read the list again. "Eh, nothing really good. Hit me up again next month."

"Okay, but we really need to have something by the time the demo is done. Can't give them a demo with no band name. And they'll need to have it in time to promote the event."

"Of course." I flipped back to the page where I'd written the lyrics to a new song. Again I wished I could just hand the notebook over so she could read it herself. If I was going to contribute to this musical experiment at all, it was going to be as a lyricist, so I had to show her what I was working on. But to do so, I'd have to tip my hand a lot further than I wanted to at this point.

The truth was, I'd been trying to write about anything but her. But she was the only thing I could think of. She was the first thing on my mind every morning, the last thing on my mind every night, and there she was every minute of the workday in between. She even invaded my dreams. The only place left for her to go was into my songs.

I cleared my throat. "You ready to jump into something new now that we solved the problem of world peace?"

She sat up straight and adjusted the guitar on her thigh. "Definitely. Hit me."

"The melody's nothing special. Yet. But I think I've got the words pretty close."

Heart pounding, palms sweating, I pressed the calloused tips of my fingers against the strings, took the plunge, and squeaked out the words.

> I met a girl one day whose soul slipped out her
>   fingertips
> And danced along the strings of an old guitar
> Didn't have to ask her name 'cause I remembered it
> From the misty dream I'd had the night before
>
> I listened as she picked those sacred notes apart
> And put them back together one by one
> Then a hurricane filled the empty chambers of my
>   heart
> And I told myself, "Be strong now, don't succumb."

"And the chorus goes something like this."

> But the wind was coming to get me, to toss me to and
>   fro
> The rain had already wet me, from my head down to
>   my toes
> The moment that I saw her, I knew I was a goner
> And you know sometimes that's just the way it goes.

I kept my eyes glued to the notebook so I wouldn't see Natalie's reaction and barreled on.

> She didn't need any words to get her point across
> Didn't rely on pretty turns of phrase
> She spoke the truth through tones 'til I was at a loss
> To extricate my heart from its malaise

"I'm not really sure about that part," I said, still strumming chords. "The second chorus is mostly like the first, but the last line is a little different. Then there's the fourth verse."

> Then she put down her guitar and said, "Come over here
> And sit with me in silence for a while."
> We let the notes float round us 'til the air was clear
> And then I turned to face her with a smile.

"Third chorus."

> I said, "The wind is coming to get me, to toss me to and fro.
> The rain has already wet me, from my head down to my toes,
> The moment that I saw you, my aching heart was run through."
> And she said, "Sometimes that's just the way it goes."

I stopped playing then. It wasn't the end of the song, but I couldn't make myself sing the last part. Not yet. "Anyway, that's what I've been working on." I finally looked up from the notebook.

Natalie's head rested at a thoughtful tilt, lips pursed, eyebrows knit. "I like it. It has lots of potential. But that's not it, right?"

"What do you mean?"

"It's not the end of the story. It needs another verse and another chorus."

"I'm working on it."

She nodded. "All right."

If Natalie knew the song was about her, she didn't say anything. But she couldn't not know. Which meant she did know—and she didn't want to talk about it. Which was fine, really. I didn't want to talk about it either.

"I think we can do a little better on some of those chords, don't you?" she said.

I plastered a fake smile across my face so she'd hear it in my voice. "Absolutely," I said. "That's what you're for."

Track Eleven

A few days after Nelson Mandela was released from prison, Natalie and I completed recording our second song. It wasn't the one I'd half shared with her. Instead, I reworked an older one I'd found in an earlier idea notebook. One of those songs where I moaned about my terrible upbringing and how alone I was in the world, the chorus of which went

> Who in the world do you think you are?
> Where in the world have you been?
> What in the world were you thinking?
> When will I see you again?

But we twisted the lyrics a bit and jazzed it up enough so that it probably wouldn't make anyone want to slit their wrists. We needed five songs for the demo—more for the gig—and March was just over two weeks away.

"He doesn't need it by March 1st," Natalie said when I insisted there was no possible way to get it done in time. "Just sometime in March."

"Even if that's true, we've only managed to write two songs in like four weeks—five weeks! We need to pick up the pace.

Write simpler stuff with fewer parts. We need a couple songs that are just you and me without backup."

Natalie slipped a record out of its sleeve. "Okay, you got some lyrics for those songs?"

We were celebrating our small accomplishment with a night off in the listening room. Valentine's night. There was no part of me that thought this was romantic, despite the fact that Natalie was playing exclusively love songs on the hi-fi. She still had shown zero signs of being charmed by me at all. I hadn't realized just how much of my admittedly minor effect on women involved them being able to see me.

"I have one or two that might fit the bill. With some work," I said. "But you know, you can write some lyrics too. No one's stopping you."

She lifted the needle and set it on the edge of the record. "Oh, I've got something I'm working on. But it's not right for the demo."

Stevie Wonder's "You Are the Sunshine of My Life" sang sweetly from the speakers while Natalie ran her fingertips over the album cover.

"Why not?" I said, but she shushed me with a finger over her lips. Talking over songs was not allowed in the listening room. This was a sacred space, dedicated to the worship of melody and harmony, voice and instrument, rhythm and beat. It was not a place to quibble or air grievances or talk about practical or pragmatic things, things of the mind. This was a haven of the heart, a place to forget everything else in the world that wasn't pouring forth from the speakers directly into your soul.

When the song ended, she lifted the needle and picked up where we left off. "It just isn't. So what have you got?"

Who could argue with that logic? "I've got most of a couple verses for a song your mom kind of inspired."

Her eyebrows shot up. "Oh really?"

"Yeah. It's a faster one. Which we need more of since the first couple were on the slower side."

"We need fast songs?"

"Don't you think so? Seems like for every slower song there should be at least three faster ones."

"Says who?"

I hesitated. "Uh, the music industry?"

"Don't you think that depends on the kind of music we're making?"

"Yeah, I'm still not clear about that. What are we trying to do here? Rock? Folk? Easy listening?"

"I don't know. I thought we were just having fun. Mixing and matching."

"But what label does it fit under? You need to fit into a clear genre to market music."

"Again, says who?"

"Again, the music industry. People who don't fit anywhere, they don't get airtime, they don't sell records."

She smiled and kind of shook her head and chose another album. "You're so concerned with fitting somewhere. Fitting in at clubs, fitting some arbitrary definition of musical genre. Let's just make some good music, whatever it's called. Take advantage of anonymity while you have it. No one has any expectations of you. You can be anyone when you're no one."

"I feel like I should be kind of offended by that." I snagged my notebook from the table as Natalie set the needle down. I hunched my shoulders to block out as much of the Beach Boys' "Wouldn't It Be Nice" as possible as I scribbled furiously, scratched out, scribbled more. I imagined what it might have been like to see Deb Wheeler in her heyday. She clearly had made a big impression on people. What sort of impression would she have made on me? Would I have been jealous of her celebrity? Would she have charmed me like she must have charmed my uncle?

The song ended, and I jumped on the silence. "What about this?"

> You ignite the room
> Just by walking in it
> But I would not presume
> Even for a minute
> To be somebody you'd take notice of
> 'Cause I'm nobody anyone could love
>
> I don't have the look
> That turns anyone's head
> But I think you wrote the book
> On knocking people dead
> You're everything a superstar should be
> I'm nothing much, but here's what you don't see
>
> Everyone wants to be someone
> To chase fame up the charts
> But when nobody knows your name
> That's where the music starts

Natalie smiled. "I like that. Did you just think of all that right now?"

"Nah. This is the song I started writing about your mom. But you helped me finish the second verse and gave me the chorus."

"Read it to me again."

As I did, Natalie's fingers mimed chords and strumming patterns.

"Gosh, I really like that," she said.

"Should we go back into the studio and fiddle with the music?"

She folded her hands. "No. Not yet. We can do that tomorrow night. Maybe you can think of some more lyrics while you're working tomorrow. Tonight we're taking a break." She lifted *Pet Sounds* from the turntable, slipped it back into the sleeve, and replaced it on the shelf. "Have you ever heard my mom's albums?"

"My mom used to play *Homeward* fairly often. I don't know if I've ever heard the other two."

"That one was definitely the most popular of the three."

"Why don't you put one of the other ones on and we can listen to the whole thing."

"Oh, none of my mom's albums are in the listening room."

I looked up at the three Deb Wheeler albums framed on the wall. Clearly they were not playable in that state, but was it possible that Natalie didn't even know they were in here?

"Why not?" I said. "You have every other album ever recorded in here."

"Hardly. You're not going to find much country in here. A bit of the old good stuff, the old cowboy songs. Patsy Cline and such. Some gospel. A little classical. But not nearly as much as is out there."

"That wasn't really my point. Why wouldn't you play her stuff in here?"

"We have copies somewhere. But Mom doesn't like to hear them. She says it fuels her pride. And as long as she's around, Dad won't play them."

"That makes no sense. What's wrong with being proud of your accomplishments? They were hugely popular records, right?"

She shrugged. "That's the problem. For her, at least. That's why she stopped putting records out. It made her think too highly of herself and crave the admiration of others."

I considered this. Who made all that effort to gain fame just to decide they didn't want it? While countless other musicians never even got it to begin with. What a waste. "I just don't get it. What's wrong with pride? I mean, aren't you proud of how amazing a musician you are?"

Natalie tipped her head from side to side as if weighing the question. "Pride's a funny thing. Not enough and you can end up thinking you're a born loser and nothing you try will ever amount to anything."

Ouch. That assessment hit just a little too close to home. I tried to push off the feeling that she was talking about me—push it over to Mike where it belonged.

"A lot of the guys we met through our work in rehabs were that way," Natalie continued. "You had to convince them they had worth in and of themselves, by virtue of being made in God's image, not because of anything they accomplished or didn't accomplish. If you could get that simple fact through, a guy had a good chance of turning his life around."

"Okay, so that makes my point. Pride is a good thing."

Natalie held up a finger. "*But* too much is not a good thing. For my mom, too much of her identity got wrapped up in other people's opinions of her. If a song got popular or an album got good reviews, she felt good about herself. If it didn't, she felt miserable. Big highs and big lows."

"I mean, I guess that's just the music business, right?" I said.

"Sure. That's why so many musicians have problems with alcohol and drugs—they're trying to hold on to those highs. You know why we got involved in rehab ministry in the first place?"

"Why?"

"Because she was in rehab. In 1969. When she was pregnant with me."

"I thought your aunt said they didn't do drugs."

"Not way back then. Not before she met my dad. Not before she got involved in the music industry."

"Wow."

"Wow, nothing. It's the most common story there is."

I thought of how many musicians had died young of overdoses, of how many had left a string of failed marriages and fatherless children in their wake, of all those entries in the red guest book upstairs. "I guess."

"She needed to get off the roller coaster. She got pregnant, got clean, and got herself out of the business. As much as she could, being married to my dad."

"So, do you ever listen to her music?"

"I mean, yeah. When I first went away to school, a friend found her first two albums in a resale shop and we listened to them. But I've actually never listened very closely to the third one. That's the one that didn't get as popular. A lot were sold because people expected it to be like her first two. But when she recorded that one, she'd already been famous for several years, and the songs just weren't the same anymore."

"Why would that make any difference?"

"How can you even ask that after the chorus you just wrote? 'When nobody knows your name, that's where the music starts.' It's easier to write with complete honesty when no one knows who you are and they don't have any expectations. Once your name means something specific, you start feeling like you have to stay within the limits people have in their heads about you. That's why everyone hated Dylan when he went electric. He was going off script."

"That's all the more reason, then, for us to figure out a core sound and genre before we start, right? So we don't end up wishing we'd started with something else that we really want to play." I knew I was violating the sanctity of the listening room by pushing the conversation ever forward, but I didn't care. It was starting to dawn on me that if any music execs did happen to get wind of this nebulous musical experiment Natalie wanted us to do, it might ruin my chance to do rock music later. The leap from Art Garfunkel to Eddie Van Halen is tough, no matter how high you can jump.

"So we never evolve?" Natalie said. "We never get to experiment? Where's the fun in that?"

How could I explain to her that I was in this more for the fame than the fun without seeming like I was using her? I was having fun—more fun than I'd ever had with Rodney and Slow—but the imbalance in our ambition was starting to concern me as much as the imbalance in our level of talent.

"Anyway," she said, "maybe just keep that in mind as you work on that song. I think it could be a good one. And I promise to keep the instrumentation simple. Simple will fit the theme."

"Sure," I said, not entirely certain what I was agreeing to.

"So," she said, officially taking back control and moving on, "what should we listen to next? Your pick."

It was eleven o'clock when I walked across the street to find a vaguely familiar car parked erratically half on and half off the gravel drive in front of the trailer. Did Mike have a girl in there for Valentine's Day? The prospect of having that to deal with almost had me walking back up to Natalie's to see if I could spend the night in the guest room. But then I saw that Mike's car wasn't there.

Inside, Brittney was sprawled out on the couch, staring slack-jawed at the TV. I could guess what was coming. I shut the door firmly, startling her upright. She let out a curse.

"What are you doing here, Brittney?"

She stood, almost toppled, righted herself. "That's a nice way to greet someone. After I drove all the way out to Hickland to see you on Valentine's night."

At least every six months, Brittney and Slow would fight, she'd get drunk, and then she'd try to get even. Her schemes always involved making Slow jealous by hitting on another guy. Usually I was the most convenient other guy because I lived with Slow. Now that I lived nearly an hour away, I was a decidedly inconvenient other guy—how did she even know where this place was?

"Oh, so sorry," I said. I pasted a fake smile on my face. "Brittney! What an awesome and unexpected treat! I can't imagine what brings you out here tonight. Surely it's not that you're angry at your boyfriend and looking to get back at him for something you've blown totally out of proportion and then made worse by getting drunk and telling him you were going to see one of his best friends."

She looked taken aback, but only for a second. She started toward me on wobbly legs. "You think you're one of his best friends? He's still angry at you for the last time you made a pass at me." She batted her eyes, her mascara notably non-tear-streaked—had there even actually been a fight?—and put a hand on my shoulder.

I shook it off. "That was you. It's always been you. You know that. I know that. Slow knows that."

She grabbed my belt with both hands. "Well, whoever started it, you know you liked it and he knows you did too."

I pried her hands away and held them so she couldn't grab anything else. "Brittney, you're drunk. It's a miracle you made it all the way out here without crashing into a tree or a ditch. Let me drive you home."

She wrenched her hands away. "No. I'm never going back there."

I sighed and played along. "What happened? What did he do to you?"

Brittney snaked her arms around my waist and squeezed. "I don't want to talk about it," she moaned. "In fact, we don't need to talk at all."

"All right, all right." I patted her head like you might a stray dog. Tentative, hoping not to get bit. "Well, you can't stay here."

She squeezed harder, her bony arms locking my ribs in a vise. "Please? I won't be any trouble. I promise."

I reached behind my back and tried to untangle her fingers. "You already are trouble."

She tipped her head up and smiled. "I am, aren't I?"

I grabbed her shoulders and pushed her back. "Knock it off, Brittney. Get your coat."

"I don't want to go back!"

I found her coat on the floor and tossed it at her. "Fine, I won't take you back, but you're not staying here."

Her face brightened. "Are we going to a hotel?"

"We're going across the street. You can stay at my friend Natalie's house."

"Who's Natalie?"

I practically dragged Brittney outside and up the long driveway to the Wheelers' front door. I winced as I rang the doorbell, thinking I should have called first, imagining waking everyone up. Even though I should have wanted her to rest, I prayed that Deb would answer the door. But when it opened, Dusty was on the other side of it in shorts and an undershirt, eyebrows raised, mouth in a hard line.

"What's this?" he said.

"This needs a place to stay tonight."

Track Twelve

Brittney's protests stopped as soon as she stepped into the Wheeler house. "Ooh, this place is *niiiice*."

Dusty's expression made it clear he was not happy about the intrusion, but he led us down the hall to the guest suite. I grabbed the guest book off the nightstand and suggested it might be safer somewhere else for the night.

He held out his hand for it, then tucked it under his arm. "Does she have an overnight bag?"

Brittney was already lying on the bed, exclaiming how soft everything was.

"I doubt she planned that far ahead," I said. "Listen, I'm really sorry about this, but she can't drive home and I can't let her stay with me."

He nodded his understanding. "Just tonight."

"What's going on?" came Natalie's voice from the doorway. She had changed into lavender pajama shorts and a light blue T-shirt, the first non-black shirt I'd seen her in.

"We have a guest tonight," Dusty said. "Though I didn't catch her name."

"Brittney," I said.

"Slow's Brittney? What's she doing here?"

"She was at my place when I got home." I was pleased to see Natalie frowning about this. "Every so often she gets it in her head that she and Slow are fighting," I explained, "and when that happens, she usually uses me as a way to get back at him."

"Natalie, could you take care of her tonight?" Dusty said. "I don't want to get your mother up."

The frown deepened. "Sure."

Dusty and the guest book took their leave, and Natalie's hands went to her hips. "What am I supposed to do with her?"

"I don't know. What do you usually do with people?"

"They're not usually drunk when they get here. This isn't a rehab center."

"Well, maybe we need to sober her up." I turned to Brittney. "Hey, you hungry?"

But she was already out cold, coat still on, mouth wide open on the pillow, one arm trailing off the side of the bed.

"Looks like you don't have to do anything tonight. I'll come over early tomorrow before I have to go to work and check on her." I took a blanket from the closet and laid it over Brittney's bottom half. "Her car is at my place, so she should be able to just drive home. Maybe you could give her breakfast?"

Natalie sighed.

"Hey, I thought that was what you guys did here. Helped messed-up people get back on the straight and narrow?"

"Yeah, well . . ."

"Well, what? What's the problem?" I wanted her to say it. To say that Brittney, specifically, was a problem. Because she was a threat. Because Natalie had feelings for me.

But she didn't. She just swept a hand toward the door and said, "Good night, Michael."

After a night of almost no sleep, I did stop by the Wheelers' before work. Dusty was drinking coffee at the kitchen counter, but Deb, Natalie, and Brittney were nowhere to be seen.

"She's still asleep," he announced before looking back at the newspaper on the countertop. "So's Natalie."

"I hope she wasn't too much trouble."

"I wouldn't know."

I snuck off to peek into the guest suite. Brittney had barely moved in the night, but she'd managed to create a sizable puddle of drool on the pillow. She'd feel terrible when she finally woke up. The thought made me smile.

All day at work, my mind switched between wondering what kind of interactions Brittney and Natalie were having and developing more lyrics for the song I'd started about Deb. Slowly, slowly I pieced together a second part of the chorus and the next couple verses and jotted them down on a strip of receipt paper. The song was really coming together. I still needed a bridge and maybe a final chorus that had a twist to it, but I figured I'd be able to get it done by tomorrow. If we kept the music simple, we could record it this weekend.

I was excited to show Natalie my progress and pulled into the gravel drive at the trailer with more speed than I should have, skidding on the new-fallen snow and nearly hitting Brittney's car, which hadn't moved from the night before.

"You gotta be kidding me," I said out loud. I ran in to change clothes, relieved that Brittney wasn't in the trailer but also horrified that she was still at the Wheelers' house, making a nuisance of herself, making Dusty more irritated with me. No doubt if Deb was up and about, she'd be making a fuss over her wayward houseguest. In my imaginings I'd pictured Natalie all but shoving her out the door in the morning after a warning to keep her paws off me. But what if they were becoming friends? What if

Brittney was telling Natalie stories about me? What if she was telling her lies?

I changed in a rush and trotted as quickly as I dared across the slick street. I'd been at the Wheeler house almost every night for weeks and had been granted status of a no-knock dinner guest, so I walked in and started taking off my boots. I could hear voices behind me in the kitchen. Deb. Natalie. But no Brittney.

"She's still here?" I said as I entered the kitchen. "Where is she?"

"Michael," Deb said, opening her arms and waiting for me to enter them for a hug. "She is just the funniest little thing." She squeezed me a little. Weaker than the last time. "She's downstairs right now giving Dusty a run for his money at the billiards table."

I was watching Natalie's face for some indication of her current feelings toward Brittney, but she gave nothing away. Just went about setting the table as usual, this time with an extra place. I wondered where Brittney would end up sitting and hoped for the first time that my leg wouldn't be within groping distance.

"They've been down there for hours," Deb continued. "Dusty was up here a few minutes ago, and I could tell he was losing."

I grimaced.

She whacked me lightly. "Oh, don't make that face. He could use a little humility when it comes to pool."

I washed my hands and waited for Deb's instructions. As the weeks had gone by, she handed more and more of the dinner prep over to me. I was happy to contribute because it made me feel less like I was constantly mooching off them the way Uncle Mike was always mooching off Carl. This time I was mashing more potatoes and whisking flour into gravy and carving pork loin. I transferred everything into serving dishes along with roasted carrots and onions, handing them off to Natalie one by one. Finally, I was sent to call everyone else up to dinner.

Dusty and Brittney appeared, he grim, she grinning like a cat and wearing what looked to be some of Deb's vintage 1970s clothes and maybe even some of her jewelry. Nothing was said about the game. In fact, except for Deb and Brittney, no one said much of anything during the entire meal. Brittney regaled Deb with stories I knew to be gross exaggerations of the truth or else outright lies. But I wasn't about to point that out. Deb deserved to be entertained for as long as she could laugh without ending up in a coughing fit. She did start to struggle a bit at the end of the meal, prompting Natalie to step in and wrap things up.

"Well, it's been really nice to have you around today, Brittney," she said.

"I bet you girls had fun," I said, wincing at the condescension in my voice. "But it is really time for you to head on home, Brittney."

Deb rallied. "Oh, no, she can't go home, Michael. Not to that man."

"Slow's fine," I said. "Brittney has a way of blowing things out of proportion."

"Certainly not," Deb said. "I couldn't live with myself if I sent her home to an abusive boyfriend."

I fixed Brittney with a look. If anyone was abusive in their relationship, it was her. Constantly manipulating him, flinging emotional blackmail in his face, and yeah, occasionally resorting to physical violence.

I stood. "If she's going to stay awhile"—Dusty and Natalie swung their heads around toward me—"she'll need to get some of her things from the old apartment. I'd be happy to drive her out there and go in with her to make sure nothing happens to her."

Deb was nodding. "That's a very good idea, Michael. Why don't the two of you go now, and Natalie and I can clean up dinner."

Brittney was about to say something, so I pulled her up from her chair, put an arm around her, and looked deep into her eyes, knowing Natalie couldn't see it. "Don't you worry. I'll take good care of her." I walked Brittney out of the room and into the guest suite, arm still around her shoulders, propelling her forward. I shut the bedroom door behind us. "Get your crap. Let's go."

"Excuse me?"

"You and I both know Slow never hurt you. He may be better off without you around, but I'm not about to watch you take advantage of the Wheelers' hospitality."

"Oh, like you are?"

"Natalie is my friend. We're in a band."

"Yeah, right. You can't be in a band with her."

"Why not?"

Brittney pointed at her eyes. "Uh, duh, she can't see anything. How's she going to play an instrument?"

"Haven't you ever heard of Ray Charles? Stevie Wonder?" I started picking up the clothes she'd had on the day before off the floor. "Put your shoes on or you're going to have to walk barefoot on the snow. I'm not fooling around. You need to get out of here."

Furious, Brittney pulled on the red heels she'd worn with her short skirt last night. They looked ridiculous with the flower child getup she was currently wearing. I almost told her to change, but I knew she'd do it right in front of me—slowly—to get under my skin and drag out the process of leaving.

"What are you going to tell Deb when you come back and I'm not with you?" Brittney asked as I helped her across the street.

"The truth. That you're a conniving, scheming, lying tease and that even though Slow would be better off without you, he would never hit you."

"What about my car?"

"What about it?"

"How are you going to get it back to me?"

I opened her car door, which she'd left unlocked in her drunken state, and dumped her into it. "Looks like the keys are just where you left them," I said, pointing at the ignition. "Sayonara, sweetie. Watch your feet."

Brittney pulled her feet in half a second before I shut the door. I stood there staring, waiting, not willing to move until she saw that I was serious and wasn't going to budge until she was gone. She cursed, started the car, and hit the gas too fast. Her back tires spun ineffectively in the snow for a moment. She stopped, changed gears, and tried again. I gave the car a shove. Then she was moving. I watched until her taillights disappeared around a bend and breathed a sigh of relief. Maybe this evening could still be salvaged.

But when I thought of telling Deb what was really going on and what Brittney was really like, an overwhelming tiredness settled upon me. Maybe it would be easier on her if I lied to her. Told her that once we were back at the apartment Brittney changed her mind and decided to take Slow back. Deb would feel bad about that too, but in a way that didn't make her look like a gullible simpleton taken in by a very convincing liar. She'd say a prayer for her, and that wouldn't hurt either.

But that meant I couldn't go back to the Wheelers' right away. Couldn't see Natalie and show her my progress on the song. I'd have to wait an hour or two, tell my lie, and then get to bed so I wasn't late for my early shift tomorrow.

At that moment, I hated Brittney. But that was okay. Because anger had fueled some incredible songs over the years. And I had nothing better to do that night than write.

Track Thirteen

The last wailing notes of "Brittney Sucks" reverberated in the still air of the live room. It had taken some explanation to get through to Natalie that I had nothing but contempt for her unexpected guest before she'd condescend to let me in Friday night to work on some music. Now as I looked toward the window into the control room, I expected to see her laughing, or at least smiling. The song was funny. She was doing neither. Instead she pushed the PA button and said, "Whose band did you write that for?"

The white Stratocaster hung impotently from my shoulders. "Are you serious? That song is awesome. It's one of the best things I've written."

"Disagree."

I sighed and threw up my hands. "What's wrong with it?"

"It's too . . . mean."

"Too mean? Too mean?"

"It's an angry rock song."

"Exactly! People will love it. Everyone has a friend who has a terrible girlfriend. It's something people will really connect with."

"I dunno."

"Would you like it better if it was about a terrible boyfriend?"
A pause. "Maybe."

I released a burst of frustration, and it came out as a growl.

"You said you had two songs, though, right?" she said.

"Yeah. I mean, I finished the one I started about your mom."

"Got music for it?"

"Some. I'm sure you'll make it better."

"Okay, why don't you play that one for me?"

So I did. The whole thing. And it was long. If "Brittney Sucks" (which was just a placeholder for the song title, but I kind of liked its simple honesty) was your typical three-minute-thirty rock song, "Anonymous" was nearing five. And that was without any of the instrumental parts Natalie would add. In my notebook, those parts were marked with *Natalie does something cool here.*

I played it on the Strat because that was what I already had in hand, and I found I liked it a whole lot better on electric than I had on acoustic. But that may just have been because when I was fiddling with it before, I was playing my thuddy Oscar Schmidt. The new strings Deb had given me made it sound a lot better, but it still couldn't compare to a high-end instrument.

Again, I looked to Natalie in the control room. Again, I didn't see the reaction I was hoping for.

After a moment of consideration, she said, "I'm not sure I believe you."

"Well, I can tell you don't believe the line about every song I make being a work of art."

She shook her head. "No, that one rang true. It was—what was it? Something about the nightmare of being on magazine covers and getting radio interviews? And 'when you're nothing much you can't be touched'? And that last one about rejecting fame being sweeter. I just don't believe you."

"Maybe that's because I don't believe me either. I was just writing it in the direction you were talking about the other day." You know, in the hour before Brittney showed up and drove this weird invisible wedge between us. I unplugged the Strat and placed it on its stand. "I'll rework some of the lyrics, but maybe for now we should call it a night," I said as I made for the door.

Natalie stopped me on the other side of it in the little anteroom before I could get out to the hall. We stood inches apart in the four-foot-by-four-foot square, her hand on my chest.

"It's no big deal," I said. "We'll start fresh tomorrow."

"Look, I know I shouldn't be so critical. Especially since we're under some pressure to get songs written." She dropped her hand, leaving a cold spot on my chest where it had been, and put both hands in her pockets. "I know I haven't been contributing lyrics, so maybe I have no business critiquing them."

My unseen body language said, *Ya think?* but my voice simply said, "Mm."

"I'm just having a lot of trouble with writing anything I like lately, and maybe that's bleeding into my attitude about your stuff."

I relaxed. "So let me help you with it."

She shook her head. "No, no. It's something I really have to do myself."

"Says who? You help me with instrumentation. Why can't I help you with lyrics?"

"Because. It's none of your business." She caught herself. "I mean, it's just something I need to work through myself."

I looked down into her scrunched-up face. I hated seeing her so tied up inside. "You know, I don't think we've been a band long enough to have an ugly breakup. I mean, we don't even have a name."

The deep furrow between her eyebrows softened, and she touched my arm, too briefly. "About that. Any other ideas?"

I put my hands in my pockets. "A few. I thought about Intersection or The Intersection, kind of alluding to the intersection between musical genres."

She brightened. "I like that. Let's keep that one in the mix. Any others?"

"Nothing as good as that."

"Intersection. The Intersection. With or without the *The*?"

"I dunno. I like it both ways."

She leaned back against the closed door of the control room. "Now, you realize that if we call the band that, it means we have to have an actual intersection of genres, right? So we don't have to worry about labeling ourselves one thing to be marketable."

I mirrored her position against the live room door. "Sure. Fine. I will concede that, if—*if*—you concede that 'Brittney Sucks' is one of the genres that is intersecting the others."

Natalie sighed. "Fine. I can tell it's a song that some people will like. But it's got to have a better title than that."

"Sure."

"And it needs a strong bass line."

"Which you can provide."

"And it needs drums."

"Right. You've got a drummer?"

"I'm working on it."

"Good luck with that," I said. "Malarial devils, aren't they?"

The corners of Natalie's mouth twitched. "Who played drums for The Pleasure Centers? Maybe we can get them."

"Who *didn't* play drums with us. Let's see, there was Pete, Troy, Chad, Marcie."

"You had a girl drummer?"

"For one practice. Brittney made sure she didn't stick around."

Natalie crossed her arms. "She is a piece of work."

"Now you're getting on board."

"So, anybody you'd recommend?"

"I can make some calls," I said. "But no guarantees."

We were still standing there, a foot apart, and we'd just run out of things to say. I wished she could look into my eyes just then. Share a moment like in the movies. A lingering look where either the tension would break with a kiss or it would get put away for later escalation by someone breaking eye contact. But she'd never look me in the eye. Never give me any kind of signal that way. You can't break a connection that hasn't been made.

"So," I finally said. "You really don't want help with your lyrics? I'm not suggesting writing them for you. But maybe if we just did some brainstorming back and forth, it would break the dam."

She shrugged noncommittally. "We'll see. For now, though, let's work on refining the music for your stuff. And you still need to finish up that song about the girl with the guitar. Remember? You need another verse at least."

"Yeah. I haven't forgotten. I'm working on it." That was a lie. It was done. It had been for weeks. So we both had some things we weren't ready to share. "Will your dad be available tomorrow to help us record these two, though?"

"Maybe. But we still need a drummer. We need a drum line for the war song too."

"Doesn't your dad have anyone he could call in to lay down all the drum lines? It would only take a day. If that. They don't have to be complicated."

Natalie smiled. "There might be someone."

Despite a late night working in the studio Friday, I was up early on Saturday, ready to lay down some tracks. It would be better if a drummer was there to start with. The Pleasure Centers had tried to record the guitars first and add the drums later on several occasions, and it was always a disaster. But Natalie insisted adding the drums later would be fine as long as Dusty was in the mix. And I did want to capture the energy of the Brittney song before too much time passed and I forgot why I was so annoyed with her. I'd decided over Frosted Flakes and an episode of *Garfield and Friends* to call the song "Satan's a Hot Girl."

Outside I was surprised to see Mike's car in the driveway. It hadn't been there when I got home from the Wheelers' the night before, and I hadn't heard him come in afterward. I was even more surprised when I entered the Wheeler kitchen a moment later and saw him sitting at the counter beside Natalie, a large piece of paper spread out in front of them.

"I had a friend who's a landscape architect draw this up for me," she was saying, "but I'm going to need you to decide if it needs any changes before you begin. I mean, he's never actually seen the backyard. I described it to him best I could from my perspective, but it's not like I had any actual measurements."

Mike was listening to her but looking at me. "No problem, Pinky."

"Thanks, Mike." She leaned over and planted a kiss on his stubbled cheek. "You're a peach."

"What's this?" I said, inserting myself into their little moment.

"Oh, hey, Michael!" Natalie smiled. "Check it out. These are the initial plans for the koi pond Mike is going to build this spring. If the weather guys are right, it's supposed to be a mild one, so he should be able to get going on it in March. Can you believe they're predicting temps in the seventies next month?"

"Crazy," I said. "Can I take a look?"

Mike rolled his eyes and spun the paper around so I could see it. I didn't care what it looked like, and I certainly had no expertise to offer. I just wanted to be included in the conversation, in the project, in everything Natalie had anything to do with. And I definitely didn't mind if I annoyed Mike in the process.

"Looks nice. I didn't realize the river was right behind your house." I retrieved a mug and poured my coffee, watching for a reaction from Mike. But then I realized that if Natalie allowed him to call her Pinky, he undoubtedly had kitchen privileges too. He'd certainly been around longer than I had.

"It's a ways down the hill, actually," Natalie said, getting down off the stool. "You can hear it from the top deck, in the spring especially. Less so in the summer when the water level is lower. Pour me a cup too, would you?" She came around the counter and then turned back to Mike. "Mom should be out for breakfast soon if you want to wait."

Mike stood and rolled up the koi pond plans in his thick fingers. "Nah. I'll just get going and draw up a materials list for this project. Tell her I'll catch her later."

"Sure." She turned to me then. "Ready?"

"Yep."

I followed her out of the kitchen without a backward glance at Mike, balancing the mugs in my hands. There were no drinks other than water allowed in the studio, but Natalie and I had developed a Saturday morning ritual that started in the listening room, where we'd play the most amazing recordings we could think of—songs that shifted paradigms, songs that did things no one had ever thought of before, songs that inspired you to be bold and break molds.

It was Natalie's idea, her way of reminding me that the point wasn't to blend in with what was already popular but to be the next big thing, to do the unexpected. A lot of the songs we listened to on these mornings were not the singles that got radio play. They were the B-sides, the deep cuts, stuff only real fans would know about. Natalie knew about all of them. Most of the time, they were either only vaguely familiar or completely new to me. It was inspiring. But it was also intimidating.

However, on this particular morning we were listening to stuff like Queen, The Beatles, Michael Jackson, and Billy Joel, acts that were anything but obscure. Specifically, we were listening to songs with distinctive key changes, like "Bohemian Rhapsody," "Penny Lane," "Man in the Mirror," and "Uptown Girl."

As the third verse of Paul Simon's "Still Crazy After All These Years" played, Natalie moaned and sank down into the leather chair. "Oh, that, right there. That's what does it. That's what breaks your heart a little. And if it doesn't break your heart a little, why bother? That's why most of the songs on the radio right now don't grab me. So many of them are just background. They don't go anywhere. Don't make you feel any particular way. They're just there. Flat."

"I don't know," I said. "I think there's a lot of emotion and movement in a lot of rock songs."

"Maybe. Some of them. But they're always playing on people's baser instincts rather than trying to elevate."

"You think good music has to bring you up?"

"Not exactly. I mean, the blues are down."

"But," I said, happy to have something astute to say for once, "they elevate being down, don't they?"

She pointed a finger in my direction. "Yes. *Yes.* You're right. Of course they do."

"So does my song about Brittney elevate anything?"

She pursed her lips. "Hmm. It does have a lot of baser instincts in it."

"But doesn't it say something positive about friendship?"

"How so?"

"It's a guy telling his friend that he should dump her, that he deserves better. She's dragging him down, but if he'd just let go and let her sink, he'd shoot back up to the surface and his friend would pull him out of the swamp of misery she'd had him stuck in."

"I'm not sure that counts," she said. "Have you actually told Slow to dump her?"

"No."

"Why not?"

"I don't really have a dog in that fight. If he wants to deal with all that crazy just because she's hot, that's his business."

"Until she makes it your business by showing up at your house."

"Yeah, but that doesn't happen all that often."

Natalie was quiet a moment. "She's hot?"

I squirmed a little, the soft leather of the chair gripping my pants. "Well, yeah. In a certain trashy kind of way."

"What does that mean?"

Careful, Michael. "I dunno. She wears sexy clothes and lots of makeup, and she's always flirting with guys."

"That's what you find hot?"

I sighed. "It's a certain type of hot. There are lots of types of hot."

She turned in her chair to face me. "What type am I?"

I smiled. "Oh, I see where this is going. Fishing for compliments, are we?"

"No," she said, unable to completely snuff out the small grin that was trying to bloom on her lips.

"There has never been a more obvious fishing for a compliment in the entire history of mankind," I said.

The smile won out and spread over her whole face. "Okay, so?"

"You think I won't tell you?"

"I think you will."

I crossed my arms over my chest. "What makes you think I think you're hot anyway?"

"Oh, come on. I know people think my mother is gorgeous. I must have gotten at least some of her looks."

"You got more than some," I said. "But your hotness is about more than just looks."

Natalie raised her eyebrows expectantly. "So?"

I hesitated. One conversation could shift the key of a relationship as easy as one chord could shift the key of a song. "You realize once I tell you this, there's no going back?"

"What do you mean?"

"The minute you know what I really think of you, it's not going to be the same between us."

She laughed. "What? You think I'll fall madly in love with you or something?"

I let her question linger in the silent room. Her smile slowly melted away, replaced with a thoughtful look that in turn melted into concern.

She stood suddenly. "Put that record back, would you? Let's get to work."

Track Fourteen

I think I may have found a drummer," I said. "It's this guy who played a gig with us at a high school dance once. It was his high school. But he's graduated and all now."

It was the first Saturday in March, and Natalie and I were in the studio getting ready to record the guitar tracks for the song I'd written about her. It would be the last song we'd need for the demo, and I couldn't put it off any longer.

"He's not the best," I said, "but he is available."

"The best would be better," she said, "but I guess someone is better than no one. He can come next Saturday?"

"Pretty sure."

"Confirm it with him this week and let me know for sure. If we don't finish up by then, we'll have to wait until after Mike digs the koi pond. Even though the walls are soundproof, the heavy machinery will send vibrations through the ground and it'll impact the quality of the recordings."

"It is just a demo."

"It is just Saint Andrew's Hall."

"I thought your name got you in there."

"Yeah, and I don't want anything associated with my name

that's not as good as it can possibly be. There's a certain reputation to uphold."

We took turns in the live room playing our parts. I played rhythm guitar all the way through, metronome in my headphones, lips mouthing the words I still couldn't release. Natalie had been bugging me for days to do a recording of the whole song so she could hear the last verse. But I stretched out the revelation of the actual words as long as possible.

Natalie took my place in the live room, and I sat down at the controls that were becoming like extensions of my own fingers. She played through the bass line and the complicated lead guitar part, which served to demonstrate exactly what the lyrics were talking about. When I'd first written the song, I'd had her fingers running up and down a piano, thinking of the first time I'd seen her at the piano with Stevie Wonder and the complex classical piece I'd heard her play the first day we got together to work on songs. But I couldn't figure out what rhymed with *piano*, so I switched it to an old guitar. Her flawless picking made it seem like the lyric couldn't possibly have been anything else.

She finished the lead line, and then I was out of time.

"Okay, moment of truth," she said. "Get in here and sing this song. The *whole* song."

I took a deep breath and hit the PA button. "Okay, but I actually need you to sing the last chorus."

"Alone?"

"Yeah."

"Won't that be weird to have just my voice come in at the end? Or did you want me to do harmony throughout the whole thing?"

"No, no harmony on this one. It's mostly me, and then you have a few lines that are just you." At her continued look of perplexity, I said, "You wanted something unexpected."

She shrugged. "Okay. But it would have been nice to get the words a little earlier than the day we're recording so I could actually have practiced them. You'll have to sing the last part anyway so I can hear them."

"Right. I know."

Then there was nothing left but to do it. To take my place at the mic while Natalie took her place at the sound board. To lay bare the way I felt about her. The way I wished she felt about me.

We met in the anteroom, passed through the opposite doors, and took up our places.

"Playback," came Natalie's voice from the control room.

I stood at the mic, sweating. Listening for my cue in my headphones. Missing it.

She stopped the playback. "You ready?"

I cleared my throat. "Yeah." The playback started up again. I coughed, waited, missed my cue.

She stopped the playback again. "Need some water?"

"No, I'm good." I cleared my throat again, tried to wet my lips with a dry tongue.

"Ready?"

"Hey," I finally croaked out. "First of all, you're gorgeous." I had to do better than that. "Your eyes are hazel, almost green. Like soft moss in a cool forest. Your skin is like a smooth stone you'd find at the lakeshore. Your lips are like satiny pink flower petals on a rose that's just bloomed." I watched her through the glass, like looking at some lovely thing in a museum. "You're beautiful."

She reached a hand up to cover her mouth.

"But that's not all. You're the most talented person I've ever met. You can play anything. Any song on any instrument. And you never look like you're even trying that hard. You're confident and smart and always say exactly what you think about everything. And you don't care what anyone thinks. And I wish I was more like you. That's the kind of hot you are. The kind that would make anyone who ever met you fall in love with you." I cleared my throat again. "Okay, I'm ready now. Roll the playback."

There was a moment of silence. She sat in the booth, immobile. Then she pushed the button. The instrumental tracks started up in my headphones. I closed my eyes. I didn't miss my cue. I sang the whole thing, better than I ever had when practicing alone at home, in my room, in the shower, in the car on the way to work. I sang it all the way through, including the last secret verse and the last chorus that Natalie would have to sing.

> Now a lifetime's come and gone since I last saw her
> Even though it's barely been one day
> Can't catch my breath when I'm stuck under water
> And I just really need to hear her say:
>
> "I am coming to get you, to pull you from the sea
> And I will never let you slip away from me
> The moment that I met you, I knew my dreams had
>   come true
> So rest now, baby, you'll be safe with me."

When I finished, I looked into the booth to gauge her reaction, glad for the moment that she couldn't see me staring at her. Her brow was slightly furrowed, her mouth closed, not smiling, not frowning.

"So that last part, the last chorus, is you," I said. "And maybe that one line earlier when she says, 'Sometimes that's just the way it goes.'"

Finally, her finger moved to the PA button. "I think you're going to have to do the whole thing again."

The floor dropped a little, like a hitch in an elevator. "It didn't record?"

Then a grin broke out on her face. "I'm just screwing with you."

A wave of relief washed through my stomach, followed closely by a wave of anxiety as I waited for her reaction.

"I like it."

"You do?" I said, trying not to read anything into that simple statement.

She nodded. "It's good. It's . . . it's good."

"You'll want to listen to it a few times. To get your parts down."

"Definitely. To get my parts down."

"And you like the idea of you singing it?" I said, leading her a little. ·

"Yeah. I get it now. It works."

Was that it? It works?

"I'll just need some time with it before I'll be ready to record my part." She seemed like she was waiting for me to say something. But I'd already said everything. "Hey," she said finally, "thanks for what you said. Before the song."

"Uh, yeah. Sure. No problem."

Natalie took a deep breath. "Need a break? Or do you want to go right into the next song?"

I wiped my palms on my pants. "Uh, no. Let's keep going."

I grabbed the Strat and started tuning the strings as Natalie fiddled with dials and slides and switches. I wished I hadn't said a thing. Wished I hadn't written that song. Wished I hadn't fallen so hard so fast.

Track Fifteen

I got ahold of my drummer the following Tuesday, but since I'd talked to him last, he'd gotten a chance at a weekend gig he couldn't pass up. I wasn't really surprised he'd bailed. But that did put us in a precarious position. Natalie said she'd make some calls. Then on Wednesday night she told me she had found someone who could do it, but only if it was on Thursday, a day when I'd be working. I wasn't exactly thrilled about not being there, but I trusted her. And we had spent some time tapping out possible drum lines, so I did have a chance to give my input.

Anyway, Mike had gotten the go-ahead from Dusty to break ground on the koi pond on Saturday to take advantage of the warm spell. The snow had been gone for a couple weeks and the ground had thawed, and Mike had a small backhoe being delivered on Friday. So the weekday drum recording was just as well. Dusty had committed to helping mix and master the tracks on Saturday, then he'd drop the demo off to the right people at Saint Andrew's and 89X when he had a chance sometime later in the month. It was hard to believe that just over nine weeks ago, I didn't know that Natalie Wheeler existed, and now I was less than a couple weeks away from having a demo for a new band.

I got to the hardware store at eight o'clock Thursday morning to open at nine. The warm weather had wound everyone up, and there were already people lined up outside ten minutes before Mr. Harmon and I unlocked the door. The ambitious homeowners of West Arbor Hills were out in droves, buying grass seed, preemergent herbicides, vegetable seeds, potting mix, gardening gloves, chainsaws, tomato cages, wheelbarrows, and bags of sand, compost, and pea gravel. I mixed countless cans of paint, measured out plastic tubing, hauled patio umbrellas and bags of mulch to people's cars and trucks. I hadn't worked this hard in months, and I was glad I didn't have to play guitar tomorrow because there was no way I'd be able to move my arms.

Despite the constant customers, I watched the clock and wondered how things were going with the recording. I itched to give the Wheelers a call, but I knew Natalie and possibly Dusty would be in the studio and I didn't want to take the chance that I'd wake up Deb, who was sleeping more and more throughout the day.

When I finally got a break for lunch, I headed out the back and through the alley toward the 7-Eleven, where I got a Big Bite hot dog and a 20 oz. Mountain Dew. I downed the dog in three bites while walking back to the hardware store and slammed half the pop in one long series of gulps without coming up for air. I replaced the cap, let out a belch that turned my own stomach a little, and sat on a stack of empty pallets by the back door. The afternoon sun felt warm and novel on the top of my head. Even in a dirty alley, spring was a miracle.

I spun the cap back off my Mountain Dew, took another drink, and imagined the summer to come. I'd be kicking it off with a gig at Saint Andrew's Hall, and my natural inclination was to assume it would all be downhill from there. But for just a minute, sitting there, the sunlight pouring over me like warm honey, I let myself believe that this could be the year it all turned around. Maybe 1990 would live up to the hype. Maybe it *was* the dawn of a new era. Maybe there'd be a scout for some record company in the audience at Saint Andrew's who would whisk me and Natalie off to New York or LA or Nashville. Maybe we'd travel the country in a tour bus, sitting close in the very back, laughing and writing music. Maybe she'd eventually fall as much in love with me as I was with her.

I knew better. It was stupid to dream. To plan out a future that would never happen. But what else can you do when it's seventy degrees in March?

"There you are," came Mr. Harmon's voice from the door.

I snapped out of my trance and looked at my watch.

"You're not late," he said. "There's some people in here looking for you. I'll send them around back."

He shut the door. I finished off my Dew and waited for whoever it was, knowing it wouldn't be Natalie but still hoping just the same. I was disappointed when I saw Rodney and Slow come around the corner of the building at a lope.

"Michael," Rodney said with a smarmy smile, "guess I should have known to look for you in the alley, hanging with the rats." He laughed at his own bad joke.

I stood up. "Not 'til you got here. What brings you out to the suburbs?"

They stopped a few feet from me, Slow slightly behind Rodney as always, his constant shadow.

"Thought we'd check out how the other half lives."

"Oh?"

"Yeah." Rodney glanced around for dramatic effect. "Can't say I'm impressed."

"What do you want?" I said, tapping the empty pop bottle against my leg. "We've got plenty of lighter fluid in there if you want to put your couch out of its misery."

Slow started to laugh, then caught himself when Rodney gave him a look.

"Well, I just thought I'd give you a visit and let you know we're considering reinstating you."

I stood a little straighter. "Is that so. And why the sudden change of heart? I thought I needed to prove to you I was worthy or some such nonsense. Had to bring something to the table."

"It just so happens that I heard you did have something to contribute and you've been holding out on us."

I narrowed my eyes, pretty sure I knew where this was going. "And that is?"

Rodney took a step toward me, so Slow took one too. "What's this I hear about you getting all chummy with this Dusty Wheeler guy?"

I took a step back. "I'm not chummy with Dusty Wheeler."

"But you are with his daughter," Slow said.

"And just why would you think that?" I asked, even though I knew the answer.

"Brittney told us," Slow said.

"She's the girl you brought to the apartment a couple months ago, isn't she?" Rodney said. "The blind one."

"So?"

"You never said she was related to Dusty Wheeler."

"Why would I? And how would Brittney even know who Dusty Wheeler is?"

"Apparently he's married to some famous singer from the sixties," Slow said. "Brittney said she was talking to her last month. At their giant house."

"That so? Did she tell you why she was at the giant house of a music producer she'd never even heard of before?"

Slow's face hardened a little. "She took off Valentine's night and said they let her stay at their place."

"And did you bother to ask her how she ended up there?"

"Who cares?" Rodney said. "All this time you could have gotten a big-time producer to listen to The Pleasure Centers, maybe hook us up with a good promoter. And you don't tell us?"

"First of all, Dusty has heard some of your music, Rod. I played him something the first night I met him. He hated it. Called it 'derivative.'" Not exactly true, but close enough. "And you know why?"

Rodney looked at me blankly.

"Because you straight-up stole the hook from *Charles in Charge*. You've stolen all your hooks. I went home that night and played through the whole set list, and you know what I heard? The theme song to *Perfect Strangers* and *Family Ties* and *ALF* and every other show on prime time."

Rodney plastered a phony smile across his face. "That's crazy, man. You're out of your mind. I never copied any TV shows."

I just stared at him.

"I mean, maybe there are a few similarities, but there's only so many melodies out there."

"There are infinite melodies out there," I said. "You copied theme songs, passed them off as your own, and had us out there on stage ripping off bad TV, and then you wonder why the band isn't going anywhere. And all that time you pushed back anytime I wanted us to do one of my songs."

"Your songs suck," Rodney said. "And anyway, everyone steals a little from everyone else. Nothing's original. Half of new music right now is just sampling some other song that's already out there. It's expected."

"It's lazy. You're a hack and you know it."

Rodney stood a little straighter, trying to match my height and failing. "Watch it, man. We came out here to take you back, but I'm not sure I like your attitude."

I laughed. "I'm not sure I ever liked you, Rodney." I looked beyond him to his shadow. "Slow, you're all right. But you gotta dump that girl. You know the reason she was at the Wheelers' at all was because she showed up at my place completely plastered and ready to party, to get back at you for some dumb thing you probably didn't even know you did. I had to take her over there because she was dead set on cheating on you with me. She's a total—"

Before I could get the word out, Slow landed a punch on my left cheekbone. It was a solid hit, and for a moment I stood there, stunned. I'd never seen Slow angry, let alone angry enough to punch someone in the face.

"Stay away from her," Slow said.

I shook myself out of my stupor. "Stay away from her? You tell her to stay away from me, man. And you better as well, because that's the only free shot I'm giving you. Next time, we're in it." I opened the big metal door that would lead me back into the store, back to where I'd have to explain to my boss the bruise that would soon be forming under my left eye. "Don't bother kicking me out of the band again either. Because I quit."

Track Sixteen

Friday night Mike surprised me by going to bed early in his own house. The next morning, he was up at seven, scrambling eggs and burning toast and making such a ruckus it was impossible for me to sleep, so I wandered into the kitchenette and asked him to deal me in.

We sat on the couch, plates in hand, scarfing down his best effort at breakfast since I'd moved in, watching the morning news.

"You getting started on that hole today?" I said.

"Yep."

"Need any help?" I wasn't sure why I said it. My shoulders were still aching from my busy couple days at work, and if Mike was using the backhoe, anything I could do to help would have to be with a shovel.

"Nope. What happened to your face?"

The evidence of Slow's uncharacteristic flash of anger had bloomed into an ugly purple stain that was already turning a sickly yellow at the edges.

"I told Slow he should dump his terrible girlfriend."

Mike chuckled. "He didn't like that?"

"Guess not."

"Hit him back?"

"Nah. Gave him a freebie."

Mike shook his head. "Shoulda hit him."

"If it was Rodney, I would have."

Mike got up from the couch, dumped his plate in the sink, and filled a travel mug with black coffee. He pulled on his steel-toed boots and grabbed the hard hat from the hook by the door. Then he was gone without so much as a backward glance.

I cleaned up the breakfast mess, watched some TV, and tried to resist Natalie's gravitational pull. I knew she was there, just across the street. But I also knew she had decided to spend the morning with her mom and her aunt, going through old jewelry and home videos and photos. I wondered how Natalie would experience them. Touch, sound, story.

Still, I could see if Dusty was working on the mix for the demo. I hadn't heard the drum tracks yet. Surely that would be excuse enough. I'd just go around back through the billiards room so I wouldn't disturb the ladies upstairs.

I took a shower, threw on some jeans and a T-shirt, and walked across the dry street and up the driveway. The mini backhoe had made two trails in the soft ground where Mike had driven it through the slalom run of trees around the back of the house. I followed it, leaving a set of my own shallow footprints between the tracks. I trotted across the stone patio and slid into the billiards room when Mike's back was to me as he outlined the position of the pond in sand.

It suddenly struck me as funny that Mike always locked his bedroom door to protect his rather worthless stuff, while across the street a house full of expensive instruments, stereo equipment, and priceless memorabilia was nearly always wide open, ready for pillaging. The lights were all off, the room empty, every bottle at the bar perfectly aligned, every pool cue standing at attention. Nothing slouched. Nothing sagged. Nothing screamed *failure*.

Dusty was a winner. What was the difference between him and Mike? Him and me? He hadn't started as anyone important. His parents weren't anybody special. We'd even gone to the same high school. But somehow he had created a reality for himself and his family that included a comfortable level of fame and fortune and had gathered a cadre of what seemed like genuine friends.

I fished the eight ball from the bowels of the pool table and rolled it gently down the green felt plane. Dusty had said that obstacles could be helpful. What obstacles had he faced? How did they compare to Mike's obstacles of gambling, womanizing, and probable alcoholism? To my obstacles of fatherlessness, bad luck, and aggressive mediocrity? What had Dusty had to overcome? Or was that just something he'd said to sound wise and take the measure of me?

I slipped into the dark, narrow hall and into the studio. Through the little window on the control room door I could see Dusty sat at the sound board, a giant pair of headphones covering his ears, his fingers slowly twisting one knob and then another. I knocked on the glass, but he didn't hear me. Waved. Didn't see me. I twisted the handle as quietly as possible and opened the door. He looked up then and beckoned me the rest of the way in with two fingers. When I didn't sit down, he pushed the second chair in my direction and handed me the other set of headphones.

A rough mix of "Satan's a Hot Girl" was coming through the speakers. It sounded good. Sharp, taut, with a driving force. Everything you wanted in a rock song about dumping a girl. Or at least, wanting your friend to dump a girl. And the drums were a huge part of it. It wasn't exactly what I'd heard in my head. It was better. Way better.

When the song ended, Dusty started it up again, tinkering

a little more with the mix, raising his eyebrows at me to solicit my opinion, and then seemed to notice my black eye. I gave him a thumbs-up and a nod. We listened to it the rest of the way through and removed our headphones.

"Nice," I said. "It sounds great. Who was the drummer?"

"Not sure," Dusty said. "Natalie took care of that. He's no slouch, though. Made it easy on me." He sat back in his chair, which creaked softly. "I didn't expect to see you today."

"Yeah, I didn't expect to be here. I know Natalie's busy. But do you mind if I sit in down here? Just kind of watch how it's done?"

"Be my guest."

"Which songs have you done so far?"

"That's the first." He motioned to my face.

"I may have upset someone," I said.

He let out a snort. "Looks like it. Last time I had a shiner like that, your uncle was the one who gave it to me."

I sat straighter. "Mike punched you?"

"Yeah. He was drunk at the time—of course—but he still landed it. You know he boxed for a while there. That's what got him into betting." He shook his head and looked lost in a memory for a moment.

"What was the fight about?"

He rolled his eyes a little. "What was it always about? Deb. I took and threw a lot of punches over her. It's not easy to have caught the eye of a woman like Deb. Makes you a little crazy, thinking you're always just one step away from losing your grip on her." He sighed and turned back to the board.

"You hit him back?"

Dusty smiled. "I hit 'em all back. Every single one of them."

It was lunchtime before Dusty and I surfaced from the studio. He showed me all the little secrets of the mixing board, had me rerecord a guitar track he thought was too sloppy, asked for my opinion and seemed to take it seriously. I'd never sat that long with an older guy, never felt the give-and-take of the creative process with anyone who'd had that much experience. With anyone at all, actually. Except Natalie. With Rodney there'd never been any sense of collaboration.

When I'd been kicked out of the band and the apartment and had to move in with Mike, I'd felt like I was just a few steps away from hitting bottom. But maybe it was more like a ledge interrupting my fall, giving me a chance to catch my breath and find some handholds I could use to reach the surface. The kind of obstacle that was actually useful.

Lunch was tomato soup and grilled cheese sandwiches, and I brought mine and Mike's outside and let the Wheeler family eat alone together. Mike had already cleared the shallowest level of the pond, a one-foot drop into the black earth, and was nearly done with the second level, which added two more feet of depth.

"It'll be eight feet at the deepest point," he said around his food. "So the fish will survive the winter."

"Eight feet?" I thought of Deb's concern about Natalie drowning.

"I thought that was a little excessive—normally they're not more than six feet—but that's what Natalie wanted." He shrugged. "I dunno. Maybe she doesn't want to think of anything being six feet deep."

The grim statement hung there a moment, settled down on us. I stopped eating. Dusty was going to lose his grip on Deb anyway, no matter how many punches he'd taken or delivered. How long would it be? I never brought it up with Natalie, even if I did wonder how much time the doctors had given her mother.

"You ever have a thing for Deb?" I asked.

Mike shrugged. "Sure. Don't know a guy who didn't back in the day. The whole crew was in love with her. She'd come by the work site once a week to just sort of wander around through the rooms as they went from frames to drywall to flooring, paint, and appliances. You practically never wanted a day off because you might miss her." He took a bite of his sandwich. "She always brought us something. Cookies, brownies, pop, lemonade." He sighed heavily.

I swallowed a mouthful of Vernors. "What happened with Dusty?"

"What do you mean?"

"There was a fight of some sort?"

He winced a little. "Oh, that." He fixed his eyes on a point in the trees that lined the river down the slope. "I guess I thought she and I had something special. Some kind of extra level of friendship she didn't have with the rest of the crew." He looked at his hands. "It was stupid. She was just a nice person is all. To everyone."

"But how'd you end up giving Dusty a black eye?"

He shook his head, which I took to mean he wasn't going to tell me, that this conversation—one of the longest and most cordial ones we'd had—was over. Then he turned and caught my eye. "Listen, kid. Don't start drinking, all right? Everything I've ever done or said that I regret was something I did or said when I was down a bottle." He finished off his sandwich in one final, massive bite, then stood up and got back to work.

The afternoon crept along, track by track down in the basement, scoop by scoop out in the muddy backyard, and, I assume, artifact by artifact in the room that Deb would likely die in. Each of us chipping away at something. Time chipping away at time left.

I thought it might be awkward to edit the songs I'd written about Deb and Natalie with their husband and father, but the more time I spent in the studio, the more it felt like I was working on someone else's songs, someone else's feelings. With each successive track I thought I felt Dusty's opinion of me go up just a little bit. Maybe these weren't all B-sides. They didn't really feel like singles either, though. And I had absolutely no idea how the typical crowd at Saint Andrew's Hall might react to them.

"It's eclectic," Dusty said when I shared my concern. "But that's not necessarily bad. It's a good test. You'll see which ones the audience connects with, and that helps you refine your sound the next time out."

"I guess that makes sense. But I'd still rather have everything perfect before getting on that kind of stage."

He nodded. "She's rushing it. For Deb's sake. I don't really have the heart to tell her that her mother is probably never leaving this house again."

There was a knock on the studio door. Mike was on the other side of it, deep furrows between his eyebrows. Dusty waved him in.

"Sorry, but I think you need to come see this."

We followed him out to the back through the billiard room, where he'd left his boots on the mat outside the sliding door. He slipped them on and led us to the edge of the hole, then jumped down to the deepest level he'd dug. It didn't look like eight feet yet.

"I can't dig anymore until we deal with this." He motioned to an area near his feet and ran some water from the hose on it. Strange shapes began to emerge from the mud.

"What is it?" I said. "A drainpipe?"

"Nope. Mastodon, most likely," Mike said. "That's the only big fossil you ever find around here."

Dusty frowned. "Better call the university." He shook his head. "But not now. It'll be a circus over here. Deb doesn't need that."

"If you get it out of there, you could sell it," Mike said. "I could see if I could find anyone who'd be interested in buying it. I know—"

Dusty stopped him with a pointed look. "Let's just keep it quiet for now. Mike?"

His face fell. "Of course."

"Michael?"

"Yeah. Of course."

"Better go break the news to Natalie," he said.

I stood there a moment before I realized he was telling me to do it. I walked back to the house, took off my mud-caked boots, and padded up the stairs. The women were back in the master bedroom, the door open a crack. I stood there listening to Natalie and Ruth laughing and waited to hear Deb's laugh join theirs. But all she could manage was some muffled coughing. I knocked lightly on the door, and Ruth answered it.

"Uh, can I speak to Natalie for a second?"

She opened the door wide so I could see where Natalie sat on the bed. I wasn't sure if I should ask to speak to her in private, if Dusty meant for me to tell just her. But the others would find out soon enough anyway.

"Mike's found a fossil of some kind in the backyard where he's digging the pond."

"A fossil?" Ruth said. "Like a Petoskey stone?"

"Um, a bit bigger. Maybe a mastodon."

Natalie shot up from the bed. "What?"

Ruth went out the sliding glass door to the upper deck and leaned over the rail to have a look. Deb stayed where she was, propped up by a tower of pillows, but leaned slightly toward the wall of windows.

"So what does that mean?" Natalie said. "Do they have to call someone to dig it all out of there?"

"I think so. Your dad said something about calling U of M. But probably not right now. Too much attention with things like this," I said with feigned authority.

Ruth reentered the room. "Should have left well enough alone."

"But what about the pond?" Natalie said.

"It looks like it'll just have to wait," Ruth said.

Natalie looked unhappy about that. She started for the door and nearly knocked me over as she said, "We'll see."

I followed her out of the house and into the backyard, where she slowed her pace considerably. I reached out to grab her arm, but she pulled away.

"It's fine," she said.

"Well, there's a giant hole now where there wasn't one before, so you may want to reconsider accepting my help."

"Oh, yeah." She stopped and jutted out her arm.

At the edge of the hole, Dusty and Mike told her basically the same thing I had.

"I don't see why you can't just call someone to get it out," she said.

"Your mother doesn't need a bunch of strangers digging up a skeleton right now," Dusty said. "She needs peace and quiet so she can rest."

"But can't Mike get it out?"

"That thing's been there thousands of years," Dusty said. "It'll keep a bit longer."

"But when will the pond get done? If you're waiting until she dies to get the bones out, that means she'll never see the pond. That's the whole point of it—that she sees it. It's her Mother's Day present."

Dusty put a hand on her shoulder. "It might have to be something else."

Natalie looked like she was going to either snap or cry. Or both. She did an about-face and tripped over a pile of dirt. I caught her from behind and held both of her arms firmly, trying not to step on her heels as she continued to stomp away. We struggled up to the patio, and then she shook me loose and made a beeline for the listening room, where she closed and locked the door before I had a chance to sneak in behind her. The little label above the doorknob said OCCUPIED in lurid red.

I knocked on the door and said her name even though I knew she wouldn't hear it through the soundproof walls. I pounded harder, thinking she of all people must be able to hear *something*. "Natalie!" But the door remained shut.

I became aware of Dusty standing just down the hall. "Let's call it a day," he said. He squeezed past me and went through the family room and up the stairs.

A moment later Mike was in the hall behind me. "Well, that's some bad luck, isn't it?"

And just like that, whatever sympathy I'd begun to feel for my uncle in light of his uncharacteristically candid lunchtime revelations and warnings about alcohol evaporated. Mike thought this was my fault. Me and my bad luck. It wasn't that he was so distracted by the sexy homeowner that he happened to build her house on top of some Ice Age butcher shop.

"I guess your days suddenly freed up," I snapped. "You can get back to watching TV and growing that beer gut."

He smiled. "Come on now, kid. Don't be like that."

"Like what?"

"You're still acting like an angry ten-year-old. And here I thought you were growing up."

"What's that supposed to mean?"

"I dunno. I thought we were bonding for a minute there outside. And I figured when you agreed to Steve doing the drum tracks for your little project with Natalie that—"

"What?"

"I just thought that showed a lot of maturity. I guess maybe I was wrong."

I felt my jaw clench. "Steve who?"

"Who do you think? Your dad. He's the one who came in to do the drums."

I looked at the door Natalie had shut in my face. I still wanted it to open, but not so I could console her. I wanted that door to open so I could tell her exactly what I thought about her calling up my no-good loser dad behind my back and telling him he could play drums on our songs. Then I had a realization and turned to Mike.

"And just how did she get his number?"

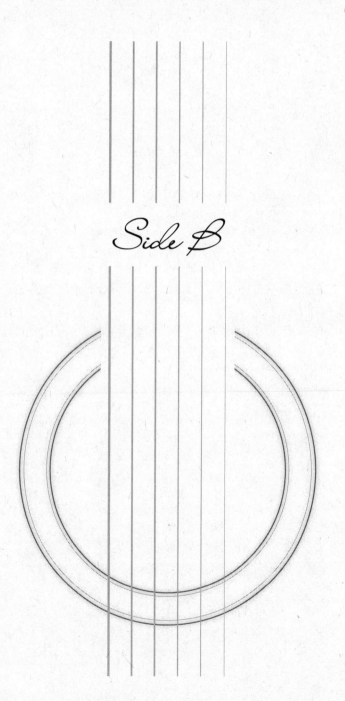

Side B

Track One

The unseasonably warm weather couldn't last forever. After a few days in the seventies, the skies turned gray, the wind turned cold, and the temps dipped back into the thirties and forties. I turned cold as well, but I was trying hard not to direct too much of that iciness toward Natalie. I decided that the mature thing to do would be to pretend I didn't know that the drums on the demo had been played by a man who'd abandoned me before I was even born. Natalie had enough going on in her life. She didn't need me to pile on. There'd be a moment for a reckoning, but this wasn't it. Can kicked.

Anyway, I didn't want to be mad at her. There were so few people in my life I wasn't mad at. It had felt really good the past few months to be on someone's side and know they were on mine. That was why the whole thing sucked so bad. I'd kind of felt like Natalie and I were slowly unearthing something really good, and now, just like with the pond in the backyard, something had stalled our progress. Some old skeleton I thought I'd buried long ago.

Mike, on the other hand, was right there in front of me with nothing better to do than bear the brunt of my anger. Which would have been more satisfying if there had been any indication that it bothered him. He didn't notice the silent treatment because he was never the one to start a conversation anyway. My passive-aggressive slamming of doors and drawers, little comments under my breath, ever-so-slightly shoulder-checking him when we crossed paths—none of it elicited so much as a glance in my direction.

Maybe he thought he'd already said everything that needed to be said when we left the Wheelers' the day the mastodon emerged. I'd covered a lot of ground on that long walk down the driveway and across the street. Most of it I don't remember since I was as close to a blind rage as I've probably ever been. I wanted to hit him, but I already had a black eye, he had at least seventy pounds on me, and Dusty's comment about how he'd been a boxer—how had I never known?—kept running through my head. And then it was over. He told me to cool off, then shut his bedroom door in my face. It didn't lock anymore—not since the crowbar—but it didn't matter. We both knew I wasn't going to open it.

The next day he was gone. I'd thought of a lot of other things to say to him, but I couldn't get a fight going without an opponent. With no outlet, my anger began to poison me. I could feel myself entering a twilight state. I went through the motions at work, sleepwalked through practices with Natalie, went to bed earlier, started thinking again how it would be so easy to just get in the car and leave it all behind—start over somewhere no one knew me, somewhere I'd never cross paths with my deadbeat dad or my loser uncle. With my luck the car would break down before I could even cross the state line.

Natalie had too much of her own stuff going on to have the energy for mine, so I kept it bottled up. When we had to speak, we did. When we didn't, we didn't. We focused on the work in front of us rather than the person in front of us. I waited for her to ask me what was wrong, and she waited for me to ask her what was wrong, and nothing was said about any of it.

Until one day, not long after Gorbachev was elected president of the Soviet congress, I came down to the studio to find her sitting at the piano with her elbows on the keys and her face buried in her hands. She straightened up as soon as she heard the doorknob turn, as though she was just about to begin playing and I'd interrupted her.

"What's going on?"

"Nothing," she said, all business.

I came around to where I could see her face. "You've been crying."

"No I haven't."

"Your eyes are red and your skin is all blotchy. You've obviously been crying."

She took a deep breath, let it out, took another. A crack formed in her mask, disappeared. A placid expression spread over her face, and the cathartic potential of the moment slipped soundlessly away.

"I was just trying to work out some lyrics in my head is all," she said, "and then you walked in and I lost them."

I could play along. "What song?"

"The one I played the first night we were down here in the studio. Do you remember it?"

Did I remember it? The melody hadn't stopped running through my head since that night. "Do you have any lyrics down yet?"

She sighed. "No. Nothing I like anyway."

"What's it about?"

"It's . . ." She hesitated. "I want to write something for my mom." Her voice broke a little on the last word, but she reined in her emotions immediately. "I want to write her something that encapsulates what she means to me, something that . . . but I'm just stuck."

I waited for her to continue, not wanting to step in too soon. She played a few quiet notes of the haunting melody she'd played on the night I met her almost three months before.

"I just can't seem to get it right. It's like, I want to write a happy song because all of my life that's what she's meant to me. She's always made me nothing but happy, and I think she'd say the same about me." She ran the closely clipped fingernails of her left hand across her right palm. "But everything I write comes out sad because . . ." She trailed off.

"Because that's what you are," I supplied.

She nodded. "All the time. Yeah."

Yeah. And here I was waiting for an apology for some petty thing that didn't really matter in the scheme of things. Or at least not on the same level.

I sat down beside her on the piano bench. "Then maybe that's the song you have to write right now. I mean, anything less than bittersweet just wouldn't be honest, right? Pretending you're not sad doesn't actually make things any less sad. And she's probably feeling the exact same way."

Natalie released a shuddering sigh but still kept it together. "She's not sad. She's looking forward to it. She says she's ready, she wants to go to heaven and see Jesus face-to-face. She keeps talking about how once she's there, she'll have no more pain, she'll get her voice back, be able to sing without pride and ego getting in the way of it. And she keeps saying that when I meet her there someday, I'll be able to see her the way she's always seen me."

I wanted to put a hand on her shoulder, but some invisible barrier stopped me. Like I'd run into one of the many walls of windows in the Wheeler house. And I realized just how much had been broken between us when she'd broken my trust. My anger was still there, even as I tried to weigh it against her sadness. It was still real, still raw.

"I don't want to see her there," Natalie continued. "I just want her to stay here."

I nodded pointlessly as the pit that had been in my stomach for days deepened. I wanted so badly to care about her pain as much as I knew I should. But all I felt was resentment. Why was I being asked to carry any of her emotional baggage when she wasn't even thinking about mine, didn't even notice I had any?

She stood abruptly, retrieved the Stratocaster, and held it out to me. "What have you got for me today?"

I took the guitar from her. "Nothing." I crossed the room and put it back on its stand. "I got nothing in me today."

She slumped back on the piano bench, and my petulant, childish thoughts of the last few moments slapped me in the face. What kind of friend was I anyway? I had to get control of this before it poisoned everything.

Before I quite knew what I was doing, I said, "Let's get out of here for a while."

"And go where?"

Good question. I glanced at the control room. "Did your dad take the demo down to Saint Andrew's yet?"

"No. But I don't think he can do it today."

"So what? You and me can do it today."

"You and I."

"Whatever. Let's go." I popped into the control room. On top of a stack of three cassettes was a Post-it note declaring "Pinky's demo—need band name." I slipped a cassette from the stack, pulled out the paper insert, and wrote in blue pen along the spine "The Intersection—DEMO." Then I crossed out "The," wrote out our names and the Wheelers' phone number on the front, and slid everything back into place in the case.

In the live room, Natalie was still seated at the piano bench.

"Go get your coat and meet me out front in ten minutes," I said.

I waited for her to stand, then followed her out of the recording studio and up the stairs, leaving her in the hall outside her bedroom.

"Ten minutes," I repeated as I headed out the door.

The drive to Saint Andrew's Hall took over an hour. The early spring had prompted a surge of road repairs. Orange barrels popped up like rows of tulips. Traffic lanes disappeared and reappeared for no apparent reason. Cops lurked on entrance ramps, following cars with their radar guns. I couldn't afford a ticket or the hike in insurance that would follow, so I took it slow and tried to ignore the silence coming from the passenger seat.

What was she thinking about? Her mom? The band? The gig? Was there any room in there for me? I tried to push back against the waves of negativity that kept crashing against my brain. Stop thinking about it. Stop dwelling on it. It'll keep. It's not the time.

I eased onto the exit ramp past Annunciation Greek Orthodox Cathedral, which seemed like it had been under construction for most of my life. I turned right onto East Congress Street, just made the green light at Beaubien, and parked illegally in the lot across the street from Saint Andrew's Hall. The towers of the Renaissance Center glittered in the sun as the clouds moved off across the river to hang out in Canada for a while. I got out of the car and patted my pocket to hear the reassuring plastic rattle of the cassette. Encoded onto its thin magnetic ribbon were our songs. Not Rodney's. Or NBC's. Ours. My lyrics. Her music. Our best efforts of the past few months.

It should have been one of those pure moments of life, when you feel nothing but pride, hope, achievement. Love. But no matter how much I wanted it to be, it wasn't. It was tainted. Because woven into everything Natalie and I had created together, everything we had shared, was a constant reminder of her duplicity. Every beat of every song bore witness to her dismissal of my feelings, her disregard for my desires. It was deceit, plain and simple.

I touched her elbow long enough to guide her across the street and up the steps, then dropped it, rubbing my fingers together as though I'd touched something greasy. A stab of pain shot through my chest as I thought of how perfect it had felt when she hooked her fingers through my belt loop at Lips, how badly I'd wanted her to touch my hair as we sat in the car outside the Thrash Factory. Then we'd seen my dad there. Was that the moment everything turned? Had she already decided then that she was going to quietly entice this man into the middle of our music? This stranger I happened to look like?

Inside, the foyer was dark except for the dusty light streaming in through the front windows, cutting its way to the floor. We went through the double doors into the concert hall, the ripping Velcro sound of our footsteps on the sticky hardwood echoing in the empty room. Natalie stopped in the vast open space and reached out for me. I took a half step away and put my hands in my pockets.

So this was what this place looked like during the day. Like a church—minus the pews and plus the long bar on the right-hand side where, on busy nights, at least five bartenders never stopped moving.

"Where to?" I asked.

"How should I know?"

"What do you mean, how should you know? You know these people, right? I mean, I've been here before, but I never got farther off the main floor than the disgusting little bathroom. Where do we go? Who should we talk to?"

She shrugged dramatically. "Why would you assume I know that? I told you it's my dad who knows people here."

"You know someone everywhere."

She laughed. "Yeah, I know bouncers and DJs. Not club owners. I tried to tell you—"

"You tried to tell me." I took a few short, sticky steps into the room and then back. The roiling waters in my head were reaching flood stage, and the levees were not going to hold. "Great. I just drove an hour to deliver a demo tape to no one for a band that doesn't exist so we can book a show we won't be ready for and that nobody will probably come to anyway."

"What's your problem, Michael?" Natalie said.

"My problem?"

"Yes, your problem. Why are you angry at me? You've been so weird lately."

"No I haven't."

"You have. You've been cold and distant and weird. I don't know what you expect from me, but—"

"What I expect from you?" I realized I was practically shouting and lowered my voice a little. "I guess I just expected that you knew how to do this sort of thing, that's all."

"No, it's more than that," she said, crossing her arms over her chest.

I didn't say anything. I thought I'd kept it all pretty well bottled up. I'd been even-keeled, spoken in even tones, never brought it up. I even had the advantage of her not being able to see my facial expressions, which otherwise might have given me away a time or two.

"Look," she said, "it was your idea to drive out here today. I told you my dad was busy. I never said I knew the owner. You're making these huge assumptions, where if you'd just listened to me—"

"Oh, yeah, that's rich." If I wasn't fooling her like I thought I was, I might as well just unleash it, right? Let that beast out of its cage. "I don't listen to you? I don't listen to you? I can't believe you have the gall to say that to me. To my face."

Natalie threw her hands up in the air. "What is going on with you?"

"Nothing! Nothing is going on with me. Not with you." I came up to within a few inches of her face. "I thought we had a partnership here."

"We do," she said. "At least, I thought we did until you started flipping out on me out of nowhere."

I laughed. "This is not out of nowhere, and you know it's not."

"Well, would you mind explaining it to me, just a little, so I know what in the world you're talking about? Because, if you haven't noticed, I'm having a little trouble following you."

"No you're not. What could I possibly be this angry about, huh? When was the last time you've known me to be this angry?"

She didn't answer, but I could see it in her face. I could see her knowing it, could see her starting to work on an excuse, something to soften what she did—what she'd done knowing she shouldn't do it. But there was nothing. No explanation that she could come up with that would maintain her innocence in the whole thing. The evidence was there. If she hadn't known I'd have a problem with it, she would have just made the suggestion. She'd have said, "What about asking your dad to play drums for us?" She hadn't asked because she'd already known the answer.

"Well?" I demanded.

"Excuse me, can I help you two?"

The voice came from behind me. I turned to see a frowning man in jeans and a sport coat crossing the room toward us. I waited for him to recognize Natalie, for her to charm him and facilitate the smooth transition of the demo tape from my pocket to his hand. But she said nothing. Just stood there, jaw set, unmoving.

"Hi," I said, holding out my hand. He shook it. "I'm Michael and this is Natalie . . . Wheeler . . . and we're dropping off a demo?" I pulled the tape from my pocket. "Um, Natalie is . . . do you know Dusty Wheeler?"

The man was still frowning. "Of course."

"Yeah, well, Natalie's his daughter and—"

"Oh, for crying out loud," Natalie said. "Just give the man the tape and let's get out of here."

I held the tape out, and after an awkward moment, the man took it.

"I'll have Dusty give you a call to sort this all out," Natalie said.

He tapped the tape against his thigh. "No need. I've already spoken to him about this. I thought he'd be coming down with it."

"So did I," Natalie said emphatically, then she spun on her heels and started toward the door with her hands out in front of her.

"Sorry," I said to the man as I hurried after her. "Thanks for listening to it."

I grabbed Natalie's arm and rushed her through the double doors into the foyer and then out into the blinding sunlight.

"What the heck was that?" I said. "Why didn't you say something?"

"You were doing such a good job in there I didn't want to overstep my bounds, because clearly you've been doing this sort of thing a long time and you know what's best. I'm sure you thoroughly impressed that guy and there will be a message for us when we get home begging us to fill a regular slot in Saint Andrew's schedule."

"Don't try to turn this around on me." I guided her down the steps and across the road. "You were just being petty in there because you can't face up to the fact that you went behind my back and asked my dad to do drums on the demo."

She fumbled for the car door handle, found it. "I didn't go behind your back."

I opened my own door. "You knew I'd have a problem with it, which is why you didn't say anything to me about it."

We both plopped onto the seats and shut the doors.

"We ran out of time and we needed a drummer," she said.

"Time? We'd have nothing but time if you weren't trying to rush this whole thing so your mom can see it before she dies. But she's not going to see it. You think she's leaving your house ever again? She barely even leaves her bedroom. She's going to die there, and soon, and you know it."

There was a moment of silence, a moment when I tried to reel the cruel words back into my mouth. But it was too late. They were out there. Forever.

After a second or two of shocked silence, Natalie whispered, "Go home, Michael." She got out of the car and started shuffling across the parking lot toward the road.

"Natalie, wait!" I tore after her and grabbed her arm. "Wait."

She wrenched it away. "Go home."

"What, am I supposed to leave you here? In some random parking lot in downtown Detroit?"

"I'm going back in there, and I'm using their phone to call my aunt."

I drew my hand roughly over my face. "I shouldn't have said that. But if you'd just stop being so stubborn about it, you'd see that—"

"You know why I called your dad, Michael?" she said, spinning on me. "Because you still have time to fix your relationship with him. But someday you won't. Someday he'll really be gone—for good—and what are you going to do with all your anger and bitterness then? Huh? Just going to swallow it all down into your gut and let it eat away at you for the rest of your life? Try to drink it away like your uncle? Is that how you want to end up? Sad and alone and beholden to the pity and charity of others?"

I stuck a finger in her face, not thinking about the fact that she couldn't see it. "Here's your problem, Natalie. You and your sanctimonious mom. You think just because someone makes decisions you wouldn't make that they need someone who 'knows better' than they do to fix their life for them. You think you can fix everyone else's problems. And maybe they're not even problems. Maybe they're just not things *you* would do. Maybe you should focus more on your own business and stay out of mine."

"What do you think I think about all day every day? You?"

She waited a moment, leaving room for me to answer. Leaving time for me to admit that yes, that was what I wanted her to be thinking about. Not her dying mother. Me. I didn't say anything, and that was answer enough.

"Wow. That's some ego you've got." She was yelling now.

"My mother is disappearing a little more every single day! And you're mad because your dad's a good drummer who, by the way, only said he'd do it if I didn't tell you it was him because—guess what—he's just as scared of facing you as you are of facing him."

I rolled my eyes. "My dad's a coward, all right, but he's not afraid of me. To be afraid of me he'd have to care about me, at least a little, and I can assure you he does not. He just didn't want to grow up and take responsibility for his actions twenty-two years ago." I took a step toward her. "We're going home. I'm taking you home, one way or another."

She pulled back. "What is that supposed to mean?"

I let out a curse. "Just get in the car. Now."

For a moment she looked like she was about to turn and walk away. Then she said, "Whatever," and shoulder-checked me—hard—on the way back to my car.

When she was buckled in, I started it up, turned out of the parking lot, and got on the highway. She leaned away, facing the window, staying as far from me as possible the entire silent ride. Just another person in my life who wanted nothing to do with me. Only this time, I couldn't totally blame her. I couldn't believe I'd said those things about Deb. About a woman who had been nothing but kind and generous to me.

But what really concerned me was just how irate I still felt. My anger bubbled just below the surface, a sick, boiling swill. I didn't want to feel this way. Not about Natalie. Not about anybody, but especially not about Natalie. I had to get home and get her out of the car before I made things even worse.

When I finally stopped in her driveway, she did not get out and rush for the house as I'd hoped.

"We're here," I said.

"You're not coming in?"

I couldn't hide the utter surprise in my voice. "You want me to come in?"

She was silent for a beat. "I thought maybe we could listen to some records," she said, opening the door to reconciliation just a crack.

One of the thousand knots in my stomach loosened a little bit. The rolling boil settled into a simmer. For just a second, I thought maybe I'd take her up on the offer. It was hard to take the first step back to being okay after a fight with someone.

Still, I did not turn off the car. Because what was this, really? This wasn't contrition. This wasn't even an admission of guilt. This was her wanting to make amends without making an apology.

I reached across her body and unlocked her door for her. "No, I don't think we can listen to some records right now."

She sat there a moment, maybe trying to get up the stones to say it. To say, "I'm sorry." Then she got out of the car without another word.

Track Two

It would have been easier if I'd said yes. If I'd parked the car and killed the engine and followed Natalie downstairs to the listening room. It would have made that night easier. It would have made the next day easier. In fact, it would have made everything that followed easier. Just pretend nothing had happened, that she didn't go behind my back, that I hadn't thrown the fact that her mother was going to die in her face, that we hadn't been shouting at each other in public.

Easy. I pretended things were fine all the time. It was the only way I knew to get by in a world where things never actually were.

The problem was, nothing ever got better. Sometimes it didn't get worse. But only sometimes. And it was never really fixed. I pretended to be satisfied with The Pleasure Centers. I pretended not to care about my mom's string of unrelentingly awful boyfriends. I pretended my dad leaving us was inconsequential and that we were better off without him. But none of it was true.

I couldn't just act like nothing had happened. Natalie and I had both said things we regretted—at least, I hoped she regretted her words as much as I regretted mine. But those things were true. As much as she wanted to believe otherwise, her mother wasn't going to see the show. And as much as it killed me to admit it, it was probably time to grow up a little and talk to my father. At some point. Maybe.

As March turned to April and the first bright green haze formed along the branches of the trees around the trailer, I continued to go to the Wheeler house a few nights each week to practice, to get things sounding tighter, more professional. But I bowed out of dinner most evenings. I didn't want to have to make conversation. Didn't want to see Deb getting thinner and slower. Didn't want to see the heartache on Dusty's face anytime he looked at his wife moving the food around on her plate across the table. Didn't want to pretend things were fine with Natalie.

Staying home more had its benefits. I figured out how to cook some meals on my own. I spent more time songwriting. I got more sleep. I even caught a couple of our songs on 89X, though I turned them off when I remembered who was hitting the drumheads.

Most of all I was able to keep tabs on Mike, who'd disappeared for a couple weeks the day after the mastodon skeleton had stalled his work on the koi pond. He showed up again on a Thursday, looking bedraggled and a bit stunned, as though he'd just woken up from hibernation. He reeked of booze and there were bloodstains on his shirt. I asked him where he'd been and what had happened. He answered with a coughing fit, then shut himself in his room.

For days now he'd been in there, sleeping mostly, though occasionally I'd hear him on the phone and look around the corner to see the phone cord stretched to its limit, bisecting the hall and disappearing through the space between the door and the splintered molding. He came out to use the toilet but not to shower. I left food for him on the floor outside his door—spaghetti, grilled cheese, nachos. He never returned the plates, so I had to start using paper ones.

It wasn't too long before the smell of old sweat and crusted-over dishes and basic rot started to seep out into the hall, and I finally had to open the door despite the fact that he'd ignored me every time I knocked. The curtains were closed, the room dark, the air heavy and stale. The sound of a fly buzzing somewhere in a corner mixed with the static from the old silver transistor radio Mike used to take to jobs, back when he had jobs.

I shuffled through the detritus on the floor and turned off the radio. "Mike."

He was lying facedown on the bed, one arm dripping off the side, his hand almost touching an empty liquor bottle on the floor. The blankets cascaded off the end of the mattress, half covering an empty pizza box from four days ago.

"Mike, you gotta get up, man. This is disgusting. Even for you." I snagged an empty bottle from the nightstand, held it near his face, and watched his breath fog up the glass. "You're not dead. You smell like you are, but you're not. You gotta get up and get out of this room and take a shower."

Mike didn't move. I tripped my way across the room, slid back the drapes, and opened the window to let some of the stink out. The evening sun directly in his face accomplished what my voice could not. Mike cursed and raised his head off the sweat-stained pillow.

"Get out of my room!" He swung his arm impotently at nothing. "Get out of here!"

I stood just beyond his reach and kicked at an empty beer can. "Nothing would make me happier than not being in this cave of filth and sadness, man, but you're stinking up the whole place. You need to clean up this mess and take a shower and put on some clothes that don't have a week's worth of BO clinging to them. You smell like an armpit that took a dump. What happened to you?"

He turned away from me, away from the light, and shoved a pillow over his head.

I grabbed his left leg and yanked it hard. "Get up!"

Suddenly he was on his feet, his face an inch from mine, his breath like a locker room at the end of football season.

I stumbled back a moment, then held my ground. "Mike, you have to pull yourself together. I don't know what's going on here, but you can't live like this. I'm going to stop feeding you unless you take a shower and make a trip to the laundromat."

He sat back on the edge of the bed, whether of his own volition or because he lost his balance, I couldn't tell. "Just leave me alone, Michael."

"Again, I'd love to. But I'm not going to."

He put his head in his hands.

"What is going on?" I asked.

His shoulders lifted as he drew in a deep breath, then shook as he coughed it out. He mumbled into his palms.

"I can't understand you," I said.

He lifted his head. "I said I did something."

"What'd you do?"

His head dropped down again, then his hands were in his shaggy, greasy hair. He groaned. "I did something, Michael. I took something, and now I can't get it back."

"What?"

He raked his fingers through his hair.

"What did you take, Mike?"

"I sold it. I needed the money." He looked up at me, his eyes like two tarnished pennies on a dirty sidewalk. "These guys out in Vegas. I couldn't put 'em off any longer."

"What are you talking about? What happened in Vegas?"

He scrubbed a hand down his face. "When Carl and I went in January, I was losing at the casinos. I was almost out of money. Someone told me about this poker table in the back of a restaurant where you could get in on credit. I had to. I was out of money. But I was still losing."

"So instead of losing what little money you had—money which was probably already borrowed from Carl—you were losing money you didn't have."

"I thought I could just bet big on this one hand. It was a good hand."

"But not good enough."

"No," he said. "They told me they'd give me ninety days to come up with the money."

I sighed. "What's the deadline?"

"It was April 1st. I had to get the money somehow. I didn't know what else to do."

I thought of how he'd been so keen on selling the mastodon skeleton. He'd probably been thinking of this then, planning on skimming money off the top of the transaction in order to pay his debt. But the fossil was still in the ground.

"How'd you get it?"

He stared down at his hands. "The Wheelers. They have this guest book."

I crossed my arms. "I'm familiar."

"All those signatures. All that dirt."

I felt my mouth drop open. "You didn't."

"I had to. I didn't know what else to do."

I cursed and threw up my hands. "Why didn't you just ask them to loan you the money?"

"I already owe them money. And Deb—she'd just give it to me if I told her I needed it. But Dusty . . ."

"I can't believe this. I can't believe you." I paced the small space, kicking trash along the carpet, then I grabbed a whiskey bottle from the floor and threw it across the room, where it shattered against the wall. "You piece of crap! How could you do that? You have to get it back."

He was shaking his head. "I can't get it back. The money's gone. I handed it over last week."

"But who has the book?"

"Carl knew a guy in Detroit who'd buy it for what I owed."

"But not what it was worth."

He shrugged.

"Well, is this guy going to keep it? Or sell it for more?"

He stood up and started shuffling toward the door. "I don't know, man. It's gone. It's done. What does it matter?"

I grabbed his shoulder and spun him around. "It matters because you need to get it back."

He shoved me, hard. "I said it's gone. And it's none of your business anyway. Get out of my face and get out of my room before I throw you out on the street." He walked into the hall, mumbling underneath his breath, "Never would have happened if I hadn't let you live here anyway."

Everyone's got a breaking point. I'm not sure why it happened just then rather than months before or years after, but that was the last time I was going to let Mike blame me for his pathetic life.

I stalked into the hall, slammed into him, and attempted to plant my left fist into his face before he had a moment to process what was happening. But even hungover, somewhere inside Mike was still a boxer. He tilted his head just enough for me to send my fist into the wall, then he answered back with a right hook that sent me reeling. If the hall hadn't been so narrow, I would have been on the ground. I shook the stars from the sides of my vision in time to see him walking away. I heard the front door slam and his car start up and tear out the gravel drive.

I became aware that blood was streaming from my nose, over my lips, and down my chin before dripping onto the matted beige carpet. I went into the bathroom to survey the damage, then stopped the bleeding with wads of toilet paper shoved up what I was pretty sure was a broken nose. I had only just gotten rid of the last remnants of the bruise Slow had given me a few weeks earlier. Now I'd be walking around with two black eyes.

I went to the kitchen for some ice, twisted the plastic tray, and nearly dropped it on the floor when something popped in my left hand. I knocked the tray against the counter with my right, tossed some ice cubes into a dirty dishtowel, and held it to my face. Then I tried to straighten the fingers on the hand I'd slammed into the wall. Pain shot up into my arm, the edges of my vision blurred and sparkled just a bit, and I let out an involuntary yell.

The phone rang. I put down the improvised ice pack and tucked the receiver between my ear and my shoulder. "Hello."

"Hey," came Natalie's voice.

There was a moment of silence.

"Yeah?" I prompted.

A sigh. "I just thought you should know we're all set at Saint Andrew's."

I shifted the phone to the other ear and put the ice pack up against my face. "When?"

"June. He tried to book us for August, but I convinced him to go with June 15th."

"Who are we opening for?"

"No one."

"What do you mean?"

"We're it."

"We're it?"

"We're it. We're the act."

My head was starting to throb. "We're it."

"The guy liked our stuff, and I guess he heard it on the radio too, which didn't hurt. The band that was supposed to play that night had to cancel. So there will be a couple shorter opening acts and then us. He asked if we could fill at least ninety minutes."

My stomach dropped. "Did you tell him we can't?"

"Of course not."

"Natalie, we only have forty minutes of material. Tops." I forgot myself and tried to grab the receiver off my shoulder with my left hand. It clattered to the floor. I dropped the ice on the counter and picked up the phone.

"What the heck was all that?" Natalie said.

"Nothing," I said. "I think I might have broken something."

"What, like a plate?"

"No. My hand."

Track Three

I hadn't planned on going to the hospital. I had no insurance. I had almost no money. And if I didn't deal with it, maybe I could pretend it hadn't happened. Just like my fight with Natalie.

But Natalie insisted I get my hand looked at. Not because she cared for me, I was sure, but because it affected our ability to play the gig she had just booked. She also insisted on paying for it. I finally agreed to go—my hand appeared to be doubling in size from the swelling—and she somehow finagled her way into the passenger seat of my car. But I wasn't about to let her pay. Not when I knew what Mike had just cost her family. And also because I sure didn't want to owe her anything.

The drive to the hospital was silent on the surface, but you could almost hear the buzzing and grinding of our thoughts as we worked through what to say and how to say it and what, at all costs, to avoid saying. There is nothing so loud as an argument that hasn't happened yet.

Natalie wasn't allowed back in the examination area when the X-rays were taken and the bones in two of my fingers were immobilized with splints, but she was sitting right where I'd left her in the ER waiting room when I was finally released, nostrils still packed with gauze.

At the checkout desk I asked the lady what I owed.

"Nothing," was her response.

I cursed under my breath. "That's what you think."

The nurse gave me a sour look, but I didn't care. It fit my mood just right.

I tapped Natalie's shoulder and told her I was ready to go, then steered her out to the parking ramp with my good hand on her elbow. We were just pulling onto the street when she said, "How long until you can play?"

"Doctor said four weeks, then they'll do another X-ray and see if it's healed."

She let out a half sigh then stopped herself, trying to make it sound like just a deep breath.

"I know it was stupid," I said. "I don't need your sighs or comments or implied disappointment. And I didn't need your charity."

"Four weeks? That's May. We're not going to have much time to practice before the gig as it is, and we have to write a bunch more songs."

"Both of those things are your fault, not mine."

"I didn't punch a wall."

I clenched my teeth to keep from saying anything more that I'd regret. Deep breath. In. Out. Drive. I guided the car past the buildings of North Campus, over M-23, and between the greening fields and forests on either side of Plymouth Road before turning toward West Arbor Hills.

"I told you not to pay my bill," I said.

"Someone had to."

"I could have done it. Eventually."

She didn't respond, and I had nothing else to say. The debt

was paid. I should have been grateful. But I wasn't. I wasn't some sad sack sitting on a folding chair in a church basement, listening to some washed-up singer and her daughter talk about Jesus between songs. I wasn't their drunk, thieving handyman. I'd thought I was a friend at least. But maybe I'd been wrong about our relationship the whole time.

We were five minutes from home when Natalie finally spoke again. "I don't know what your problem is with your family, but you have to deal with it. Before it gets worse. I know that Mike's probably not the easiest person to live with. And I know your father—"

"My father is none of your business. My uncle is none of your business. I am none of your business, okay?" I squeezed the wheel with my good hand. "I'm not in some twelve-step program and you're not my sponsor, and you're not my spiritual guide or my guru or my shrink or whatever you imagine yourself to be. I'm not your patient. I'm not your charity case. I'm just some shmuck you tricked into being in a band because you needed someone who could write lyrics. Which seems to be the one thing in life I can sort of do without completely screwing it up, and which is apparently the only thing you, Miss Perfect, can't do at all."

I could feel my adrenaline start to pump, my blood start to rise, my face getting flush. I took a slow, purposeful breath and tried to tamp down the anger.

"Stop being such a child, Michael. No one forced you to do anything. Who's really using whom here? Let's see. What do I bring to the table but top-of-the-line instruments and equipment, a recording studio, a well-respected producer, connections in the music business, talented musicians—stop me whenever you get bored. And what do you bring to the table?" She paused for dramatic effect. "Fistfights, a bad attitude, and that giant chip on your shoulder that I'm surprised hasn't crushed you yet under its colossal weight. Can you write lyrics? Sure. So can lots of people. Even me."

I made the turn into Natalie's driveway too fast, sending her right shoulder into the car door.

"Watch it! I can't afford to break any bones. Because clearly I'm on my own from here on out, just like your pal Rodney said would happen. Hoo-boy! How will I ever manage all by my lonesome?"

The car screeched to a stop. Natalie immediately released her seat belt and opened the door, then slammed it shut behind her. I threw the car in reverse, looked over my right shoulder, and struggled to back down the long driveway using just my right hand. The tires left the pavement for the grass a few times as I weaved my way back to the road, then I just kept going backwards across the street and down the gravel drive. I stopped just inches from a car that shouldn't have been there.

My mom's car.

Feeling monumentally exhausted, I pulled the keys from the ignition and reached over to open the car door with my right hand, dropping the keys on the ground in the process. I wanted to sit there and cry. Instead I got out, scooped them up, and dragged myself inside. My mother was on her knees, washing the kitchen floor with a dish towel, the bowl Mike used for popcorn next to her, full of dirty, sudsy water.

She looked up at me but did not stop scrubbing. "This was all I could find." She glanced at my splinted hand but didn't bother asking about it. She must have already talked to Mike. Was he at her place sleeping it off while she was here cleaning up his mess?

"What are you doing here?" I said.

"Mike came by. Thought you guys could use my help."

"I guess." I sat at the kitchen table and relaxed just a little. There was something about a mom, just her presence, that gave a person a moment to breathe. Mine would be the first to admit she hadn't always done the right thing for me. That too often she was more concerned with her own loneliness than mine. But for a few minutes, as she scraped a bit of the grime off the floor of my life, I could breathe freely.

She stopped scrubbing and sat back on her heels. "Heard you saw your dad."

My chest tightened. "Not really."

She placed the filthy towel in the bowl and stood up, then she began rinsing everything out in the sink. "Mike said he was playing drums for your band."

"I'm not in a band."

She adjusted the water temperature, saturated the towel, wrung it out, rinsed it again, twisted it into oblivion. "He's not so bad, you know."

"I'm sorry, who are we talking about?"

"Who do you think?"

"Don't start that."

"What?"

"Don't be another person in my life telling me to give him a chance. You've done nothing but complain about him for twenty years, and for good reason. He's a piece of human garbage. Don't pretend he's a decent person now. I'm not interested."

She turned off the water, wrung out the towel once more, and laid it over the edge of the sink. "There's a lot you don't know, Michael. About him. About that time." She sat down at the table and placed her left hand on my right. Her palm was warm and damp. "I don't care if you ever talk to him again. That's your business. There were certainly times in my life I felt the same way." She sat back. "I just thought you were playing with him, and I thought that was nice."

I shook my head but offered no details about the goings-on of the last few months. There was little to tell anyway. Everything that had been building to something was falling down around me.

She pointed at my hand. "I guess you can't play for a while anyway."

I shrugged. "Doctor said it would be fine in a few weeks."

She nodded. "Mike said you're playing with that Natalie girl across the street."

"I was."

She raised her eyebrows, waiting for more.

I sighed. "It's not working. Her mom's dying, our styles are different, she's not involving me in the big decisions at all. We're not going to be ready for this gig she booked. I said some things. She said some things. It's kind of a disaster."

"When's the gig?"

"June, but I'm sure it will get canceled. Why?"

She shrugged. "I'd like to go is all."

I laughed. "You've never come to any of my gigs."

"I know."

"So—"

"You don't want me to come?"

"No, it's just . . . there's not going to be a gig, okay?" I stood up. "I'm going to go take a nap. You can stay if you want. But you don't have to clean. Mike should clean up his own messes."

I kissed her forehead and left her there at the table. I closed myself into my room, pulling the covers over my head and letting consciousness slip away to the rhythm of the pulsing pain in my left hand.

When I reemerged sometime later, Mom was gone. The kitchen, bathroom, and living room were clean. She'd even collected all of the trash out of Mike's room, changed his sheets, and made his bed. She put the dirty clothes and linens into a laundry basket by the door and left a roll of quarters on top. On the kitchen table she'd left a note scrawled on the back of an envelope.

Mikey,
   Come by sometime soon. I miss seeing you.
   Love you.

   Mom

At the bottom she'd written out my dad's phone number. "In case you need it," the note said.

I tore it up and tossed the pieces into the trash can.

Track Four

It turns out that having just one functioning hand is a pain even if you're not playing guitar. For the next four weeks I stood behind the cash register at work, trying to punch in the prices and bag the merchandise and take the money without taxing my healing left hand. I couldn't stock, couldn't haul stuff to customers' cars. I could barely even open my own pop on my break now that everything was a twist top. At home I dragged bread around with a knife full of peanut butter when I tried to make a sandwich one-handed. My hair was always in my face because I couldn't put it in a ponytail.

But the worst part of it was that, while my bones were healing, my guts were completely tied up in knots over what had happened between me and Natalie. I couldn't stop my brain from running over every sentence, every gesture, every twitch of her facial expressions as our emotions boiled over into words neither of us could take back. And even as I held tight to my righteous anger, I ached to see her face, to hear her voice, to watch her draw music from her instruments. All I wanted was to rewind the tape, back to before the moment everything turned. It felt like we were on an alternate timeline, like the bad 1985 in *Back to the Future II*, which I'd seen alone in a packed theater

Thanksgiving weekend. If I could just get back to that moment before old Biff stole the DeLorean—before she'd contacted my dad, before I'd so callously pointed out what she already knew about her mom—everything would be fine.

I picked up the phone a dozen times a day and hung it up again without dialing. Sometimes it was because I was thinking of Natalie and wanting to make things right. Sometimes it was because I was thinking of Brittney. Of how easy it would be to just forget my sorrow for a while with her. She'd used me. Maybe it was my turn to use her a little.

Each time I hung up the phone, I felt like a little more of me was being emptied out. Like water from a tub with a slow drain. Filth clung to my insides and crusted over, while everything good trickled down into some dark labyrinth beneath my feet, where it was whisked away.

Instead of practicing at the Wheeler house or in my room, I spent nights watching the news, slack-jawed and half zoned. Watching people dying in earthquakes and ferry disasters. Watching the space shuttle *Discovery* place the Hubble telescope into orbit. Watching a truce end Nicaragua's civil war. Watching the slow, incremental steps that East and West Germany were taking toward one another after decades apart. As I sat on the couch, the world kept marching relentlessly on toward the future. I had nothing to do with any of it. Nothing to do with anything at all.

Mike had come home a few days after my mom cleaned up his room. It took him less than a week to completely trash it again. The roll of quarters disappeared from the top of the overflowing laundry basket, but the contents of the basket were never washed. Mike probably wasted every coin on the slots at Soaring Eagle Casino, where he and Carl went to try their luck the weekend before Tax Day. I eventually dumped the laundry basket out on his bed. I wanted to light the whole mess on fire. Watch it burn and spread and erase the trailer and everything in it from the earth.

On the 3rd of May, X-rays showed my bones had healed. The splints came off and I was encouraged to return to normal activity, but my fingers were stiff and uncooperative. Holding a pencil was tricky. Forming certain chords felt impossible. But after all, did it really matter? Natalie hadn't called. I hadn't called her. The way we'd left things was pretty clear. The band was dead on arrival. There were no wrecking crews tearing down our wall like there were in Berlin. She'd have to find someone else to play and sing my parts for the gig at Saint Andrew's.

But . . . they were still my songs. Or at least partly. They were my words. My feelings. My heart. She had no more claim to them than Mike had on the Wheeler guest book, which, after calls to every pawn shop and antique dealer in the phone book, I still hadn't located. Mike had been so drunk when he sold it, he couldn't remember the name of the guy Carl had hooked him up with. Finally I called Carl myself, which got me a name, an address, and a warning that these guys were not to be messed with and I should probably just leave it alone.

And probably I should have. I hadn't stolen the book. Mike wasn't my responsibility. The Wheelers should have known not to let him get his hooks into their lives as deeply as he had. Certainly Dusty knew better.

But somewhere in the back of my mind was the absurd idea that if I could get the book back and restore it to its proper place in the guest room, that would fix everything. For me. I didn't care what they thought of Mike. But until I could get my hands on it, I knew I wouldn't be able to look Dusty or Deb in the eye.

This idea had burrowed itself so deep into my brain that when the phone rang that Saturday, I wasn't prepared to hear Natalie's voice on the other end of it.

"My mom wants to see you."

She hung up before I could respond.

Fifteen minutes later, I entered the Wheeler house through the open garage. I peeked into the kitchen, the dining room, the living room. All empty. I crept into the hall. Twenty feet away, Natalie's door stood closed. I knocked lightly on the master bedroom door and thought I heard a whisper beckon me in.

Deb's drawn face smiled weakly among the mounds of pillows and blankets that enveloped what was left of her. I hadn't seen her in a month, and I was shocked at the transformation. She had looked thin before. Now I could see the topography of her skull lurking just beneath her skin.

I took a few slow steps into the room and attempted to smile. "Hey, Mrs. Wheeler. Long time no see."

She tipped her head toward a chair next to the bed, and I came around and sat on the edge of the seat. Her thin hand rested on top of the bedcovers. A small wave of her fingers told me she wanted me to hold it, and I slipped my newly healed hand under hers, drawing a small smile from her lips.

"Michael," she said, her voice hoarse. "I've missed you."

"I've missed you too."

She swallowed with some effort. "Where have you been?"

"You know. Busy. Working."

"Not at night."

"No." I shifted a little in the chair. "Nat and I had a bit of a falling-out."

"Mm."

"My fault. But . . ." I trailed off. I couldn't very well tell her what I'd said. Because I'd said it about her.

Deb nodded slightly. "You don't have to explain yourself to me. But you better patch things up before the gig." She took a wheezing breath in. Out.

I sighed and was suddenly aware of just how much air my lungs could move with ease. "I'd like to."

"But?"

"I don't know." I covered Deb's fingers with my other hand. It was like I was holding on to a small, naked baby bird. "I'm not sure I really deserve her forgiveness. I . . . I said some things—"

"Psh," Deb said quietly. "No one deserves to be forgiven. The very nature of forgiveness is that we don't deserve it."

"Yeah, I guess."

"Michael, everyone's said things. Everyone's done things they regret. Natalie has. I have. Dusty has. Your uncle has."

Did she know about the guest book? Had he fessed up?

"We can never get rash words back," she whispered. "We can't undo the things we've done. All we can do is repent of them. Be sorry, and say you're sorry."

I nodded even though I knew that wasn't enough, couldn't be enough.

"And when other people tell you they're sorry," she continued, "believe them. Forgive them and move on."

I thought of all the people who owed me an apology. Rodney. My dad. Uncle Mike. Natalie. Even Slow could stand to apologize for punching me in the face. "And if they aren't sorry?"

"Well, just because someone hasn't apologized yet doesn't necessarily mean they aren't sorry. After all, doesn't that describe you?"

I closed my eyes and sighed. "Yeah, I guess."

She smiled. "So?"

I smiled back. "Is that why you wanted me to come over? So I could apologize to Natalie?"

"Pinky needs you. She's going to need you even more soon. And I'm not talking about the gig."

My smile faded as quickly as it had appeared. "I know you're not."

"I'm not going to make it to the show, you know."

My throat tightened. "I know."

"I was hoping maybe you'd do one for me here. Just you and Pinky. I know she's got big plans with a bunch of her musician friends for the performance at Saint Andrew's, but I just want to hear the two of you play. Can you do that for me?"

I nodded. "Of course. I know she'd do anything for you." I hesitated, testing the truth of what I was about to say. "And so would I."

She closed her eyes. "Okay then."

I stood up.

"Michael?"

"Yeah?"

"Go get my guitar over there." She pointed weakly at the guitar on the stand in the corner of the room. The guitar she'd played so beautifully until her pride got in the way.

I picked it up and brought it back over to the bed.

"Sit down," she said.

I settled back into the chair.

"Play me something."

I made a weak fist with my left hand. "I'm a bit out of practice."

"That's okay. Just play me something you've been working on, and if you mess up we'll just both chalk it up to that."

I thought for a moment. "I do have something. But I'm still missing the last verse and chorus."

"That'll do."

I hesitated. "Only it's not my song, exactly. The words are, but it's Natalie's melody. She's been trying to put words to it for a while. I offered my help, but she didn't want it."

"Mm. Kind of like you didn't want your dad's help with the drums."

I sat back. "She told you about that?"

She opened her eyes and looked into mine. "She tells me most things."

I swallowed hard and sighed. "It's not the same thing."

"No, it's not quite. But you've gone ahead and worked on the song even though she asked you not to, right?"

"Yeah. Just like she went ahead and contacted my dad even though she knew I wouldn't want him involved."

"So maybe you both could use a little mercy from the other, eh?" She smiled to take the sting out of her words. "But there's time for that later. Right now, play me that song."

I scooted to the edge of the chair and positioned Deb's guitar on my knee. "I told you it's not finished."

She nodded and closed her eyes again. I cleared my throat, pressed newly healed fingers to the strings, and played a D chord. I tuned the B string. Played the chord again. Then sang.

> The truest feeling is an ache
> A vague, insistent pulse of pain
> Carving out a piece of flesh
> Internal wound that's never dressed
>
> The good, the bad, it's all the same
> The love, the hate, the pride, the shame
> The sweet young thing who caught your eye
> The lover who's about to die
>
> It's a life that is ending
> A shroud that's descending
> The time that you're spending

How you keep pretending
The world's not caving in
You're not dying within
Slowly . . . slowly . . .

The deepest canyon is the hole
That sorrow dug out of your soul
The one you thought you'd always hold
Is growing distant, growing cold

Mistakes you were afraid to make
And chances you would never take
Roll through your mind like tumbled stones
Convince you that you're all alone

In a world that's contracting
A part that you're acting
A price you're exacting
A smile that's distracting me
From my heart caving in
You're saving me again
Slowly . . . slowly . . .

And you can't recall
Ever not feeling this way
It's like you were born with this pain
Stuck behind the eight ball
With no way of escape
And here in this pit you'll remain

After the bridge, I played a few more measures where the instrumental interlude would be before trailing off and letting the last note ring in the still, closed air of the bedroom. When it died down into nothing, Deb opened her eyes and spoke.

"That's really lovely."

I cleared the emotion from my throat and stretched my

fingers, surprised that as I played the stiffness had drifted away. "Thanks."

"But how will it end?"

I looked into Deb's fading hazel eyes and hugged her guitar. "I don't know. That's the problem."

"Will it be a sad song?"

"It is a sad song."

She shook her head slowly from side to side. "Not necessarily. It all depends on that last verse. That's what determines what kind of song it is. That last turn. You could live your whole life a scoundrel until the last verse. And that's when it can all turn around. I still have hopes that your uncle will experience that. He's had such a hard time of it since his baby died. But death's not the last word."

For a moment I couldn't form a coherent thought. "Mike had a baby?"

"You didn't know that?" She paused. "I'm sorry. I didn't realize. Yes, when I met your uncle when we were having this house built, he had a baby on the way, just like I did. You never saw a man so excited, never saw a man work so hard to make sure he could provide for her—he was sure it was a girl. Then his girlfriend changed her mind. She went to New York to have an abortion and didn't tell him for over a month. She was three months along when she left, and when she came back she started losing weight and finally had to tell him what she'd done. He was devastated. He's never gotten over it."

Suddenly Mike's devotion to Natalie and entanglement in the life of the Wheeler family all made sense. His excessive drinking made sense. His inability to get his life together made sense. Even his dislike of me followed a certain kind of twisted logic. He'd lost a child he wanted while his identical twin abandoned a child he didn't want. A child who looked as much like his uncle as his father. My uncle didn't really resent me. He resented his brother. Just like I did.

"But I still think God's not done with Mike yet." Deb lapsed into a short coughing fit but recovered soon enough to keep me from running out of the room to get help.

"I should go. Let you rest."

She held up a hand, collected herself, then spoke in an even quieter whisper. "Please talk to Pinky. I want to hear the two of you playing together."

I went to put the guitar back on its stand.

"No," Deb said. "That's yours."

I turned to face her. "No. I can't take this. You can't give it to me."

"It's mine to give to whomever I please."

"But it should go to Natalie."

"No, it's yours. The case is there in the closet."

"But—"

"Michael, I want you to promise you won't sell it, and when it comes time to pass it on, you'll give it to someone who needs it. Not someone who deserves it. Someone who needs it."

I nodded slightly, fighting the tears that were looking for release. Gut churning, I retrieved the guitar case and tried one more time. "Natalie—"

"She'll understand. Now go make up. There's no time to lose. You never know what day will be your last chance to make amends."

Kneeling on the floor, I inserted Deb's guitar into the soft gray lining of the case and wondered what color satin would line her casket. Then I closed the lid and clicked the metal fasteners shut.

"Michael?" Deb tapped her cheek with her finger.

I leaned over and pressed my lips to her gaunt face, then

hurried out of the room, shutting the door behind me. I stood there a moment in the hallway, trying to get my bearings, trying to flesh out my own emaciated understanding of death and Mike and what had transpired between me and Natalie. I leaned back against the wall and sank down to the floor, guitar case standing at attention between my feet. I tipped my head against it and closed my eyes. I felt like I wanted to say a prayer, but I didn't know how.

All at once, I realized that someone was beside me, slipping down onto the floor next to me. For a long time, neither of us spoke.

Then Natalie said, "That was my song."

Track Five

I fiddled with one of the clasps on the guitar case. "Yeah, well, I couldn't get it out of my head." Just like I couldn't get her out of my head.

Natalie let out a slow breath. "She gave you her guitar?"

I dropped my hand from the clasp. "I told her not to." I tipped the case toward her. "Here, you take it."

She pushed it away. "She gave it to you."

We sat there in silence for another minute. Two.

"Nat—"

"Is that what she wanted? To give you her guitar?"

"Partly." I chose my next words carefully. "She wants us to give her a preview of what we're playing at Saint Andrew's."

"What *we're* playing? You mean you'll be there?"

"I was planning on it." Was that a lie? I wasn't sure.

"You'll be there no matter what?"

"What does that mean?"

"Rodney said—"

"Never mind what Rodney said. I'll be there. If you want me there."

She got to her feet. "When does Mom want us to do this preview?"

I stood up. "She didn't say." I thought a moment. "What about next Sunday?"

"That's Mother's Day."

"Might be a nice present. Since you can't give her the pond."

She sighed. "Maybe. But won't you be with your mother that day?"

Oh, yeah. "I mean, not the whole day."

Can a blind girl give you a withering look? If so, Natalie gave me one right at that moment. "Fine. Come over at five o'clock that day." She started down the hall to her bedroom.

"Shouldn't we practice before then?"

"Practice yourself. I'm always ready to perform." And with that she disappeared through the doorway and shut the door.

I went back through the living room, dining room, and kitchen to avoid passing Natalie's bedroom on my way out. I was nearly out the open garage door when I heard my name. Dusty was standing just outside under the eave, smoking a cigar.

"Hey," I said.

He pointed his cigar at the guitar case. "You keep an eye on that."

I knew he meant Mike. Did he know about the guest book? "I tried to refuse."

He rolled the end of his cigar against the stone wall, sending an inch of ash tumbling to the concrete. "I know you did. You're a good kid."

Was I? Would he say that if he knew what I'd said about his wife? What I'd said to his daughter? "I don't know about that."

He pulled another cigar from his breast pocket and held it out to me.

"Nah, thanks. Maybe another time."

He tucked it back in place. "You talk to Natalie?"

"A bit. We'll be doing a little private concert for Deb. On Mother's Day. If that's all right with you."

"Whatever Deb wants, she gets. Always been that way. No sense in changing things up now."

I leaned the guitar case against the wall. "Can I ask you something?"

He motioned for me to continue.

"Is Deb the reason Mike lives across the street? I mean, did she set that up for him?"

"Well, you know I didn't." He sucked thoughtfully on his cigar. "She and Ruth had a brother much older than they were. Died of an overdose a few years before I met her. So she's always had a soft spot for guys down on their luck."

I thought of Esto and Ronnie at Lips. "Natalie said they sang at rehabs."

"Rehabs, jails, hospitals. Anywhere the sad and desperate people were hanging out."

Sad and desperate. Perhaps the most accurate descriptors I could think of for my uncle.

"And Natalie always went with her?"

"Since she was a little girl."

I leaned back against the wall and crossed my arms. "Deb seems like a really forgiving person."

Dusty nodded. "Easiest thing in the world for her. Not so easy for most of us, though."

I picked at a piece of ash that had dislodged itself from Dusty's cigar and landed on my shirt. "What about Natalie? She get that from her mom?"

He looked me square in the face. "Why? What'd you do?"

I pulled at the stubble I'd let grow on my chin. "Just said something stupid I wish I could take back."

He raised his eyebrows and went back to smoking. "We all do that now and again."

"Yeah."

"Pinky's . . . well, she's a tough one. She's good at giving strangers a lot of grace. Maybe not so good at doing the same for people she really cares about. Love keeps no record of wrongs. Or it shouldn't. But no one can hurt us quite as bad as the ones who're supposed to love us." He clapped me on the shoulder. "So I guess take solace in that. If she's angry at you, it probably means she cares about you."

"How reassuring."

Dusty laughed. It was the first time I'd heard him laugh in the four months I'd known him. He looked up at the fading light through the trees. "I better get in there and find something to eat. You're welcome to join me, but it will probably just be a sandwich."

I picked up Deb's guitar. "Thanks, Dusty. I think I'll pass for tonight. Just had an idea and I better get it down before I lose it."

"You bet, kid."

About halfway down the driveway I heard the garage door close. Though I should have been deflated from my time with a dying woman and a daughter who could forgive felons easier than she could forgive me, I felt strangely energized walking down that ribbon of concrete in the cool twilight. When I got to the trailer I went straight to my room and shut the door. I pulled out my notebook and removed Deb's guitar from its case. For just a moment, I chewed on the end of my blue BIC pen.

Then I wrote the best song of my life.

Track Six

Mother's Day dawned cold and clear with frost edging every weed along the gravel drive. I brought in the paper, made half a pot of coffee, and riffled through the news without much interest. Abortion, birth control, gays being pushed out of the closet. All kinds of controversies that didn't seem to fit with the smooth sailing we were promised back on New Year's Eve and also didn't seem to involve me at all.

It was weird to think of the rest of the world being out there beyond the thin walls of the trailer, beyond the little hamlet of West Arbor Hills, somewhere across the vast freshwater seas that hemmed Michigan in on three sides, set us apart. All those people out there dealing with their own lives, their own heartaches, their own losses, their own limitations. I wondered how many people were sad at that very moment. How many were happy? How many were somewhere else along the continuum? How many of them were dreading the day to come? How many were excited about it?

I was all of it. I was happy for the opportunity to play my music and sad about the circumstances of playing it. I both desired and dreaded to see Natalie. I was trying at the same time to psych myself up about it and tamp down my expectations as I tuned Deb's guitar and ran through the set list I had in my mind, which I had not discussed with Natalie. I put on a fairly decent pair of pants and a button-down shirt. Then I headed out.

Before I could see Natalie's mom, I had to see my mom, which meant driving to Redford. The house I'd mostly grown up in had been sold a year before I graduated high school in a misguided attempt to help Mike with his money problems. Since then, Mom had lived in a series of apartments that declined in square footage and increased in sketchiness with each move. Sometimes her name was on the lease. Sometimes it was not. After breaking up with the guy whose house I'd attempted to visit on Christmas, she'd slept on a friend's couch for a week or so. At the moment she was living in a tiny one-bedroom over a local video rental place that was closing—a casualty of the big chains cutting into their customer base. As far as I knew, Mom still hadn't bought a VCR.

When I knocked on the door, it took longer than it seemed like it should before I heard the deadbolt being unlocked. When the door finally opened, I was momentarily disoriented to see not my mother but my uncle.

"What are you doing here?" we said almost simultaneously.

"It's Mother's Day," I said. "Where is she?"

"She went to church." He took a step to the side to allow me to enter.

"Church?" I set the grocery store flowers I'd gotten her on the kitchen counter beside an ashtray and tried to remember if I'd heard Mike in the trailer last night.

"Yeah, apparently she's going to church now," Mike said.

"Every week?"

"So she says."

I put my hands on my hips. "So what are you doing here?"

"I can't visit my sister-in-law?" He sat back down on the couch where he must have been when I knocked on the door. There were no blankets, no pillows. He hadn't slept there.

"She's not your sister-in-law. Never was."

"Yeah, well, it's easier to say than my illegitimate nephew's mom or my brother's ex-girlfriend he knocked up."

I bit my tongue and felt a twinge in my left hand. "When's she supposed to be back?"

"Soon." He picked up the comics section of the *Free Press*. "You know the lady who does these Cathy cartoons is from Midland? She went to U of M."

"Fascinating." I sat in a tatty plaid wingback chair that listed slightly to the right.

"What's your problem today?"

I rubbed my hands down my face. "Nothing. I just thought that maybe when I stopped by to wish my mom happy Mother's Day, I'd be sitting here talking to my mom, not you. Where have you been lately anyway? I thought you and Carl might have gone back to Mount Pleasant or something."

"I've been here. Mostly. Your mom and I are . . . helping each other out."

I felt a shard of rage settle between my eyes as I considered the implications. "You mean she's helping you out."

He put the comics section down. "Boy, you are a piece of work. Everything anyone says, you've got to argue with it."

"Nah. Just the stuff you say." I stood up to go. "Tell her I came by, would you? And maybe put those flowers in a glass of water before they die."

Just then the door opened and my mother stepped through it. She wore a long floral dress, tasteful makeup, and understated jewelry. Her hair had been teased, her shoes were free of scuff marks, and she was carrying a purse she used to take only on dates.

"Oh! Michael, what a nice surprise!" she said, smiling. Then she seemed to notice Mike behind me and suddenly couldn't look me in the eye. She put her purse on the counter and picked up the flowers. "Are these for me? They're so pretty. Let me get them in some water." She fussed in the kitchen, opening cupboards, running the faucet, snipping the ends off each green stem with a pair of kitchen scissors. "I guess I didn't expect to see you so early. You usually come by pretty late on Mother's Day."

I caught the barb—that I came by at night because it took me all day to realize what day it was. It was not untrue. She'd never get an award for World's Best Mom, but I certainly wasn't knocking on the door of World's Best Son either.

"I've got a . . . thing later." With someone else's mom.

She tipped her head up and kissed my cheek. "Well, I'm glad you're here now."

She placed the flowers on the small kitchen table and sat in one of the two chairs. I sat in the other, unsure of what to say. If Mike wasn't six feet away, we'd probably talk about him. I'd ask her why he was hanging around, tell her what he'd done with the guest book, make sure she remembered what a scumbag he was. Maybe I'd ask her why I never knew he was supposed to have a kid. As it was, I realized that I had very little to say to my mother on Mother's Day. She'd done her best considering what she had to work with. Whatever resentments I had about the way I'd grown up weren't directed at her.

"You're going to church?" I said.

She looked a little sheepish. "Trying it out. A friend at work invited me. She was kind of persistent."

I nodded. "You like it?"

"It's nice, yeah. Feels kind of good to dress up and sing and sit and listen to the pastor talk. It's encouraging."

"Sounds like hell," Mike said from behind the paper he'd picked back up.

"I invited Mike to come with me," she said. "Told him it would do him good." She glanced to where he lounged on the couch. "He's not convinced."

"Bunch of chumps and hypocrites," Mike said. "Every one of 'em."

"Which am I?" Mom said.

"Both," he said without looking up.

I pushed away from the table, ready to make him take it back.

Mom covered my hand with hers and shook her head. "Maybe," she said. "But I think it's good for me."

"Then you should keep doing it," I said, settling back down. "And maybe you should cut some of the dead weight out of your life while you're at it. You know? People who drag you down. People who bleed you dry."

"I heard that," Mike said.

"I hope so."

"All right, all right," Mom said. "That's enough. I guess I'll keep Mike around awhile yet. See if maybe someone can save him from himself."

"Good luck with that," I mumbled. I rubbed my hands together and stood. "Listen, I gotta go get ready for this thing I have tonight."

"Of course," she said, standing. "What is it?"

"Uh, just this music thing."

"A gig?"

"Sort of."

She was waiting for more.

"It's Natalie's mom. She won't be able to come out to see

229

the thing at Saint Andrew's we're doing in June, so we're going to play her a few songs at their house."

"Oh." She smiled, but it didn't reach her eyes.

Guilt twisted my stomach. "Why don't you come?"

She brightened a little. "Really? You don't think she'd mind?"

"Of course not."

"I've always kind of wanted to meet her. I used to listen to her records."

"And you could meet Natalie," I said.

She frowned. "Oh, but then what will you do tonight?" she asked Mike.

My eyes drifted to my uncle on the couch. Why did she care what he was doing? Did they have plans? What was really going on here?

"You could both come," I said, imagining Mike having to look Deb in the face, knowing what he'd done. "Deb would like it, I'm sure. She's known Mike a long time." I couldn't resist getting in a jab. "He's kind of got the run of the place. Knows where all the secrets are hidden."

My mom looked at him hopefully. "What do you think?"

He kept his eyes glued to the newspaper. "Yeah, maybe."

She clapped her hands together. "Well, then maybe we'll see you there."

"About 5:30," I said, already knowing that they wouldn't show.

Deb was wedged into the corner of one of the white leather couches, practically buried in blankets that Ruth continually and needlessly retucked in order to have something to do. Dusty and I had moved the other couch against a wall. In its place we had set up two stools, two guitar stands, and four mics—one for each guitar and one for each voice. There was no need for amplification in the intimate space, but Dusty wanted to record the proceedings.

If I thought about it too hard—the fact that what I was about to play and sing would be recorded for posterity, labeled "Mother's Day 1990," and pulled out and played someday by Deb's descendants—my hands would start to shake a little. This informal concert with an audience of three felt more significant than anything I'd ever done. It was certainly more important than any gig I'd played with The Pleasure Centers. It even felt more important than the gig I'd play a month from now at Saint Andrew's Hall. It was like I already knew that when I was old and looking back on my life, this would be one of the standout moments. One of those visceral memories that would be more than simply recalling that something had happened—it would be like reliving it.

I was already nervous about seeing Natalie, trying to feel out whether her attitude toward me had softened at all since we'd sat on the floor outside Deb's bedroom. Trying to figure out if I was forgiven. By the time we settled on a set list and sat down on our stools to tune and give Dusty some levels, I still couldn't tell. No matter. I would focus on Deb, do my very best for her, and hope that somehow my genuine love and affection for this remarkable woman would get through to her daughter.

I took a sip of one of the glasses of room-temperature water Ruth had set out for us and cleared my throat as Natalie spoke into her mic.

"Mom, as you know, I'd hoped to give you a koi pond for Mother's Day this year, which didn't exactly work out as I'd planned."

Deb smiled and Ruth chuckled.

"Instead," Natalie continued, "Michael and I would like to give you the exclusive gift of being the very first person—along with Dad and Aunt Ruthie—to hear The Intersection live."

"Intersection," I said quietly. "It's just Intersection."

The muscles in Natalie's jaw tightened momentarily. She quietly counted us into "Chasing Clear Skies," and after a short intro, we started singing our alternating parts, harmonizing more and more as the song built to its last saccharine sentiments. I tried to stay mentally present, tied to the song, but the lyrics meant nothing to me. I'd written them not out of my own experience, my own emotions, but out of a sense of what might hook others in. I didn't actually know what I thought of what was going on over on the other side of the world. I just knew what I *should* think about it.

When it was over, Ruth clapped politely, and I knew she could tell I didn't believe what I was singing.

"Oh, lovely, lovely," Deb whispered, also out of politeness I was sure, and a pang of sorrow hit my gut as I realized that her voice, weak as it was, would not show up on the recording. "What beautiful harmony."

She wasn't wrong about that. More than ever—despite weeks of me not practicing as my hand had healed, followed by a week of practicing alone—my voice and Natalie's had felt like one during that song. For a few minutes, even though I didn't know what I was saying with the lyrics, we'd been completely in sync musically. It was an incredible feeling, one voice buoying the other the way water held up a boat, the way a wind current lifted a bird. Only I couldn't tell if I was the boat or the sea, the bird or the air. And even though nothing was said about it, Natalie had to have felt it too.

"Anonymous" was next. I explained how I'd written it with

Deb in mind, how I didn't know if I truly believed it but maybe there was a small part of me that was coming to understand it.

As we barreled through the first several verses and choruses, I watched Deb's smile grow on her face and had the deep satisfaction of feeling that even if I didn't quite get it, maybe I'd still managed to get it right. Then we came to the bridge.

> You long for lost obscurity
> For days when only you could see
> The beauty and the purity
> The hope, the grace, the light, the glee
> The way this broken world should be
> Holding hands in harmony
> But now you're stuck on the marquee
> Playing to the bourgeoisie

Though her smile held, a tear slipped down Deb's cheek. Ruth reached for her hand and squeezed. Natalie and I headed into the last chorus and final verse.

> So, girl, you got to make a choice, you got to take a
> stand
> And I'll be there right by your side to take you by the
> hand
> You only got one life to live, one chance to be yourself
> Don't let 'em tell you what to do to stay up on that
> shelf
>
> Step out into the dark with me and hope that they
> don't follow
> We'll write our songs where no one sees, give no
> thought to tomorrow
> And someday soon you'll come alive again
> And find out that you're more than just a trend

The last chord rang out. Ruth clapped for real and Deb put her hands together.

"Yes," Deb said softly. "Yes, exactly, Michael. You got it right. You know I never did stop writing songs. Or recording them." She and Dusty shared a look. "It's one of the reasons when we built this house that we put a studio in it."

"It's part of why I made the switch from musician to producer," Dusty said.

There was nodding all around. I was the only one in the room for whom this was news. I wondered why Natalie hadn't told me about these secret recordings when she'd told me about Deb's reluctance to put out any more records. The night I'd written most of this song.

"Audiences are great," Deb continued, "but they do bring along with them their own expectations and opinions. I lost the joy of singing when I became fixated on how people responded to it, good or bad."

Was that my problem? Why I had been so angry about the possibility that people had caught on to Rodney's theme song rip-offs? Why the gigs I'd missed over the years always seemed to be the ones with the biggest audience, the most potential for people to see me, hear me, judge me? Why I was so worried about not being good enough for Saint Andrew's? Why I didn't really want my mom to be there?

And why was I stuck in an endless loop of making everything—even a dying woman's personal revelations—about me?

For the next half hour, we played through our meager set list. Ruth and Deb shared a knowing look or two during "The Way It Goes," the song I'd written about Natalie. They laughed—or tried not to—at "Satan's a Hot Girl." They both let a tear or two run down their cheeks at "The Truest Feeling," especially as we came to the last verse and chorus, which I'd written after

Deb had explained how the last part of a song decided whether or not it was sad.

> But every time you're feeling low
> There's something I think you should know
> You're never on your own out there
> I'm right beside you, don't despair
>
> I'll answer when you're calling
> I'll catch you when you're falling
> I'll push you when you're stalling
> No matter what's befalling you
> I won't let your life cave in
> You can count on me, my friend
> Always . . . always . . .

I couldn't keep myself from looking at Natalie then. And despite her initial displeasure at me writing my own lyrics to the special song she had been working on for her mother, she leaned over to me when it was done and said, "It kills me to admit it, but it's kind of perfect."

I was glad she couldn't see the big dumb smile that took over my face for a moment. I couldn't put my finger on how or why, or how it could happen so fast, but it was clear to me that my happiness was inextricably wrapped up with hers. That if I couldn't make things right between us, I would be miserable for the rest of my life.

We filled in the set with a few covers of some of Deb's favorites and ours. Natalie sang her rendition of "Landslide." I sang "Don't Think Twice." We dipped into some Paul Simon and John Denver and Joan Jett, even a hymn or two. The last song on the set list was the hymn "It Is Well with My Soul," which Ruth had suggested Deb would most appreciate.

But before Natalie could introduce it, I pulled my mic a little closer and said, "Before we do our last song, I have something I'd like to play. Not for you, Deb—no offense—but for Natalie."

Deb nodded for me to continue. I turned a little on my stool, adjusted the mic that was picking up the beautiful round tones from Deb's guitar, and began picking out the first notes of the song I'd written the night she gave it to me. Then the words poured out like a spring in the desert.

> I want to live inside the moment I first met you
> When I didn't know just how much hurt there'd be
> And how many sleepless nights I'd have to go through
> Thinking you'd be better off not knowing me
>
> It seems like everything I touch
> Has a way of getting broke
> You may not think of me much
> Since the day that we last spoke
> But I'm never alone with my thoughts
> 'Cause you are always in them
> Your memory's calling all of the shots
> And my heart's a helpless victim
>
> I want to reach into the moment it turned sour
> And pluck out all the words that I regret
> Every lie, half-truth, and lapse in my willpower
> Slices through my gut like a rusty bayonet
>
> It seems like everything I touch
> Has a way of getting broke
> You may not think of me much
> Since the day that we last spoke
> But I'm never alone with my thoughts
> 'Cause you are always in them

Your memory's calling all of the shots
And my heart's a helpless victim

Please tell me there's a moment called tomorrow
When I won't be dwelling on the pain I caused
When I won't be suffocating in my sorrow
When you won't be counting up my many flaws

Although I don't deserve your mercy
Your forgiveness or your love
And I'll never prove myself worthy
Of a pardon from above
I can't survive a lifetime
Of exclusion and rebuff
Won't you toss to me a lifeline
And say "I'm sorry" is enough

Won't you toss to me a lifeline
And say "I'm sorry" is enough

Silence hung heavy in the room after the last chord dissi-
pated, and I realized that I hadn't thought this far out. Hadn't
thought of what might happen, what might be said after the
song was done, after Natalie had heard the most heartfelt apology I could muster. It only occurred to me in that very moment
that her answer might be, "No, sorry is not enough."

I covered the strings with my hand and leaned toward her.
"Listen, I know I have been stubborn and callous and childish
and even a bit vindictive. I know I hurt you with how I acted
and what I said and by stealing your song. But—"

"Michael," she interrupted. "You already apologized."

I swallowed down my anxiety with effort as I waited for her
to finish. To actually answer the question I had asked her in
the song. She reached her right hand out toward me. I placed
my left in it, gingerly.

"And I forgive you," she said.

The clenched fist of my heart loosened its grip, and relief spread through me like blood reentering my veins.

"The question is," she continued, "do you forgive me?"

I squeezed her hand. "Of course I do."

She smiled. "Good. Now, we have an audience waiting patiently for the last song."

I straightened up. Deb caught my eye and winked. We started into "It Is Well with My Soul."

And it really was. Perhaps for the first time.

Track Seven

A week later, I sat in my car on Outer Drive in Bright-moor, shifting rapidly between confidence and anxiety, Carl's warning to me throbbing in my head like a cartoon stubbed toe. I reminded myself that there was nothing to worry about. This was a reconnaissance mission, nothing more. All I was doing was confirming that it was here.

The sign above the cracked glass door of the storefront declared Gun's Jewlry Electronics Memorabilia in poorly spaced, hand-painted letters. I didn't know if it was the name of the store or just the pawn shop equivalent to the party store's ubiquitous Beer Liquor Wine Lotto. I also didn't know why they knew how to make one word plural by simply adding an *s* but felt the need to add the apostrophe in the other. Or how they had managed to spell *memorabilia* correctly but got *jewelry* wrong. But all of these little details reassured me that I was at the right place.

A short string of sleigh bells tinkled as I entered, and the large bald man behind the counter raised his head. It looked like it took some effort to do so, like his thick neck had a limited range of motion. He quickly took stock of me, seemed to deem me *easy to subdue*, and looked back to the crossword in front of him on the countertop. "Lemme know if you need help finding anything."

"Thanks," I said, starting a circuit around the store.

Despite its less-than-professional presentation outside, inside it was well organized. The guns and jewelry were locked up in glass cabinets. Books, records, videotapes, and cassettes were alphabetized. The electronics were relatively free of dust. One wall held several decent-looking guitars and a tenor saxophone. Another was covered with artwork that looked a little better than what you'd see in a hotel, but it was certainly a far cry from what you'd see at the DIA.

Looking around, I quickly realized that it was extremely unlikely that anything so valuable and portable as the Wheeler guest book would be on a shelf somewhere readily available for shoplifting, no matter how big the goon at the counter was. It had to be in one of the glass cases somewhere.

I approached the register, and the guy lifted his bulldog face once more. "Hey, do you have any rock memorabilia?"

He raised his eyebrows and pursed his lips. "Whatcha lookin' for?"

"Autographs?"

"We got an autographed poster of Hall & Oates on the wall over there. It's just got one of their signatures, though. Oates's, I think."

I followed the trajectory of his pointed finger. "Uh, yeah. That's . . . cool. But I'm looking for something a bit smaller."

"Like a signed record?"

"No. Maybe like a collection?"

"An autograph book?"

"Something like that. I have pretty wide taste. Rock, pop, blues, country. Love Detroit musicians." I kept talking, waiting for his facial expression to change, for some indication that he was connecting my needs with a particular red book full of exactly what I was talking about. "I'm looking for something no one else would have. Something totally unique."

He shook his head. "Sorry, kid. I don't think I have what you're looking for."

"Money's no object," I said.

He regarded me doubtfully.

I put all my cards on the table. "I heard someone might have sold you a red guest book full of entries written by a ton of different musicians."

He chuckled. "Maybe. But you wouldn't be able to afford that, pal."

"Do you have it, though? Like, if I got together the money, would it be available?"

He narrowed his eyes. "You think you could get together $5,000?"

The breath left my body.

He read the shock all over my face. "I didn't think so."

"But you do have it? If I could get the money together?"

"Oh, I have it."

"And you'd sell it for that price?"

He shrugged. "Sure."

"Would you take $1,500?"

He laughed and shook his head. "You're dreaming, kid. I'm already taking a hit on the price. I could get a lot more if I cut it up and sold the signatures off piecemeal, but it's got writing on both sides of the pages."

The thought of this guy even turning the pages with his sausage fingers, let alone taking an X-ACTO knife to it, made me ill. "I want to buy the whole thing. Intact. I can get the money. It just might take me a while."

"I can't hold it for you. Especially since I doubt you can get your hands on that kind of scratch."

I nodded and picked up the pen from the counter. "Can I at least leave you my name and number so if anyone else comes sniffing around it, you can give me a call?" I spun his crossword book around and scrawled out my name and number on the top of the page before he could say no. "Thanks, man." I put down the pen and headed out the door.

In the car I took two huge breaths. I'd never be able to get even half the money I'd need. There was really only one thing to do. Tell the Wheelers what Mike had done and let them buy the book back themselves.

But I couldn't tell Deb about yet another of Mike's dumb moves after hearing about the disappearance of Glen Campbell's guitar. And I didn't really want to tell Dusty. He was getting a little old for fistfights with former boxers, and I couldn't quite see him just shrugging the whole thing off. Plus it seemed so childish to go tattling to someone's dad. I cared what Dusty thought of me. A lot. And I thought maybe he had a pretty decent opinion of me at this point. I didn't want to mess that up.

Maybe I could tell Natalie, though. She knew who Mike was, the heights of stupidity he was capable of reaching. No matter how careless he might be, she cared about him. And she had trouble forgiving people she cared about. Which suited me just fine in this case.

Still, it wasn't the best time. Deb was spending her days in bed, most of that time asleep. Natalie's time with her was running out. Plus the gig was in just three weeks. The first of the backup musicians would be arriving in town soon. Natalie and I needed to buckle down and write some more songs, learn some more covers, and finalize a set list. I couldn't have her chasing after something that should be safe in her house.

But I also couldn't wait. What if the book was sold in the meantime?

On the drive back to West Arbor Hills, it struck me that I had another option. I could report it stolen. I could turn Mike in and tell the cops where it was and then wash my hands of it. Maybe the Wheelers would press charges, maybe they wouldn't. If they did, I might be able to get Mike out of my life—and my mom's—for a little while. If they didn't, what more could Mike do to me? Kick me out? If he did, my mom would surely let me sleep on her couch for a while, which might discourage Mike from making any more visits. Or I could stay at the Wheelers' in the guest room. I could start every day making Natalie breakfast and end every night listening to records with her. Either way, the book would be returned, no money would have to change hands, and Mike would have to suffer some sort of consequence.

By the time I turned onto North Dixboro Road, I was resolved. Unfortunately, I could see from Mike's car in the drive that I was not alone.

I expected Mike to be watching TV with a beer in hand despite it being only eleven o'clock in the morning. So I was not prepared when I walked into the trailer to see him hunched over on the couch, face buried in his hands, shoulders shaking as a low sob escaped his body.

Deb.

I rushed over to him. "Is she dead?"

He kept crying.

I wanted to shake him. "Mike, what happened?"

He rubbed his eyes hard and snorted a load of snot back into his sinuses.

"Mike!"

He cursed. "Can't you just give me a minute here? Geez, Michael. She's still alive."

I took a deep breath, relieved. "Then what happened?"

He pulled his hands over the back of his head and down his face and neck. "I just got back from talking to her is all. And I'm sure it will be the last time." He looked at me. "She looks just . . . she looks like she's already dead."

I sat down next to him on the couch, my plans to turn him in to the police in tatters. Deb would never do something like that. "What did you talk about?"

He sniffed. "Old times. God. Pinky. You."

"Me?"

"She told me I needed to be nicer to you." He scoffed, but the look on his face held no derision. He actually looked . . . sad. "She said I should place a higher value on my family."

I sighed. "I guess you're probably not the only one." I swallowed my pride and clapped him on the shoulder. "Sorry if I've been a pain to have around."

He shook his head a little. "It's actually not bad to have you around. Most of the time."

I chewed the inside of my mouth a moment, considering. "How hard do you think it would be to get that mastodon skeleton out of that hole?"

Mike frowned. "Probably take a while. And some more hands. But it's doable. Why?"

I stood. "Because you need $5,000 to buy back that guest book. And you're going to do whatever you have to do to get it."

Track Eight

"No heavy equipment," Dusty said.

The three of us—Dusty, Mike, and me—were standing in the Wheeler garage, Dusty just inside, Mike and I just out. I wished I was standing by Dusty rather than Mike, aligning myself with the man I was beginning to wish was my father rather than the man who merely looked like my father.

"And I don't want you guys listening to any loud music or tromping in and out of the house or swearing or anything else that might disturb her, understand?"

"Of course." Mike rubbed his hands together. "And you're fine with me selling it?"

Dusty shook his head. "I don't really care what you do with it."

"Thanks," Mike said. "I owe you one."

Dusty fixed Mike with a look that said that was the understatement of the century and then headed back into the house. "Just keep the noise down and tell whoever's helping you to keep their mouths shut."

"No problem." Mike turned to me after Dusty closed the door. "You hear that?"

"I'm helping you?"

He started walking down the driveway. "Obviously."

"But Natalie and I have a lot of work to do," I said, following.

"You'll have to make time for this too if you want to get that book back."

I thought again of just calling the police. "Well, you need a few more guys if you want to get this done fast."

"I can get a couple."

"Who, Carl? That guy's useless."

"Just leave it to me."

I stopped following and let Mike make the rest of the trip home by himself. I walked back up to the house, through the garage, and down to the studio. The first of the backup musicians was scheduled to get into town soon. I needed to make sure I could play my parts as professionally as possible. That meant that every spare moment I had—fewer now that I'd been roped into an amateur paleontological dig—had to be spent practicing. If I didn't feel absolutely confident in my performance, there was a decent chance I wouldn't be able to make myself walk onto the stage at Saint Andrew's Hall in three weeks. And chickening out was not an option.

"It's a shovel, not a teaspoon," Mike said. "Put your back into it."

Carl put no more effort into scooping dirt in his quadrant than before Mike said it. If anything, he put in less. "When are we breaking for lunch?"

It was weird. On the phone, it always seemed like Carl was the alpha wolf—the man with the connections, the man with the plan—but when a job required more than just smooth talk, when it required some muscle and some sweat and some stick-to-itiveness, Mike was a force to be reckoned with and Carl fell down a rung on the ladder.

We'd been at it all morning, and Carl wasn't the only one who wanted a break. I was sure he didn't need one like I did—my left hand was starting to feel like the handle of the shovel was covered in thorns—but he asked for one about every eight minutes. It was slow going with just the three of us, which really amounted to just the two of us. Mike checked his watch every so often and assured me that more help was on the way, but I was beginning to have my doubts. Was this how Rodney felt when I didn't show up?

We did finally break for lunch, scarfed down some sub sandwiches Carl had picked up from a gas station on the way over—his greatest contribution to the cause thus far, which wasn't saying much—and hit the shovels again after only twenty minutes of rest. So far, not one bone had been removed from the pit, though the outline of a large jaw, skull, and tusk was now clearly discernible. I had expected the bones to be white, but they looked like the clay we used to make coil pots in art class in high school. The tusk looked like the teeth of a lifelong smoker. The thing wasn't very pretty.

"I'm running across the street to make a phone call," Mike said. "You two keep working. Carl, I don't want to catch you leaning on that shovel when I get back."

The moment Mike was out of sight, Carl stopped pretending to work. "What do you think we're going to get for this thing?"

"We? We aren't getting anything. Whatever Mike gets, he's handing over to the pawn shop guy so we can get that book back. I can't believe you helped him sell something he stole."

Carl raised his hands in surrender, and the shovel dropped

to the ground. "Hey, I was just helping a friend out of a sticky situation."

"Not so loud," I said, pointing up to the deck outside Deb's room.

Quieter: "He asked me for help, and that's what I gave him. Anyway, Mike can do whatever he wants with his cut. I'm thinking I might buy a car."

"A car?" I was ninety percent sure Mike had not told Carl we were splitting the profit on the mastodon skeleton, and if he had, it was just a ruse to get him to lend a hand in its extraction. "I doubt there would be enough split three ways or more for you to buy a car. And if your portion is a reflection of the amount of work you actually do today, I'd say you're not even going to be able to afford a bike. Maybe a skateboard." I thrust my shovel into the ground, ignoring the increasing numbness in my hand.

A moment later, Mike was back.

"So is this other guy ever coming?" I said.

"He didn't answer the phone, so he must be on his way." Mike motioned to Carl. "This one do any work while I was gone?"

"Just working his jaw."

Mike looked at Carl. "Come on, man. It's not that hard."

For the next half hour, I kept my head down, chipping away at the task at hand, stopping only to move and stretch my fingers. There was something a little satisfying about a job like this. It required almost no thought, just consistent, plodding effort. It left room for the mind to wander. Maybe that was why Carl didn't like it. Not enough deep thoughts to fill the giant void between his ears.

My thoughts were of Natalie. Of her talented friends who were even now packing their suitcases to make the trip to Detroit. Of the songs we needed to fill the set list. Of the vast room at Saint Andrew's Hall filled with people hoping to have a good time, hoping to discover a hot new band. I was so focused on my thoughts that it barely registered when someone said my name. Then, like waking up from a deep sleep, I heard it again, closer.

"Michael?"

I looked to the source of the voice, the source of my name, and for just a moment I wondered how I hadn't noticed that Mike had shaved when he ran back to the trailer. And wasn't he wearing a U of M cap before? Since when was he a Spartans fan? Then I was seeing double. This wasn't Mike. Mike was a couple steps behind him, beard intact, big maize *M* on a blue ground on his forehead. This was my dad.

I knew he was waiting for me to say something. They were all waiting for me to say something. But I couldn't even get "hello" past my lips.

Steve frowned, then turned to Mike. "Got a shovel for me?"

Mike took Carl's shovel and handed it to his brother.

"What am I going to use?" Carl asked.

"You weren't even using that one," Mike said. "Why don't you take off."

"Am I still getting my cut?"

"Beat it, Carl," Mike said. "There was never any money on the table for you."

Carl crawled out of the hole and walked up the slope amid a steady stream of mumbled curse words, then disappeared behind the house.

Without another word, the three of us Sullivan men got to work. Just as before, I kept my head down. But unlike before, my mind was not exploring the days to come. It was stuck rehashing the past. It was seeing the cards my mom clumsily forged to try to convince me that my dad knew it was my birthday. It was seeing empty doorways I hoped he would walk through, empty bleachers where I hoped he would sit and cheer me on. It was seeing the yellowed photo of me in my mother's arms when I was a month old, my mom smiling for the camera, my dad nowhere to be found.

Then I could feel it coming on. The same feeling I got when I had to make a game-deciding free throw in seventh grade basketball. The same feeling I got when I had to go onstage at a gig. My heart started pounding uncontrollably. My hands started to sweat. My breaths came in gulps that seemed devoid of oxygen. I dropped my shovel and climbed out of the hole.

"Where you going?" I heard Mike say.

"Be right back," I managed to respond. I was up the slope and on the Wheelers' front porch with my head between my knees in a matter of seconds. I could feel the panic spreading out inside of my body, the way creamer snakes through hot coffee when you pour it in. I tried to slow my breathing, to keep any tears from squeezing out between my tightly closed eyelids. Get a grip, man. Breathe in. Breathe out. Slower. Slower.

"Um, excuse me?" a voice said.

I glanced up to see a young man and a young woman, black instrument cases in tow, looking down at me. I snapped to attention and stood up, wiping my dirty forearm under my nose. "Sorry. Allergies." I held out my still-gloved hand. "I'm Michael."

The guy looked at my hand and grimaced a little. I saw the muddy glove and pulled it off.

"Sorry, I'm helping with something out back."

He shook it as quickly as possible. "I'm Cory and this is Carrie."

Carrie waved.

Cory held up his instrument case. "Violin."

Carrie raised hers an inch. "Cello."

I put my hand to my chest and dropped it when I could still feel my heart thumping hard. "Rhythm guitar."

They seemed to be waiting for something.

"Oh, sorry." I went up the steps to the door and opened it. "The studio is just downstairs. I'll let Natalie know you're here."

They descended the steps to the basement level, and I quickly removed my boots and the other glove and left them on the floor of the foyer. I peeked down the hall, then knocked lightly on Natalie's bedroom door.

"Natalie?"

No answer. I checked the kitchen, the dining room, the living room. No Natalie. I headed downstairs myself. The family room was empty. The listening room was empty. The billiards room was empty. In the studio, Cory and Carrie were alone, tuning their instruments.

I poked my head in. "Natalie knew you were coming today, right?"

"Of course," Cory said.

"Of course," I repeated. "It'll just be a minute."

I went back upstairs and looked down the long hall to the door that led to the master bedroom. Was Natalie in there with Deb and Dusty? Were they even home? One of them had to be. They wouldn't leave Deb here alone.

I peeked into the garage. The Mustang was gone, which meant Dusty was gone. But Natalie must still be here. Then I noticed the guest room door was ajar. I hadn't thought to check there. I opened the door the rest of the way. Natalie sat on the foot of the bed, her face expressionless.

"There you are," I said. "A couple musicians just arrived. Cory and Carrie. I sent them downstairs. Did you want me to clean up and join you guys, or—"

"Michael, do you know where the guest book is?"

My stomach lurched. "It's not here?"

She turned in my direction. "Michael?"

"What? I don't have it."

"That's not what I asked."

I let out a weary sigh. "Yeah, I know where it is."

"Did Mike take it?"

"Yeah."

"Does he still have it?"

"No."

"So where is it?"

"He sold it. To a skeevy pawn shop in Brightmoor. To settle a debt from his Vegas trip New Year's Eve."

She nodded, unsurprised. "My mom wanted to look at it. Read some of those notes one last time. She asked me to get it twenty minutes ago. I searched for it everywhere in here." She sighed. "I should have known the minute it wasn't in its regular spot."

I sat down next to her on the bed. "Do you want me to tell her what happened?"

She tipped her head against my shoulder. "No. I figure if I stay in here long enough, by the time I get back she'll either be asleep or will have forgotten she asked for it. She's in and out a lot."

I didn't want to move from this spot. Ever. But Cory and Carrie were downstairs, and my father, I was remembering, was in the backyard.

"You smell like dirt," Natalie said.

"We're digging up the mastodon skeleton so Mike can sell it and buy the book back from the pawn shop."

"I wondered what you were doing out there."

"Are we being too loud?"

"No. I was just out on the deck earlier and heard the shovels."

"Oh, good. Dusty told Mike it had to be quiet."

"I heard three people."

"Yeah, Carl was there earlier. Guy's useless though. Mike sent him home."

"Who's the other one? The guy out there now?"

I strained my ears to hear what she did. I couldn't hear a thing. I let out a long, slow breath. "My dad."

She sat up. "Is that why you're in here?"

"No. I'm in here because while I was having a panic attack on the front porch, two of your classmates showed up looking for you."

"Right." She stood. "I'll get down to the studio." She hesitated. "You're okay, right?"

"I am now." I wanted so badly to pull her into my arms. "Anyway, I can clean up and come downstairs with you. I'm assuming we should all be practicing together."

"We will. Soon." She started toward the door. "But you don't have to be there right now. You should go outside. Spend some time with your dad. It'll make it easier when you have to share a stage with him in a few weeks if you can clear the air a little first."

Share a stage? "What are you talking about?" But even before she answered, I felt the plain and unavoidable truth of it hit me like a Lake Huron wave on a red flag day.

How had the thought never even crossed my mind? Of course he would be at the gig at Saint Andrew's. He'd done all the drum tracks on the demo. He knew the songs. We hadn't found anyone else in the meantime. The panic started creeping back into my chest, and it took all of my will to beat it back.

I followed Natalie to the top of the stairs and watched her begin her descent. "Did you tell Mike to get me and my dad together?" I said, dreading her answer. Dreading the prospect of being at odds with her again.

"No," she threw over her shoulder. "But I bet my mother did."

I sat down hard on the bench in the foyer and stared at nothing out the wall of windows for a solid minute or two. Then I looked at my boots. I had a sudden urge to see Brittney. To drive to Plymouth, pick her up, and make out with her to get Slow back for punching me. It would be so easy. She would be so easy. And at that moment, I just wanted something to be easy.

I laced up my boots, picked up my gloves, and headed back out to the pit.

Track Nine

I paused in the deep shade of a maple tree at the corner of the house and watched my uncle and my father digging in the earth, the maize *M* of Mike's blue cap bobbing down as the white *S* on Steve's green one bobbed up. They moved in exactly the same way, though Mike, his body broken down by a couple decades of construction work, was about a beat slower than his brother. Still, there was a steady, syncopated rhythm inherent in the two of them. I wondered if that was the way I moved too.

My grandmother once told me that the way she kept Mike and Steve straight when they were first born was to always keep them in either Wolverine or Spartan colors. A flip through any of her photo albums could confirm this. Little Mike was always in blue, little Steve was always in green, and usually their first initial could be found somewhere on their person—on a shirt, a hat, a watch. It helped people tell them apart, but almost from the beginning, like the schools they represented, it had also made them competitive.

I wondered . . . did Steve know how much time Mike had been spending with my mom lately? Did she leverage their inclination toward competition to get Steve to sit up and take notice? Did she actually like Mike, or was she like Brittney, playing on men's natural jealousies, pitting them against one another to suit her own ends?

I dropped down into the pit and picked up the shovel I'd left.

"What'd you take a nap or something?" Mike said.

I didn't answer. Just started digging. I hadn't noticed until that moment that my left hand was no longer numb and tingly. Somewhere between the pit and the guest bedroom, it had come back to life.

For almost an hour, the three of us kept at it, silently, stubbornly. With Carl sent packing and Steve in the mix, we managed to free most of the skull and all of one tusk, which curved upward out of the dirt, as long as I was tall. The other one remained packed in the heavy clay soil. Exhausted, sweaty, and covered in smears of mud and grime, we stared at the huge fossil, drinking Mountain Dews from Mike's cooler.

"There's no way we're getting this thing out of this hole by ourselves," Steve said.

I silently agreed. Mike would need a crane and a crew—a real one, with scientists and people who knew what they were doing—if he was going to get the fossilized skeleton out without destroying it. This was beginning to look less and less like a solution to the problem of the pawned guest book and more like just another one of Mike's failed gambles, with a healthy helping of bad luck on the side.

I could read the defeat on Mike's face. Then I glanced at Steve. He was looking at Mike, his brow furrowed in a mixture of pity and a complete lack of surprise. Just like Dusty, he must have known to expect this sort of thing when Mike was involved.

I felt a sudden, fierce, and inexplicable sympathy for my uncle. No matter what he did, things just didn't seem to work out. But at least he tried to do things. At least he tried to hit it big in Vegas. At least he tried to find love, even if he looked for it in self-destructive ways. At least he tried to experience some semblance of family by treating the neighbor girl like the daughter he'd almost had.

And what did his twin brother do? Knocked up a pretty girl right out of high school, left her and their baby, and didn't have the decency to also leave town so they'd never have to see him again. Instead, he drifted in and out of their orbit just enough to give them a little bit of hope, just enough to keep the longing for a husband and a father alive, just enough so that people like Natalie and Deb felt somehow honor bound to try to glue the broken parts together.

It was like the skeleton beneath our feet. It would have to come out in pieces, bone by heavy bone. Then someone in some museum would put it back together the way it was supposed to be. The only difference was, all these bones had been part of a single living creature before. Joined by muscle and sinew and animated by blood and breath, they held together, worked with each other, propelled the whole organism along. But my so-called family? We'd never been a single unit. Never joined by law. Never joined by love. We'd never be put back together because we'd never been together to begin with.

I pulled off my gloves and stretched the fingers in my left hand, which had started tingling again. "Well, I guess that's it."

Mike's head swung my way. "No, that is not it."

"Mike, look at it," Steve said. "That thing must weigh half a ton. You need heavy equipment to get this job done."

I nodded my agreement with the man I hated more than any other.

"I can get a few more guys," Mike said.

"A few more guys?" Steve said. "You'd need at least twenty."

"I can get twenty."

"For free? I don't think so. The kid's right. We're done." He dropped his shovel and removed his gloves. "I'm out." He climbed out of the hole.

"Sorry, Mike," I said. I climbed out as well, keeping a few steps behind Steve as we walked up the slope.

As we entered the shade of the big maple tree, I heard the blade of Mike's shovel strike the ground again. I felt bad leaving him there in that pit, digging ever deeper but never reaching his goal, the very picture of futility. But there was little point in continuing. Hopefully Deb would die ignorant of Mike's sin, but it was looking increasingly likely that the guest book might be gone for good.

When we reached the driveway, Steve stopped to let me catch up to him. "You know you're not responsible for him, right?"

I grunted.

"Really," he said. "You're not responsible for anyone but yourself. That's the only way to live."

"No, it's not," I said, crossing my tired arms over my chest. "In fact, that's a pretty selfish way to live."

He mirrored my stance. "Okay, let's have this out now so we don't have to deal with it later."

I uncrossed my arms. I didn't want to stand like this guy, move like this guy, be like this guy in any way. "There's nothing to say, really."

"No?" he said. "Not 'You ruined my life'? 'You're why I don't trust anyone'? Or 'All my friends' dads coached their Little League teams and taught them how to drive, and I was just this weird kid with no dad'? Maybe you want to tell me how I missed your first steps and your graduation and all that 'Cat's in the Cradle' crap? Nothing? Nothing to say to me?"

I wanted to punch him, to leave a mark on that smug, unrepentant face. The only thing keeping me from doing it was the thought of hurting my hand again, of letting Natalie down by not being able to play. So instead, I shrugged. "I don't need to say any of that stuff. You just said it." I walked up the porch steps, opened the Wheelers' front door, and paused. "You're a really good drummer, Steve. You're just a really horrible father. I'll see you at practice next week."

I went inside and shut the door behind me. I stood there a moment, breathing, letting the adrenaline dissipate. Then I took my boots off and headed for the bathroom in the guest suite. I filled the white sink with hot water. I removed my shirt and scrubbed my hands, arms, neck, and chest with a wet washcloth. The water clouded with dirt until it looked like the filth in the popcorn bowl when my mom was washing the floor in the trailer kitchen. I pulled the plug and watched it all drain away. I put my dirty shirt back on, ran some cool water over my hands and through my sweaty hair, and tied the wet mess back with a rubber band.

Then I headed downstairs. I didn't have Deb's guitar with me—it was stashed deep under my bed at home, a place I really didn't want to go right now. I'd just play the Martin today.

When I got down to the studio, Natalie, Cory, and Carrie were in the midst of playing "The Way It Goes." It sounded so full and round with the cello and the violin playing the counterpoints to Natalie's precise guitar picking. They were all real musicians. And I was just a poseur, just a guy who wanted to be a rock star, who wanted his signature to be worth something someday. But who, if he accomplished anything at all, probably wouldn't even manage to be up on the pawn shop wall next to Hall & Oates, half-mocked, half-forgotten, not worth much of anything.

Still, I had to at least try.

I entered the live room, grabbed the Martin, and pulled up a stool next to Natalie.

"I'm glad you're here, Michael," she said. "Why don't you teach us how to play 'The Moment.'"

"Absolutely." I tuned the Martin, pressed my fingers to the strings, and played.

As I sang my apology to Natalie, I wondered if sorry would have been enough if Steve had said it. If he'd actually apologized and actually meant it, would I have forgiven him? Was I really expected to?

Working through the song with Natalie and Cory and Carrie, I decided it didn't really matter. He'd had the chance to apologize and he didn't. He wasn't sorry at all. Even Deb couldn't fault me for not forgiving him.

Track Ten

The next day, as a precaution, I pulled Deb's guitar out from under the bed and stored it at the Wheelers' house when I wasn't using it, which wasn't often. Every moment I wasn't at work, I was there—practicing in the studio, preparing meals in the kitchen, cleaning up the dining room table, scribbling lyrics in the billiards room. Practically every day another musician showed up. Don on the mandolin. Benji on the bass. Violet on the piano. Of course, Natalie could have played every instrument that her friends played, but she had decided that for the Saint Andrew's gig, she was going to stick to lead guitar. I would play rhythm. And, of course, Steve would play drums.

We would practice three official times as a whole band— Tuesday, Wednesday, and Thursday—leading up to the gig on Friday. That meant I'd have to be in a small room with Steve Sullivan three more times. Then the gig. Then that was it. I wouldn't have to see him ever again if I didn't want to.

I decided I wasn't mad at Mike for inviting his brother to help with the dig. And I wasn't mad at Deb, a peacemaker to the end, for pushing him to get me and my dad together. Even if it didn't result in the reconciliation I knew Deb wanted for us, a couple good things had come of it. First, it made Mike seem better by comparison, despite his many flaws. Second, it had sparked another song—one I'd play at the gig, though Natalie didn't know that yet.

I was actually starting to get excited for this thing, actually starting to think it might not be a disaster—despite the fact that the kind of music we were making was mostly not in line with what a Saint Andrew's crowd would be expecting. Natalie's friends were as nice as they were talented, and I didn't get the feeling any of them were judging me. On the contrary, they were supportive and encouraging and shared their knowledge and skill without pretension or condescension. Benji had a wicked sense of humor, Violet developed great harmonies, Don could improvise incredible solos. Even Cory and Carrie, who'd seemed rather stiff and no-nonsense at first, could roll with on-the-spot changes and laughed easily. I was even on the receiving end of a number of compliments about the songs, which everyone seemed to love. I could see that this team-up would feel cohesive, that it had potential. Just two things marred it—Steve's imminent involvement and Deb's swiftly deteriorating condition.

On the Tuesday before the gig, hospice was called in. While the rest of us got ready downstairs, Natalie was upstairs with her father and her aunt, saying goodbye just in case Deb should fall asleep and not wake up again. When she finally appeared in the door of the live room, she looked like she was the one who was sick.

I met her at the door and grasped her hand. "You don't have to do this today."

"I know." She took a deep breath. "But maybe it will take my mind off it for a while."

I led her to her mic, handed over her guitar, and waited for instructions. None came.

"Okay, everyone," I said. "Let's play the set list straight through, troubleshooting as we go. We move on to the next song when there are no mistakes and no questions."

The group followed my lead—even Steve, with whom I'd not made eye contact up to that point—and I really did feel like a front man with great backup. But with each successive song, I realized that what I really wanted was to feel the way I had on Mother's Day, when it was just me and Natalie. Just two voices and two acoustic guitars. And though Natalie played her parts without making any mistakes, I could tell she wasn't really there.

When it was time to play "The Way It Goes," I suggested Violet sing Natalie's part, just for today, and Natalie made no argument. Violet also sang for the covers Natalie was going to take lead on. As we neared the end, there was a song on the list we'd never played, one I'd never heard of.

"What's this 'Feet Made of Wheels' thing?" I asked the room. Shrugs and blank stares. "Natalie?"

"Hmm?"

"Is this something you added to the set list?"

"What?"

"'Feet Made of Wheels.'"

"Oh, yeah. But it's just me. Let's skip it for now. You can hear it later."

I couldn't grudge her the last-minute addition. After all, I had plans for one of my own, and we were pushing it to fill ninety minutes. But second to last was a prominent place on the set list. Ideally, the crowd would be ramped up at that point, and a solo with a single acoustic guitar playing would be way too quiet. I'd ask her about it later when everyone had gone home or to their hotel.

For now, we moved to the last song on the set list—"Chasing Clear Skies." Best to end the night on a high note. We got it on the first try. Probably because it was quite purposely on the generic side to increase the probability of earworms.

"Okay, that about does it for tonight," I said.

"What about something for an encore?" Cory said.

"I've got that covered," Natalie and I said in unison. Our heads swiveled toward one another.

"Looks like you two better figure that out," Steve said from the back of the room. They were the first words he'd spoken all night. He laid his drumsticks on the snare, shrugged on his jacket, and left.

The room slowly emptied out until only Natalie and I were left. I put a hand on her arm. "Are you going to be okay?"

She ducked under the shoulder strap of her guitar and handed it to me. "Yeah. This was just bad timing. I'll be totally present tomorrow."

I put our guitars on their stands. "So, what did you have planned for an encore?"

"Something for my mom. What did you have planned?"

"Something for my dad."

She snickered. "I guess we'll have to flip a coin for who goes first."

"I guess."

Only, I knew that wouldn't work. Her song for her mother would be sweet and loving. The one I'd been working on for my dad was . . . not. Anyway, the chance of anyone demanding an encore seemed slim. We had great material. Most of it just wasn't great Saint Andrew's material.

"How about we save the encore for you and I'll just stick mine in the set list earlier?" I said.

"Sure. The first half would be good. There's no solo that early. You could stick it after"—she sighed—"'Satan's a Hot Girl' before we do 'Anonymous.'"

"Hmm . . . maybe," I said, though I knew I was not going to put it there. Or anywhere in the first half. If I did that, there was really no guarantee we'd have a drummer for the second half of the show. No, it had to be as close to the end as possible. "We'll talk about it tomorrow. You should get some rest."

I made sure everything was turned off in the studio and led Natalie upstairs. Her bed was waiting for her around the corner. My boots were waiting for me in the foyer. Before I could sit down on the bench to put them on, Natalie put her arms around my waist and pressed her face to my chest. It took a second for me to realize what was happening. Then I wrapped my arms around her and squeezed her close.

Beneath my arms, her shoulders shook as she tried to suppress her grief. I didn't say anything, because everything I could say would be either obvious or untrue. I just held her. A couple minutes later, she stilled, sniffed, and pulled away. I held her face in my hands and wiped the wetness from her cheeks with my thumbs. I wanted to tell her right then and there that I loved her, that I'd be there for her, that every time she needed to cry, from that night until eternity, I wanted her to cry on me. But then every time she thought of the first time I told her I loved her, she'd think of her mom dying.

So I kissed her forehead and said, "I'll see you tomorrow night."

There was still some light lingering in the sky as I walked back to the trailer. The whole time I'd known Natalie, the days had been stretching out in both directions. Not long after the gig, they'd start getting shorter again. Time ebbed and flowed in imperceptible increments. Day to day, it never really seemed any different. Yet the seasons kept changing. We could never know as it was happening what the summer solstice of our lives would be. When our days started getting shorter and night began closing in.

As I opened the trailer door, I wondered what Deb's personal solstice was like. Was it the day she'd met Dusty? The day she'd married him? Some day in between? Had it been a significant day or one long forgotten?

I shut the door and took a step inside, and immediately I knew something was off. Mike wasn't home, which wasn't unusual. But that wasn't it. I'd seen that his car was missing, so I'd known that going in. No, it was something else. I turned on the lights, started looking around. Everything was where it always was. I flicked on the light in my room. Everything seemed normal. But back in the hall I noticed that Mike's door was wide open, which certainly was not normal.

I stepped into the room. Bare mattress. Dresser drawers emptied and not pushed back in. The closet was open and empty but for Mike's black leather jacket I'd worn to the New Year's Eve party six months ago. A yellowed envelope stuck out of the pocket. I pulled it out and removed the equally yellowed paper inside. As I unfolded it, a photo fell to the ground. I picked it up.

In the photo, younger versions of the Deb and Dusty I knew flanked a skinny man with disheveled hair who had his arms around both of them. All three smiled for the camera. The man in the middle was wearing a jacket that looked just like the one hanging in the closet. And that man was Mick Jagger.

I tucked the photo behind the letter. The penmanship was obviously a woman's, and it reminded me of the penmanship on the envelope of the party invitation.

Dear Mike,

    I wanted to thank you for your fine work on the court-yard tiling—it is stunning! We've been enjoying some lovely summer nights out there with friends, some of whom forget to pack up all of their belongings when they fly back to their homes halfway around the world. I asked Mick if he wanted me to ship this jacket back to him after I discovered it on the back of a chair in the billiards room, but he said he'd already replaced it with another and that I should give it to someone special. So I'm giving it to you as an extra token of my appreciation for the work you continue to do for us.

With gratitude,
Deb

P.S. Pinky is wondering when "Unca Mike" is going to take her on a motorcycle ride. How is your Saturday looking?

At the bottom of the letter, Mike had added his own note.

Michael,
Every rock star needs a leather jacket. Maybe this one will bring you some good luck up on stage.

Later,
Mike

I refolded the note, reinserted it into the envelope along with the photo, and placed it on the nightstand. Why hadn't Mike sold this when he needed money rather than stealing from his friend? Why hadn't he tried to work out a trade with the pawn shop once he'd come to his senses?

Why did I know without a doubt that I wouldn't have done that either?

I pulled on Mick Jagger's leather jacket. Like all of Mike's stuff, it smelled like Camel cigarettes. Mike must have worn it when he was my size. When his life was nothing but possibilities. I didn't know if he'd squandered whatever portion of potential he was given when he came into this world or if he'd just gotten some hard breaks. I didn't know if Deb's belief in him was misplaced or if all the second chances she'd given him would ever amount to anything. I didn't know if he'd manage to turn things around by his last verse. I didn't even know where he'd gone or if he intended to ever come back, though I certainly understood the impulse to run and leave your troubles behind you.

All I really knew at that moment was that I wasn't going to let life defeat me. I wasn't going to run when things got tough. I was ready to make things happen instead of just letting them happen to me.

And I was going to wear Mick Jagger's leather jacket while doing it.

Track Eleven

At five o'clock on Friday, I drove up the Wheelers' winding driveway and got out of the car to retrieve Natalie. We'd spent the morning setting up at Saint Andrew's Hall, and now we were meeting up with the rest of the band for a little food, then we'd do the final sound check before the doors opened at eight o'clock for the opening acts.

Before I got up the porch steps, I heard Dusty call to me from the open garage. I met him behind the Mustang.

"You all set for tonight?" he said.

"Yeah, looks like it. Everything sounded pretty decent this morning."

He smiled sadly. "I wish I could be there."

"Nah. Don't worry about it. And hey, I probably need to thank you. For getting us in there. I know that Intersection is not really their normal fare."

He chuckled. "You might be sorry you got in at all." He motioned to my jacket. "At least you'll look the part. Seems like I've seen that jacket before. Nice of Mike to let you wear it again."

I still hadn't told anyone that Mike had left town. "Said he thought it might bring me good luck."

Dusty nodded, and I could tell he was trying to decide if

I knew whose jacket it really was. "Well," he said, "a man wearing that jacket should not pull up to a gig in that car." He pointed at my crappy Citation leaking oil on his driveway, then produced a set of keys attached to a black leather key ring emblazoned with a shiny Ford Mustang logo.

I smiled. "Really?"

He held the keys out to me.

I took them and shook his hand firmly. "I'll take good care of it."

"Take better care of what's inside it," he said, raising his bushy eyebrows.

"Of course. I will. Thank you, Dusty."

He turned to go back into the house. "I'll send her out."

I ran a hand along the perfectly polished driver's side door. The top was already down, and every inch of the car shone like it had just been waxed. I wondered if it had. If while we were getting things ready at Saint Andrew's, he'd been getting things ready here.

"Hey," came Natalie's voice from the door Dusty had just gone through.

She was dressed in flared jeans with a sharp crease running down each leg, a cream-colored knit top, and a brown suede vest with beads and fringe. She wore the large silver hoop ear-rings she'd had on at the New Year's Eve party, and a necklace of turquoise stones laid in silver hung around her neck. Except for her short hair, which had gotten a bit shaggy over the past several weeks, she looked exactly like her mother used to.

"Hey yourself," I said, walking over to her. "You look amazing."

She smiled that golden smile and touched my arm. "Mike's jacket?"

"Yeah. He gave it to me."

"That was generous."

"Yeah, it was."

She fiddled with the fringe on her vest. "This is all my mom's stuff. I guess it probably doesn't really go with what you're wearing. I should have stuck to black."

"Nonsense. We don't have to match. We're not Sonny and Cher. This is perfect, really. Represents the intersection, right? A little rock, a little folk."

She smiled again. "You're right."

I caught myself staring at her and snapped to attention. "We better get going." I took her arm, led her to the car, and opened the door.

"Wow. Dad's letting you take the Mustang?"

"Yep. I feel like I'm borrowing Dad's car to take you to prom or something." I shut her door and came around to the driver's side. "Not that I'd know what that feels like. I didn't go to my prom, and if I had, I sure wouldn't have had the option of using Steve's car. I don't even know what he drove then."

"All right," she said after I shut my own door. "That's enough of that. Let's both promise right now that tonight is not about your dad and it's not about my mom. It's about our music. Let's just focus on that."

"You're right." I turned the key in the ignition, and the engine roared to life. "Tonight is all about the music."

As we made our way back to downtown Detroit, back to the stage at Saint Andrew's Hall, back to our moment in the spotlight, I took stock of my life. I wasn't where I had thought I wanted to be at this point—touring with The Pleasure Centers, signing autographs for throngs of fans, feeding off the admiration and jealousy of others. I wasn't sleeping in swanky hotel rooms where food and drinks and women just appeared out of nowhere to fulfill my every need. I wasn't a superstar.

I was still a nobody—but I was happier than I'd been in a long time.

I parked in the alley next to Saint Andrew's Hall, helped Natalie out of the car, and stared at the back entrance. Through that door was everything I'd been working toward. I expected to have that sick swirling feeling in my stomach, that pounding in my chest that I always felt getting up on stage with Rodney and Slow. But all I felt was gratitude.

"Ready?" Natalie said.

"Ready."

It wasn't until nearly ten o'clock that the second opening act finished up. I held my palm out flat to slap their hands as they squeezed past in the cramped backstage area, which was as full of people as it was of equipment and couches that looked like they'd been picked up off the side of the road after a few years of enduring hard rains and bleaching sun.

They'd done a good job. So good, in fact, that the crowd was primed for more. Which is what a good opener did for the headliner. I felt my newfound confidence falter. This audience was ours to lose. And I knew that we were not going to fulfill the promise the opening acts had just made to them. They were expecting dirty garage band rock. And we were . . . well, it was hard to say. Some of our songs might fit the mold if we kept the tempo fast enough. But even the sight of a violin and a cello and a mandolin was going to set people against us right off the bat.

I handed Natalie over to Violet to help her to her place on the dimly lit stage and slipped to the back. Steve was settling himself behind the drum set, and I leaned in close so he could hear me over the crowd. "Hey, if you ever wanted to make it up to me after missing my childhood, you could be well on your way if you'd speed up the tempo on everything tonight."

He met my eye. Nodded. I knew he must have the same feeling as I did: that this group of musicians did not actually belong on this stage. That we had, in a sense, bought our way into a club that others had to earn their way into. And that we were probably going to pay for it tonight.

I took my place next to Natalie, slung the white Stratocaster over my shoulders, and forced my breaths into a steady in-out rhythm, waiting for the stage lights. It couldn't have been more than a few seconds before they blazed forth, but in that short time I managed several distinct thoughts.

First: It's a decent-size crowd. Maybe the venue wasn't full—why would it be when some random band no one had ever heard of was the headliner?—but it was a lot of people. A lot of people looking at me, taking stock of me, deciding whether or not they would be on my side. These people expected something from me. Something I wasn't going to be able to deliver.

Breathe.

Second: They're here. They're actually here. Among the general din of talking, clapping, and shouting, I easily picked out Brittney's distinct "Woo!" somewhere down near my feet from years of hearing it at each gig The Pleasure Centers played. So she at least was here, which meant that it was pretty likely Rodney and Slow were here as well. And they were all near the front of the crowd, where they'd have the best view of me crashing and burning.

Breathe.

Third: Never forget, you're wearing Mick Jagger's jacket.

The lights came up.

I said into the mic, "Thanks for coming out tonight, everyone. We're Intersection."

Steve clicked his sticks together—fast—and we started into the first song on the set list. I avoided glancing at Natalie or anyone else up on stage. They were professionals. They could keep up. They might not like it, but they'd keep up.

In an era dominated by men in tight pants screaming into microphones with fireworks going off in the background, and synth-driven bubblegum pop sung by girls who looked like they'd just stopped by on their way home from the mall, Saint Andrew's Hall had been making a reputation for itself presenting bands with a rough edge. Stuff out of the mainstream. Stuff that hinted at a new, less produced, more spontaneous-sounding direction that music was taking. And if that's what this crowd wanted, that's what I would give them.

As the first song ended and I was about to start playing the opening riff of the next one, Natalie turned to Steve and said, "Hey, slow it down. It's not a race."

I looked back, made eye contact with him, and rolled my finger in the air. Keep it up.

I played the opening riff—fast—and felt the crowd coming along with me. Steve backed me up. We barreled on through. But it didn't feel as good as I thought it would. I could sense the rest of the people sharing the stage with me pulling back. They kept the tempo I'd set. But it reminded me of the first and only time I'd gone horseback riding in eighth grade. I did what the guide had told us to do—say this to make the horse go, kick him here to make him go faster, yank up on the reins if he starts eating grass along the side of the trail—but the whole time I was on that huge animal, I could feel his resentment toward me, toward this kid who thought he was in control. That's what I felt from Cory, Carrie, Violet, Don, Benji—and especially Natalie.

When the song ended, she was at my side. "What are you

doing, Michael? This is way too fast. This is not how we practiced these songs."

I hit the distortion pedal with my foot. "We can't play them how we practiced them. Not for this crowd."

"Why not?"

"They're draggy. They'll hate them that way." I turned to the mic. "You having a good time tonight, Detroit?"

The audience responded with shouts and woos.

"You think we should slow it down?"

Boos.

"You think we should speed things up?"

Screams.

"See?" I said to Natalie.

"But—"

I started into "The Way It Goes" at practically double its normal speed. When I'd written it, it had been a ballad. Now with the syncopated rhythm Steve was pounding out on the drums and the screech of the distortion effect on the Stratocaster, it sounded like something I could play at the Thrash Factory. We pulled the rest of the band along through the first couple verses and choruses. When I got to the line "and then I turned to face her with a smile," I looked at Natalie as I always did at that moment in the song, and the expression on her face made me drop a beat. I recovered and sang on, but I felt like I'd been gut-punched.

Then I realized—that was probably how she felt too.

Going into the bridge, I sang over and over, "I'm drowning, I'm drowning, I'm drowning in you." But I wasn't exactly. I was drowning, all right. But it wasn't in her. It was in my own shame. My own ego. What was I doing up here? Why was I doing this to her? Why did the opinions of all these strangers, along with a few bad former friends, matter more than her opinion of me?

I came up on the line "Can't catch my breath when I'm stuck under water, and I just really need to hear her say . . . ," and I was not surprised that instead of singing her part, Natalie actually stopped playing entirely. Just dropped her hands from the guitar and put them on her hips. One by one, the others followed her lead, until it was just Steve and me, keeping the beat, repeating the riff. Drowning up there.

Finally, I stopped. Steve stopped. The crowd started murmuring to each other and booing. I heard someone—maybe Rodney—shout, "Choke!"

I had to do something. Had to say something. We were losing them.

I was losing her.

"All right, all right," I said into the mic. "That's not really how that song's supposed to go. We're going to play it again." I turned to Natalie but still spoke into the mic. "The right way."

I clicked the distortion pedal off and started the song over at the speed I'd written it. The speed we'd practiced it. Steve reverted to the original drum part. One by one, my backup came back to me. The instruments filled up the space, took full advantage of the incredible acoustics of the venue.

And what space the sound from the cello and the mandolin and the piano and all the rest didn't take up did not remain empty. The audience filled it. With boos. They hated it. It wasn't what they came there for. It wasn't what the first couple acts had primed them for. It wasn't going to win me any adoring fans.

But I didn't care anymore. Because I could feel Natalie coming back. And I was beginning to see that her opinion of me mattered more than anyone's ever had. Ever could.

When Natalie's voice cut into the song for the last chorus,

the boos died away. Mostly. I heard Brittney still voicing her displeasure. But when Natalie and I harmonized on the last refrain of "I'm drowning, I'm drowning, I'm drowning in you," the last of the booing stopped. And when the song ended, there was some tepid clapping. They'd give us that one. They'd give us a chance to win them back.

I looked at the set list. Perfect.

"This next song is about a girl who might be here tonight," Natalie said into the mic before I could. "It's called 'Brittney Sucks.'"

I laughed out loud, then plunged into the song, backed by the driving force of Steve's pounding drums.

> She's the kind of girl who shows up drunk and kisses
>   your best friend
> A tornado, a no-good punk, relationship dead end
> She'll lie to get your sympathy, then laugh right in your
>   face
> She'll make off with your dignity, flip out when you
>   need space
> She spies, connives, and robs you blind, she rinses and
>   repeats
> Insists on being wined and dined, then turns around
>   and cheats
>
> You don't need her hanging around
> You can't defeat her, she'll take you down
> You don't need her casting her spell
> You can't defeat her, she'll drag you to hell
>
> The first time that you saw her, she didn't even look
>   your way
> Your friends all said don't bother, she won't give you
>   the time of day

She finally went out with you when you promised her
  the moon
But careful what you wish for, dude, 'cause you'll regret
  it soon

You don't need her hanging around
You can't defeat her, she'll take you down
You don't need her casting her spell
You can't defeat her, she'll drag you to hell

When you took her on your first date, she only had eyes
  for you
But when you brought her to our place, well, she had
  eyes for me too
Whenever you are out of sight, she puts the moves on
  me
Any time of day or night, don't know why you can't see

You don't need her hanging around
You can't defeat her, she'll take you down
You don't need her casting her spell
You can't defeat her, she'll drag you to hell

I swear she has it out for you
I wish that you could see it too
She's gonna break your heart someday
And you know that I'll have to say
I told you so, so many times
But you wouldn't listen, such a crime
You let a pretty girl come steal your soul
Just cut her loose, don't you know

You don't need her hanging around
You can't defeat her, she'll take you down
You don't need her casting her spell
You can't defeat her, she'll drag you to hell

She'll drag you to hell . . .
She'll drag you to hell . . .
She'll drag you to hell . . .
She'll drag you to hell . . .
She'll drag you to hell . . .

And just like that, the crowd was back. Well, all except for three of them.

Track Twelve

A few original songs and two covers later, we crested the halfway point of the set list. Soon it would be time to make a decision. Was I actually going to do the song I'd written about Steve? I glanced back at him behind the drums. He'd never been there for me. But he was there now, ten feet away, and he'd backed me up. Even though my decision to hijack the band and do what I wanted to was a bad one, he'd backed me up.

The anger and resentment that had fueled the writing of the song were still simmering—being there for me one stinking time didn't erase twenty-two years of neglect. But laying like a warm blanket over top of my bitterness about the family I never had was the family I was finding. Natalie, Deb, Dusty— even Mike. And just knowing how circumstances had formed them into the particular people they now were—Mike's lost child, Deb's lost career, Dusty's constant fear of losing his wife, Natalie's soon-to-be-lost mother—made it possible for me to pause a moment and allow for the possibility that something might have happened in Steve's life to contribute to making him the person he was. Maybe he too had lost something. Maybe he didn't deal with it very well. Maybe it haunted him to this day. And maybe, like Mike, he kind of hated himself for it.

I put the Strat on its stand and pulled the strap of Deb's guitar over my shoulder. "Natalie and I are going to play you all a song we wrote for her mother. I don't know if you know who Deb Wheeler is"—a smattering of people clapped and one yelled—"but Natalie here is Deb's daughter."

I looked at Natalie, hoping to see a positive reaction to this last-minute substitution. We hadn't planned on playing "The Truest Feeling" tonight, thinking maybe it was just too raw, too personal. But she smiled and gave the crowd a little wave, so I pushed on.

"We've all got challenges to face in this life. Deb's challenge is cancer."

Sympathetic sounds rippled through the crowd. A few boos. I chose to believe those were for cancer, not us.

"But even when we face dark days, we've got friends on our side, and that's what this song's about."

Stagehands appeared from the wings with two stools and repositioned our microphones as Natalie and I sat down, nearly facing each other. The lights on the rest of the band dimmed as the spotlight rose on us. The crowd hushed. Natalie began picking out the intro. I came in with the rhythm and the first part of the first verse.

> The truest feeling is an ache
> A vague, insistent pulse of pain
> Carving out a piece of flesh
> Internal wound that's never dressed

Natalie took the second part, improvising on the last line.

> The good, the bad, it's all the same
> The love, the hate, the pride, the shame

The sweet young thing who caught your eye
The mother who's about to die

Though we never planned it and never practiced it, I came into the chorus singing the melody while Natalie improvised a perfect harmony that put me in mind of one of our first nights in the listening room when she introduced me to the Indigo Girls.

We traded on and off for the rest of the song, Natalie transitioning easily between melody and harmony, even throwing in a countermelody as we repeated the last chorus at the end.

I'll answer when you're calling
I'll catch you when you're falling
I'll push you when you're stalling
No matter what's befalling you
I won't let your life cave in
You can count on me, my friend
Always . . . always . . .

The last note faded. The moment hung heavy and silent in the air for as long as it could. Then the audience cheered, the spell was lifted, and the stagehands appeared again to remove the stools.

The next forty minutes flew by in a moment, a swirl of sounds and sweat. Strings singing, vocal cords vibrating, drums and cymbals shivering. We plowed through the rest of the set list, inching closer and closer to the end of the gig, the end of the night, the end of this particular crowd of people who, when all was said and done, didn't seem to love us but also didn't seem to totally hate us.

After this night, all of Natalie's friends would head back to their homes in other states. Steve would presumably head back to the Thrash Factory and whatever else he did to fill his time. Natalie would head back to her mother's bedside, and I would head back to the trailer I now had all to myself.

I wished I could make it stop. If I could pause it right here, hit the replay button, loop this night over and over for a while, I'd do it. But I couldn't. I could stop the sound coming from my guitar with a hand on the strings, but no one could stop time.

"You guys are great," I said to the audience as we began to wrap things up. "You know, I used to be in this other band, and I don't think we ever had this great of an audience." A few people clapped. "But maybe it's because we weren't that great of a band." Laughter and woos. "This next song goes out to my old band. Or at least to the guy who thought he was the front man, thought he was the next Mick Jagger or something." I looked at Natalie, who was smiling broadly. "But really he was just the next Uncle Jesse from *Full House*. Only with worse hair."

The crowd erupted in more laughter. I nodded at Steve, who counted us in by smacking his drumsticks together. Benji's bass line came in loud and strong. I strummed the first dirty chords and spit the words into the mic.

> You like the girls, you like the look
> Can't sing in tune, can't write a hook
> What they don't know won't hurt 'em none
> Turn on the tube, you're halfway done
>
> Those catchy themes stick in your brain
> Like *Who's the Boss?* and *Growing Pains*
> Your *Happy Days* are 'bout to end
> It's no *Small Wonder* you got no friends
>
> The jig is up—you're drinking from someone else's cup
> The verdict's in—you're claiming prizes that you didn't
>   win

The time is now to just come clean and let it out
Say it out loud: "I'm just a fraud, not a rock god."

The *Facts of Life* that you should know
Nobody wants to see your show
If *Three's Company*, then four's a crowd
I'm jumping ship, I'm bailing out

Perfect Strangers could see right through
the not-so-*Diff'rent Strokes* you use
In *A Different World* you might be "it"
But in Detroit you're just a counterfeit

Natalie's lead line came in like a banshee's wail, at the same time technically proficient and full of emotion that felt like it was being pulled straight from my own nerve endings. The rest of us played along, kept the beat, kept the drive, but it was her time to shine. In that moment, backing her up, the crowd pulsing and jumping and yelling to the beat, I felt like a rock star for the first time. Like I didn't have to try. Like this moment belonged to me from time immemorial and I had finally grasped it. Like life was all laid out for me.

Then we headed back into the chorus.

The jig is up—you're drinking from someone else's cup
The verdict's in—you're claiming prizes that you didn't
    win
The time is now to just come clean and let it out
Say it out loud: "I'm just a fraud, not a rock god."

You're just a fraud, not a rock god
You're just a fraud, not a rock god

When the song ended, I felt like I was flying. Maybe I didn't say everything I'd wanted to say to Steve tonight—maybe I didn't even really want to say it anymore—but I finally said what I'd wanted to say to Rodney. And Natalie, for all her kindness and counsel to just let it go, had said it with me, had supported me with every angry note. I looked at her then and knew that whatever might or might not happen between us, whether she could ever feel about me the way I felt about her, I had found a true friend—perhaps for the first time in my life.

"Okay, let's give Michael here a break after that," Natalie said into the mic. "Michael, take a seat."

A stagehand appeared behind me with a bottle of Evian and the stool he'd brought out earlier. I leaned back and took a long drink. I was sweating inside the leather jacket, so I was glad for the respite.

"So, Michael writes the lyrics for almost all of our songs," Natalie told the crowd, "and I write most of the music. This next song, though, I wrote for you, Michael. I've been working on it since the night I met you."

She pressed her fingers to the strings and began to play. Then she opened her mouth and let her gorgeous voice pour forth.

> When you've got no past that you want to remember
> You blow soft and low 'cross the glowing red embers
> Of what little of worth they left there on the pyre
> And you toss on your dreams and build up the fire
>
> 'Cause what's happened 'fore now, it don't matter
>   much
> The clock's running forward and they're out of touch
> Thinking you're still the boy sitting sad and alone
> Just wishing the future would pick up the phone
>
> Today ain't never been yesterday
> And tomorrow is coming fast on its heels
> I know it's easier when there's someone to blame

But they can't hold you back, you got feet made of
  wheels

So the people you counted on just let you down
And that chance you were banking on never came
  round
You can lash out at others for keeping you stuck
But everyone knows that you make your own luck

Today ain't never been yesterday
And tomorrow is coming fast on its heels
I know it's easier when there's someone to blame
But they can't hold you back, you got feet made of
  wheels

When will you decide that you've had enough?
If you look at my face you'll see I'm calling your bluff
You'll never move forward when you're looking behind
Don't you want your tomorrow to be one you designed?

Today ain't never been yesterday
And tomorrow is coming fast on its heels
I know it's easier when there's someone to blame
But they can't hold you back, you got feet made of
  wheels

No, they can't hold you back, you got feet . . . feet
  made of wheels

I wanted to cry. It was so beautiful and she was so beautiful, and I had never loved anything more than I loved her at that moment. I stood up, took her face in my hands, and kissed her. She put her fingers in my sweaty hair and kissed me back. A long, soft, perfect kiss. The crowd hooted and cheered. And I knew my life was never going to be the same.

I pulled back and looked into her eyes. I wished so desperately that she could look back at me. That she could read the love in my eyes the way I read the love in her smile.

"Thank you," I said close to her ear. "Thank you."

She sniffed back her emotions. "I'm glad you liked it. But you know we have one more song to play."

"Right." I strode back to the mic one last time. "We've got one more song for you tonight. This is called 'Chasing Clear Skies.'"

After the real and unmanufactured emotion of "Feet Made of Wheels," "Chasing Clear Skies" felt more syrupy than ever, the difference between an actual piece of fruit and its fake candy counterpart. Even so, the audience came along for the ride, just as we knew they would when we were writing it. The room lit up with the flames of cigarette lighters swaying to the beat, and the crowd eagerly joined in the last chorus when I motioned for them to sing along.

When it ended, I said into the mic, "You've been amazing, Detroit. We're Intersection. Hope to see you again soon. Have a great night."

I took Natalie's hand and led her offstage behind the rest of the band to the cheers of the crowd. In the tiny and cramped offstage area, there were broad smiles and claps on the back and a few hugs. The applause continued, and I began to make out a chant of "One more song! One more song!" coming from the concert hall.

I'd been waiting for this. Waiting for this moment when a crowd of people couldn't get enough of me. It occurred to me then that this was my last chance to sing the song I'd written about Steve. When I could tell him and everyone else in no uncertain terms just what a dirtbag he was. When I could feed off the shared resentment of hundreds of other people who'd also had horrible childhoods and terrible parents, and we could all be smug about how far we'd come despite it all.

But I didn't want to chase that bitter feeling anymore. I didn't want to publicly punish my dad. I didn't want to live so tied to the past when my future was right there in front of me.

"Well?" I said to Natalie. "You ready to do your last song?"

She hooked two fingers through my belt loop. "Only if you come with me."

"I don't know the song."

She gripped a little tighter. "Please?"

I put my hand on her shoulder. "Of course. I'd go anywhere with you."

We walked back onstage, just the two of us, to the cheers of the audience. Natalie sat down. I handed her guitar to her.

"No," she said. "I need my mom's."

I replaced the guitar on its stand and gave her Deb's instead, then adjusted two mics to pick up the guitar and her voice. She cleared her throat. The crowd hushed.

"This is for my mom."

Natalie scooted her mother's guitar a little higher on her thigh. Then she began.

> Play me a sad, slow song
> One that breaks my heart a little
> One that starts with love and ends with loss
> Play me a mournful tune
> One that makes me ache a little
> One that starts too quick and ends too soon
>
> Because I feel it in my bones
> I won't always be alone
> So it's now or never for my grief
> I'll miss you if you like

But I won't miss out on life
Don't you know how hard it is to watch you leave?

Give me a reason why
One that calms my fears a little
One that proves I don't need you to survive
Give me a clear blue sky
One that cheers my soul a little
One that dries up all the tears that leave my eyes

Because I feel it in my bones
I wasn't meant to be alone
And I don't think you would disagree
Though I'll think of you each day
I'm gonna give my heart away
To that next true love God sends to me

Since the day I was born
You've been there for me
Now your body is worn
And you yearn to be free
So take off your dusty shoes
And cross that river wide
And when my life on earth concludes
I'm gonna meet you in the sky

And I feel it in my bones
I will never be alone
Because I carry all your love inside of me
And I'll think of you each day
My love will never fade away
I'll be okay because you helped me see . . .
That everyone I meet is family

There was a moment of silence as the audience let out its collective held breath. For some reason I looked at my watch,

I guess to check if we had filled all ninety minutes we were supposed to. It was 11:47 p.m. We'd done it and then some.

Amid the clapping—subdued at first but growing as Natalie stood up and gave a nod of thanks to the audience—I walked her offstage, where a few audience members were already chatting up the rest of the band. Slow was one of them.

"Oh, great," I said under my breath.

"What?" Natalie said.

"Hey, Michael," Slow said.

"Hey, Slow."

"Oh," Natalie said.

Slow smiled and held up his hand for a high five. "That was awesome, man." He gripped my hand, then released it and went to shake Natalie's. It took him a second with his hand stuck out to realize he had to just grab hers. "Really great. Your voice is beautiful. And the instrumentation? You wrote all those parts?"

She nodded. "Thanks."

"I mean it," he said. "It was really a great show. I mean, it was a weird show. And I'm thinking you're probably not going to be invited back here, but I thought it was great. Even Rodney had to admit it. I mean, up until that one song." He laughed. "He didn't like that one so much."

"I guess not," I said. "He take off?"

"Yeah. Kind of stormed out, but he's my ride so I hope he's out in the car."

"Hope so," I said. "I don't have room for you in what I'm driving tonight."

Slow rubbed his hands together. "Listen, I just wanted to apologize. For punching you, you know?"

"Forget it," I said. "Maybe I deserved it." A few more people were pushing their way backstage. I stepped aside. "Speaking of Brittney, I thought I heard her out in the crowd."

"Yeah, she was here. She didn't really like the song you wrote about her any more than Rodney liked the one you wrote about him. I think she called a friend to come pick her up."

"Sorry, man."

Slow waved my apology away. "Nah. You're right. She's bad news. I've known that for a long time. Just didn't have the guts to do anything about it."

"You gonna dump her?"

He shrugged. "I dunno. Maybe. We'll see. Anyway, I'm glad you didn't write a song all about me."

I laughed. "There's still time."

Slow scratched his head. "I think Rodney might regret kicking you out. Though I don't think he could ever admit it, and I know he'd never apologize for it."

I put my arm around Natalie's waist. "Best thing that ever could have happened to me."

Natalie spoke up. "We could use a bassist. Benji's headed back to New York tomorrow."

For a moment, Slow looked like he was considering it. Like he was imagining a life without Rodney and Brittney and all the drama inherent therein. He smiled. "I'll think about it."

We said our goodbyes, and Natalie and I turned to find a dozen or so people stuffed into the backstage area. People who wanted to meet us. We talked and laughed and shook hands with them, their names forgotten almost the moment they were uttered.

It took a good half hour or so to come down from the high we were all on. But as the celebration wore on, I could see that Natalie was increasingly somewhere else in her mind. It was time to take her home.

The small cadre of fans we had gathered dispersed, either downstairs to The Shelter or upstairs to what sounded like a rave. We gathered up our equipment, each toting away our own instruments into our own cars. Don and I helped Steve load up his van with the drum set. He shut the doors and turned to face me.

"Nice job," he said, then he held out his hand.

In my back pocket I had the lyrics to the song I'd written about him, the one I'd decided not to play. There was still a small part of me that wanted to slap the paper into his outstretched hand. But now I knew that song was just for me. Something I needed to say, but not necessarily something I needed to say to him or to anyone else.

I gripped his hand with mine. "Thanks for keeping the beat."

He nodded and looked like he wanted to say something else. I waited, giving him an empty space to fill.

"You know," he finally said, "I didn't leave because of you. Or your mom." He broke eye contact, looked off to the side. "It was a bad time. For a lot of us. Mike joined up after . . . well, he had something he needed to get away from."

"The baby," I said.

Steve looked surprised. "Yeah. His number hadn't been called up, but he enlisted anyway."

I couldn't figure out where this was going. What did Mike's time in Vietnam have to do with anything?

"My number did get called up," he said.

I felt my brow crease in confusion. Was this the answer? Was it that simple? "Mom never said you served."

He shifted his weight. "I didn't."

"Then how—" I shut my mouth. Took a beat to run through a dozen distinct thoughts, just like when you're about to hit a deer with your car. Only this time it felt like I was the deer.

"I was gone for a while," he said. "Just across the river."

He motioned vaguely in the direction of Canada, which sat

placidly on the other side of the Detroit River, ready to receive its neighbor's cowards and conscientious objectors. Which one, I wondered, was my dad?

"By the time I could come back in '77, you were half-grown. I was no more than a stranger. Your mom and I tried a few times to start something up again. But there was just nothing there between us."

He waited for me to say something. But what could I say? If he'd gone to Vietnam, been captured as a prisoner of war, and finally been released and made his way home years after the war ended, I could have grown up with some measure of pride mixed into the pain. I could have believed that he'd had no choice but to leave. That he'd been longing all that time to be home with his son. That when he got home, he'd been so damaged and broken by his experiences he couldn't manage a normal life with a family. Even if he'd been killed in action, I could have conjured a picture of him that accounted for his absence in a way that would have allowed me to grow up happier and more whole.

But this? What was I supposed to do with the knowledge that my father had been a draft dodger?

"I'm not proud of any of it," he said to fill the silence. "But I thought maybe if you knew the truth, it might help you understand."

I felt myself glaring at him and purposefully relaxed the muscles in my face. I tried to put myself in his shoes, tried to imagine what I would have done if my number had been called up. Finally, there was only one thing to say. "Did you know she was pregnant?"

The look on his face said it all, but he still said aloud, "Yes."

I nodded. Took a long, slow breath. Then I walked away. There was more to say. But not right then. I kicked that can way down the road and went to find Natalie and take her home.

The drive back to West Arbor Hills was chilly with the top down, so when we stopped at a red light, I slipped out of the leather jacket and laid it on Natalie's torso and arms like a blanket. She gripped it and snuggled in.

"Gosh, this thing stinks," she said. "You need to take it to the dry cleaner before you wear it again. See if you can get some of the sex, drugs, and rock 'n' roll out of it."

I laughed. "I don't mind getting rid of the first two."

"They could at least get that stale smoke smell out maybe." She was quiet a moment. Then, "You didn't play the song for your dad."

"Nope." I could have said more. But all that Steve had told me that night would keep.

The rest of the drive was mostly silent, but it was a comfortable silence. A weary, job-well-done silence. In my mind I went through the highlights of the night, culminating in the kiss Natalie and I had shared in front of hundreds of onlookers cheering us on.

I couldn't say exactly what occupied Natalie's thoughts, but the drawn look on her face told me it wasn't as pleasant as mine. As I pulled into the garage at her house, I was acutely aware that though the night may have started off feeling like I was taking her to prom, the fantasy ended here. There'd be no make-out session in the car, no professions of love, probably not even a good night kiss. Natalie was already mentally back in the bedroom with her mother, and that was where she'd be for as long as it took Deb to pass from this life to the next.

I turned off the engine and got out to retrieve the guitars from the trunk. "I'll just take these inside for now, and we can put everything else away where it goes tomorrow, okay?"

Natalie nodded, then the door to the house opened. Ruth stood on the other side of it, her eyes rimmed with red, her hand clutching a crumpled tissue.

"Ruth." I set the guitars down, and she immediately walked into my arms. Natalie got out of the car and pushed past us, disappearing into the dark house.

"When?" I asked.

Ruth sniffed back her tears and rubbed her nose with the tissue. "Not too long ago. We didn't want to call Saint Andrew's and have her find out that way. Didn't want to dampen the mood or affect anyone's performance. Deb wouldn't have wanted that." She pulled back and lifted her wrist. "I stopped my watch so I'd be able to tell Pinky. I knew I wouldn't remember."

I took her wrist and gently twisted it around so I could see the watch face. It read 11:47. The very minute Natalie had finished her encore.

"I guess Deb made it through the concert after all."

Track Thirteen

The sanctuary at Bright Hope Presbyterian Church was already packed with people when I arrived twenty minutes before the service was supposed to start. I looked around for a familiar face, someone to whom I could attach myself for an hour so I wouldn't feel so out of place. Though I saw a number of people I recognized, they were not people I knew. Some of them I'd seen at the New Year's Eve party. Some of them I'd seen on TV and in magazines. There were even several people whose names had appeared in the irretrievable guest book.

I wanted to curse Mike for stealing that book, for skipping town, for missing this. He should have been here. He owed it to Deb for all of the years of friendship and attention and all the prayers she'd wasted on him. Just the fact that I knew Mike, that I looked like him, that I lived in his place, made me feel like his shame was somehow mine. I was nearly certain that everyone in the room could sense it emanating off my skin, like the stale cigarette smell that would probably still linger in the leather jacket even after I picked it up from the dry cleaner later this week.

I had taken my share of the money we made at Saint Andrew's and bought a black suit, a black shirt, and a black tie. I was going to go with a white shirt, but I didn't want to risk looking like the Blues Brothers. Instead, I looked like Johnny Cash if he'd had longer hair. Which was just fine with me. In fact, I thought I spotted him way up in the front of the church, though from as far back as I was, still standing by the door, I couldn't be sure.

I was just resigning myself to sitting alone when I spotted someone I thought I knew. I shuffled through the crowd and tapped the large Hispanic man on the shoulder.

"Hey, are you a bouncer at Lips?" I said in the hushed tone I thought was appropriate for a church.

The guy turned to me, brow furrowed. "Yes."

"Esto, is it?"

He let his guard down a little, and I could see he was trying to place me. "Yes, and you are?"

"I'm Natalie's friend Michael."

"Oh, Michael," he said, still trying to make the connection.

"It's fine if you don't remember me—you probably see hundreds of people every night."

He stuck his hand out. "Sorry, buddy. You know how it is. But any friend of Natalie's is a friend of mine."

I shook his hand. "Thanks, man. I don't really know anyone but the Wheelers, and I can't really sit up there with the family when they come in."

Esto scooted over in the pew, bumping into the guy next to him. "Well, sit down, Michael. There's plenty of room."

There really wasn't, but I wedged myself between Esto and the arm on the end of the pew anyway. "Thanks."

"Anytime."

The church organ started up, people took their seats and quieted down, and several heads craned to see the back of the church as though waiting for a bride to come up the aisle. The minister came first, followed by a white casket edged in gold and flanked by men in suits and ties. It put me in mind of that white and gold dress Deb was wearing the first night I met her. Dusty was next with Natalie, back in black, holding on to his arm. Ruth followed, along with some older folks I presumed were Natalie's grandparents and other members of the extended family. The whole dark procession made its way to the front of the church and filed into the first few rows of pews that had been reserved for them.

It looked like they were all settled and the minister was walking up to the pulpit when Dusty stood up again and scanned the crowd. His eyes locked on me, then he walked down the aisle to where I was, in nearly the back row.

"Come on," he said. "You belong up there."

I started to shake my head, then realized that any delay I caused would steal attention away from Deb. I stood, buttoned my suit jacket, and kept my eyes glued to the floor as I followed Dusty up the long aisle to the front of the church. The guy next to Esto was probably glad to get his elbow room back, but I was mortified, imagining all the important people scattered throughout the sanctuary all thinking the same thing: *Who is THAT guy?*

Dusty pointed to the spot between Natalie and Ruth, and I sat, only to stand back up immediately when the minister called for everyone to rise for prayer. When we sat back down, Natalie gripped my hand and did not let go the entire time.

After the funeral, I found myself a number of places I shouldn't have been. Walking down the aisle with Natalie on my arm. Standing next to her in the back as she received condolences from people both notable and obscure. Sitting in the back of a long black limousine on the way to the cemetery. Helping her keep her footing on the unfamiliar turf at the graveside.

Afterward, the mortuary staff dropped us off at the church, and I drove my own car back to the trailer alone. I stopped inside just long enough to grab Deb's guitar because I was certain there was someone in the Wheeler house right that minute who deserved it more than I did. Someone who had played with her back in the sixties. Maybe someone who had given her that very guitar. But as I scanned the cars on my way up to the porch, I wasn't so sure anymore. Where were the Cadillacs, the Corvettes, the Lincolns, the Mercedes? These were Buicks and Chevettes and old trucks. These had not been waxed in a while. These were trimmed with rust rather than chrome.

I went in through the garage, leaving my shoes and the guitar by the utility room, and found the kitchen full of women. Ruth was closing the fridge with her hip, a bottle of Perrier in each hand.

"Take these out to Pinky and Ronnie in the courtyard."

I took the water, trying to remember if I knew who Ronnie was. I found Natalie easily and recognized the big man next to her as the guy from the back door of Lips. They were deep in conversation beneath a flowering tree, which had already dropped most of its pink petals across the tiles that had earned my uncle Mick Jagger's jacket.

I held the waters up. "Ruth said to bring these out to you."

Ronnie took a bottle, and I placed the other one in Natalie's hand.

"Michael, you remember Ronnie?"

"Yeah. Lips, right?"

"Not anymore," he said. "I just got a new job doing night

security for a guy named Manny, runs this pawn shop on Outer Drive."

My ears pricked. "Really?"

"Yeah, they had a break-in. Wanted to beef up security. I knew Manny when I was doing a stretch up at Kinross a few years back. Pays good money."

I recalled the inventory of the store. Jewelry, guns, electronics, a half-signed poster of Hall & Oates. "What was stolen?"

Ronnie shrugged. "Not much. Left everything alone except for some book. Obviously came in there looking for it because it wasn't even out on the floor. Had it in the back room or something."

"Wow. Must have been some book." I glanced at Natalie. She appeared to be trying to repress a smile. "Do you mind if I steal her a moment?" I tugged Natalie a few steps toward the sliding door that led into the living room. "Do you know something I don't?"

She took my hand and led me through the living room, the dining room, and the kitchen, which took twenty minutes at least because she stopped to talk to a dozen people along the way. Finally, she pulled me into the guest suite and shut the door. She dropped my hand, crossed over to the nightstand, and pulled a red book out of the drawer. At my stunned silence she said, "It just appeared. The cleaning ladies found it when they were getting the house ready for today."

I took it from her hands and flipped through the pages. "Did Mike . . . ?"

"He must have. I'm glad it wasn't you."

"That must be why he left town," I said.

Natalie frowned. "I was wondering why he wasn't here."

"Yeah, sorry. I should have told you. He left last Tuesday, the first day the whole band practiced together. Took all his stuff and just disappeared. The only thing he left behind was the leather jacket. Well, that and the giant hole in your backyard."

"Right. Dad's real thrilled about that." She crossed her arms. "So he stole this from the shop and took off to avoid the repercussions?"

"I guess so." I handed it back to her. "Apparently the guy is not to be messed with."

She sighed. "He shouldn't have stolen it from them."

"He shouldn't have stolen it from you. Anyway, he was going to try to buy it back. Just couldn't come up with $5,000 fast enough."

Suddenly I remembered writing down my name and phone number in the clerk's crossword book, right after expressing a keen interest in procuring the book while also admitting that I couldn't afford it. And my name was the same as the guy who actually stole it. What an idiot I was. Had they called the number? I'd been spending practically every minute that I wasn't working at the Wheelers' house. I could have easily missed them. Could someone find out where you lived if they had your phone number? Was the pawn shop owner even now tracking me down? Had he contacted Carl?

Natalie shook her head and put the book back in the drawer. "We'll have to make that right."

She was right, of course. The only way to fix this was to pay the guy. But that had to wait. There were more important things to attend to at the moment than the beating I was likely to receive if these guys figured out where I lived.

I pushed my anxious thoughts out of my mind and put my hand on her shoulder. "*You* don't have to make it right. You didn't steal it. And they were the ones who bought stolen property to begin with. It's back with its rightful owner. Let's just leave it at that for now." I let my hand slide down to Natalie's elbow. "How are you holding up?"

She groaned and flopped down on the bed, arms splayed to each side. "I'm fine."

I sat down next to her. "Sounds like it."

"I'm just tired is all. All these people."

I pulled at my tie and undid the top button of my shirt. "It's kind of a different crowd than I expected."

"How so?"

"I mean, I saw all sorts of musicians and maybe even a couple actors at the funeral. But none of them seem to be here."

"No. The people we invited back to the house are mostly people Mom ministered to in rehab or prison. A lot of them are people she led to Christ. I know most of them, and I love them dearly. But every one of them has a story. A good one. And they want to make sure I know it, that I know how important my mom was to them. And I do want to hear them. It just takes a lot of energy to hear them all at once. I mean, I want to be able to remember them all." She turned away from me onto her side and drew her knees up to her chest. "I just wish I could stretch it out a bit."

She sighed as I ran my fingers through her short, shaggy hair. Her brain was attempting to process a zillion details—the words of the minister, the smell of the flowers, the feel of the hymns, the memories of all those people. It was a lot to hold on to all at once, let alone hope to recall later.

"You stay here." I dragged her farther up on the bed and stuffed a pillow behind her head, then threw the same blanket over her that I had thrown over Brittney on Valentine's Day. "Just lie here for a bit. Take a nap. No one will miss you for twenty minutes."

Natalie made no argument, so I slipped out of the room

and shut the door. I found Ruth in the dining room. "Where's Dusty?"

"Probably downstairs," she said.

I started for the stairs then stopped. He had just as many demands on his mind as Natalie did, and he couldn't hide out in a bedroom for a while.

I went into the living room and stood by the fireplace. "Excuse me, everyone?" The few people nearest me looked my way, but most people hadn't noticed. I raised my voice and my hands. "Sorry. Excuse me? Can I have your attention for a moment, please?"

The crowd quieted. From the dining room, living room, courtyard, and deck, heads swiveled my way and people pressed in.

"Hi," I said. "I'm Michael. I'm a friend of Natalie's. She was just telling me what great stories you all had about Deb and about how much she affected your lives. It's funny. The first time I was in this house, it was for a party, and there were a ton of important people here and I wasn't one of them. But I still wanted to tell someone my story. How I was trying to be a rock star and I got kicked out of my band and had to move in with my uncle and all the obstacles I was facing and stuff like that. But no one asked me anything about myself. Except Deb."

Around the space, people smiled and nodded in recognition. They knew what it was like to feel alone in the world. And because of Deb, they knew what it was like to feel that they'd finally been found.

"Deb listened," I continued. "She made me laugh. She introduced me to Natalie. She made sure when Natalie and I had an argument that we didn't leave it that way, that we said we were sorry and we forgave each other. She helped me a lot." I tried and failed to clear the emotion from my throat. "She even gave me her guitar."

I had to stop then. Breathe. A rough-looking character with a Fu Manchu mustache put his meaty hand on my shoulder, squeezed it once, then let go.

"There's a studio just downstairs," I said, recovered for the moment. "Why don't we record some of these great stories for posterity? Kind of an audio guest book. So Dusty and Natalie can listen to them again and again. So we can keep Deb's memory alive. So that someday Natalie's kids will know what an amazing grandmother they had."

My chest was pounding. Heads were nodding all around, and there was a general murmur of agreement.

"Great. I'm going to get set up downstairs. If you've got a story to share, I want you to come down and say it into the microphone before you leave today." I saw Ronnie standing near the open sliding glass door to the courtyard. "Ronnie, you're first. Follow me."

Several hours later, the last of the guests walked out the front door, leaving just Dusty, Ruth, Natalie, and me. Even Natalie's grandparents had gone home. Ruth took Natalie's place in the guest suite. Dusty thanked me for the idea to record people's memories and stories about Deb and for taking the initiative to execute the project. He shook my hand and kissed his daughter, then shuffled off to sleep alone, probably for the first time in a quarter century.

Without even deciding to do it, Natalie and I made our way to the listening room.

I ran my finger along the endless spines of albums. "What do you want to hear?"

"My mom. But I don't know where those records are."

"I think I might." I took the first framed record off the wall and pulled a guitar pick from my pocket. Using the edge, I sliced through the brown paper backing, then bent up the tiny nails that held the board. I removed the album and slid the record from the sleeve. I placed it on the turntable, turned it on, and lifted the years from the vinyl with the velvet brush. Then I carefully set the needle down in the first groove and sat in the chair next to Natalie.

Deb's guitar—my guitar—sang out clear, joined a moment later by her once- and now-once-more ethereal voice. Song by song, we remembered her. I had far less to remember than Natalie, but every memory was sweet. Deb had changed my life, maybe more than any other human could. She had found me worth spending time with when no one else had. She had taught me that everything was better when people treated one another with forbearance and forgiveness. She had encouraged my musical pursuits. She had given me her guitar. A guitar I didn't deserve, but one I needed.

Most importantly, she had introduced me to Natalie.

I had originally come to the Wheeler house because I thought knowing Dusty would get me back into my old band. Now I could see that some other plan had been put into motion long before I accepted an invitation that was not addressed to me.

The last song ended, and I got up to flip the record over. "We should have covered a couple of her songs at the concert," I said as I cleaned side B and set the needle down. When Natalie didn't answer, I turned to find her fast asleep. I turned the volume down, settled deep into the leather chair next to her, and allowed myself to drift off, hoping to see Deb, happy and healthy and singing, in my dreams.

Track Fourteen

I suppose it only made sense for the crew to come remove the mastodon skeleton from the pit in the backyard on the day of the summer solstice. The longest day for a long, dirty, arduous job. Dusty had contacted a paleontology professor from the University of Michigan who had experience with these sorts of digs and knew the right techniques and the right people. The plan came together quickly, and with someone other than my uncle in charge, the job ran smoothly.

A crane lifted the largest parts out. The skull with its long, curved tusks. The pelvic bone and leg bones and ribs. Smaller pieces were brought out by hand by a battalion of the professor's current and former students. Everything was meticulously tagged and photographed and numbered so it could be put back together again, something Mike would never have thought to do.

I thought it might be kind of cool to put the thing in the courtyard. Quite the conversation piece for the next party—if there would be any more parties now that Deb was gone. But I guess Dusty had the right idea by donating it to the West Arbor Hills Historic Society for their struggling museum. After all, Deb did love lending a hand to the underdog.

The removal of the skeleton inspired me to take care of a few skeletons of my own. The day after it was trucked away for cleaning and storage until the museum could arrange a space for it, I drove to GUN'S JEWLRY ELECTRONICS MEMORABILIA with $3,000 in an envelope—$1,500 of my own savings and $1,500 I'd strong-armed from Carl. I considered just shoving it into the mail slot with a note explaining what it was for and that I would pay the rest later, then hightailing it out of there, but that wasn't the right way to do things.

I parked the car and left it unlocked in case I needed to make a fast getaway, then I pushed through the pawn shop door with my heart in my throat. But the meathead with the thick neck was not at the counter. Ronnie was. I looked up at the ceiling and whispered a thank-you. Natalie had been right—it was nice to know someone everywhere you went.

It didn't take long to explain the situation to Ronnie. He knew what it was like to be as desperate as Mike had been. He knew that if Deb had seen something worth working on in him, then he deserved another chance. He knew that I would make good on my promise to cover the remaining debt as soon as I was able. We shook hands, and I left with another friend.

The next day I bought some wood and a can of paint while I was at work so I could finally repair the splintered molding around Mike's bedroom door. I was toying with the idea of turning his room into a music room. Someplace I could write and play and store my equipment. Of course, who knew if he might just show up one day demanding it back. In the meantime, it was just sitting there, empty, waiting to be filled.

On the way home, I stopped by the dry cleaner to pick up the leather jacket. I handed over the ticket and took the plastic-draped hanger from the lady behind the counter.

"Oh," she said, "and this was in the pocket."

She handed me a business card sporting the name Vince Reinhold followed by the job title Talent Acquisition. I flipped it over, but nothing was on the back. I'd made sure to empty the pockets before I wore the jacket to the gig. I could picture the photo and the note sitting in my top dresser drawer. So where had this come from?

All at once it came back to me. In the hubbub backstage at Saint Andrew's, I had shaken a man's hand, pretended to hear him introduce himself, then promptly forgotten him. He must have slipped the card into my pocket then.

When I got home, I set the paint on the kitchen counter, propped the wood in a corner, and picked up the phone. I dialed the number on the card, then hung up before it had a chance to ring. I picked up the receiver again. Put it down. Thought of Natalie calling Steve without asking me. I couldn't have this conversation without talking to her first. I stuffed the card in my back pocket and headed across the street.

After some searching, I found Natalie in the listening room. The door had been left unlocked, and as I opened it, Deb's voice came pouring out, bathing me in its soft glow. I turned the light on low, touched Natalie's hand to let her know it was me, then sat in the chair to her left.

As per listening room rules, I said nothing as the song played. I closed my eyes and let the sound wash over me, that beautiful voice backed by the guitar that was now mine. It seemed to me that every note pointed forward, toward a future in which I could actually grasp what I had wanted for so long—plus infinitely more. I could make a living by making music. Something I created would go ahead of me over the airwaves into every town I entered, preparing the way. And when I arrived, Natalie would be there beside me. The world was ours for the taking, and Deb was giving us her blessing on all of it.

When the song ended, I looked to Natalie, ready to share my vision of the future with her. She did not get up to stop the record. The next song began. I held my peace. I could wait a little longer. We sat through three more songs until the soft scratching at the end of the record prompted Natalie to rise, lift the needle, and turn off the turntable.

She finally spoke. "What do you think?"

"Gorgeous," I said. "Where did those songs come from? I've never heard them."

She headed back to her chair. "Those are just a few things she recorded in the seventies but didn't release. Dad pulled the mother plates out for me to listen to."

"Mother plates?"

"No vinyl records were ever stamped from the masters, so the mother plates are all we have that can be played at the moment."

"I guess I don't know much about stamping records."

"It's this whole long process. I really shouldn't be playing the mother plates at all. You're just supposed to listen to them to make sure the recording is the way you want it before you use it to make the stamper. But Dad said it was okay just this once."

"Surprised he isn't down here listening to them with you."

She pressed her lips together. "I don't think he's ready for that yet."

"Oh. Yeah. I guess that makes sense." I scratched my chin. "So how's he been?"

"He's been . . . pretty quiet. Doesn't quite know what to do with himself."

"I don't blame him."

Natalie nodded.

The wheels in my head began to turn. "How many songs did she record and not release?"

"Not sure. Quite a few, I think. He has several records' worth."

"What will you do with them?"

"What do you mean?"

"Well, is your dad thinking of producing a posthumous album or two?"

Natalie's brow knit. "I don't know why he would."

"I don't know why he wouldn't," I said. "It would give him something to do. And if her reason for not releasing more records was that she felt too wrapped up in how they were received, it seems like now would be the perfect time. Give the world another album without hurting her. You could pick her best work from two decades of songwriting. It'd be a killer album."

She looked like she was considering this. Then, "I don't know. I'm not sure what she'd think of that."

"You could use the proceeds to fund cancer research or AA or one of the rehab centers you used to go to."

Natalie tipped her head, considering. "That's actually a pretty good idea."

"Anyway, it's just a thought." Time to get to what I was really here for. I pulled the business card from my pocket. "So, I have something I need to talk to you about."

Natalie twisted in her seat to face me. "Oh? Sounds serious."

"Maybe." I squirmed a little, unsure of the best way to approach the subject of what came next for us. "Um, so, you remember at Saint Andrew's when—"

"Wait, Michael," Natalie said. "Before you say anything, I feel like I should tell you something."

"O-okay," I stuttered.

"I'm going back to New York. To finish school."

The breath left my body. She was leaving? Now? Just when the needle was finally starting to move? Just when things were happening? Just when the future actually was calling me, or at least suggesting I give it a call?

"I talked to my dad about it last night. You know I was going to drop out because I didn't want to miss any time with my mom. But now . . . I mean, there's no real reason for me to stay home now."

I squeezed the card in my left hand and felt a twinge of pain. "Um, yeah. I mean, I guess." This couldn't be happening. "What did your dad say?"

She hesitated. "He said it was up to me."

"Uh-huh," I said. "You don't think maybe you should stay for him? For a while at least?"

"Well, I'll be here through the second week in August. So he wouldn't be alone right away."

I counted up the time in my head. Just seven weeks. In seven weeks, she'd be gone?

"Anyway, I just wanted to let you know as soon as possible."

"Yeah," I croaked out. "No, yeah. Thanks for, uh, cluing me in."

Neither of us said anything for a moment. Just sat there. Listening to the silence. Listening to life rearranging itself around this new reality.

"So, what did you want to tell me?" she finally said.

I looked down at the card in my hand, smoothed out the wrinkles, and put it back in my pocket. "Oh, nothing much, really. I was going to say . . ." I trailed off.

"About Saint Andrew's?" she prompted.

"Right. Uh, I was just going to say that I think maybe Slow and I might start playing together. Just us. Without Rodney." Without you.

"Oh," she said. "That's cool. I'm glad you two patched things up."

"Yeah," I said. "Me too." Then I went on the offensive. "Actually, he might be moving in with me."

She looked surprised. "Really?"

"Yeah." I pushed a little further. "Maybe him and Brittney."

She narrowed her eyes. "Really."

It wasn't a question. I could tell she was trying to decide if she was going to allow me to think she believed me.

"Patched things up with her too?" Natalie said.

"Ah, Brittney can't stay mad at me. She's always had a thing for me, you know?"

"Mmm," she said, her mouth in a hard line. "I sure hope that works out for you."

I stood up. "Well, I have to go. I've got some stuff to do tonight."

She nodded.

I took three strides to the door, turned off the light, and left the room. It took the entire walk from that door to mine to get my breathing and heart rate back under control. When I was sure I wouldn't throw up, I picked up the phone in the kitchen and dialed the number on the card, doubting that anyone would pick up this late in the day.

"Vince Reinhold's office," said a woman's harsh voice after one ring.

"Hi," I said. "This is Michael Sullivan. Vince gave me his card last week when I played at Saint Andrew's Hall in Detroit."

"Hold," the voice barked.

There was a click, then a moment of silence during which I thought she'd hung up on me. Then a man's voice said, "This is Vince."

"Vince," I said, pushing as much professionalism into my voice as I could muster. "This is Michael Sullivan."

"Who?"

I hesitated. "From Detroit. I met you when I played at Saint Andrew's?"

"Sullivan. Oh, from—what was the name of the band? The Intersection, right?"

"Well, just Intersection."

"Right. Hey, I didn't think you were going to call me. Usually people are so excited someone's interested in them, they hit me up the next day, but not you. Playing it cool? Lots of offers?"

"Yeah, sorry about that," I said. "There was actually a death in the family." I almost didn't get the last word out. For a little while, that's what it had felt like. A family. A real family. The family I'd always wished I'd had.

"Oh yeah, I think I heard about that. Sorry."

"But I'm ready to talk now."

"You both on the line?"

"Both?"

"Yeah, kid. You're not a solo act, are you?"

"Uh, no. But I can speak for the band. Most of the musicians you saw that night were studio musicians, you know?"

"Sure, sure, but I'm talking about you and the other vocalist. The chick who played the guitar. The one you were playing tonsil hockey with."

I recoiled a little and looked at the receiver. How effortlessly and completely this guy had cheapened the first kiss I'd shared with a girl that had meant anything. Or at least, that I thought had meant something.

"You mean Natalie."

"That's the one. The cute one in the hippie getup. I want to talk to both of you."

I considered my options. Tell the truth? That the cute one in the hippie getup was going back to Juilliard and would not be available for fortune and fame at this time? Take a chance that this guy would still be interested if it was just me? That seemed unlikely. Natalie was the talent. Natalie was the reason I was talking to this guy. Natalie was the reason this band existed at all.

Which left only the second option.

"Natalie said I should speak to you on behalf of both of us."

Track Fifteen

That night, I couldn't sleep. Pick your reason. Natalie was leaving me, leaving us. My conversation with Vince Reinhold made it clear that she and I were a package deal—all or nothing. And starting at around 1:00 a.m., the skies opened up, sending down a relentless barrage of rain, hail, thunder, and lightning.

Bleary-eyed and headachy, I dragged myself out of bed the next morning and opened up a brick of Folgers. I tossed out the old filter and grounds and filled the coffeemaker with water, but when I pushed the button, nothing happened. I pushed it again. Unplugged and replugged the thing. Then it hit me. No power.

I flipped a few light switches on and off to confirm. Nothing.

The lack of lights wouldn't bother Natalie, but the lack of music might. I wanted to check on her—it seemed like the thing to do, and spending some time with her in the dark wouldn't be so bad. But she had her father there. He'd take care of her. If she even needed taking care of. Besides, I was supposed to be getting ready for work. If work had power.

I couldn't turn on the news to see how widespread the outage was, so I picked up the phone. The line was dead. If I were Mike, I'd just haul my butt back to bed and plead ignorance if it came down to it. But I wasn't Mike, and God willing, I never would be.

So life wasn't going my way for the moment. So what? Except for the past few months, it never really had. Maybe I'd been fooling myself when I thought that things could turn around, that success was within my grasp, but that didn't mean I should just quit, just give up and run away. A real man didn't do that. Dusty wouldn't. He'd hit back.

I got dressed, ate a cold Pop-Tart, and started the car on the third try. The trip to Rogers Hardware normally took less than fifteen minutes, but with the downed trees and flooded streets and dead traffic lights, it took me nearly forty. As I suspected, the store was dark, as was every other building downtown. The power was there somewhere, at one of those fenced-off electrical hubs, I supposed. But the path to get it where it needed to go was strewn with obstacles and breaks in the chain. So there it sat, buzzing with potential energy, impotent nonetheless.

I pulled back onto the street, slowly making my way through a couple inches of standing water. I wasn't the only one out. Other cars were cruising through the flooded streets. A few pedestrians in high rubber boots surveyed the damage, pointing at a large branch that had crushed the windshield of an Oldsmobile. A Consumers Power truck, lights flashing, lifted a man in a bright vest and hard hat up to the junction of several lines to fix the broken connections. With a small chainsaw he cut through a branch that had cracked and sagged and rested on three power lines.

I imagined the scene from last night, the electricity arcing from line to tree. Sparks igniting a fire that burned and blackened the parts of the branch that touched the wires.

It was just too much. Too much stress. Too much energy. Too much weight. The lines had been happily going along beside one another, close in proximity yet still independent, fulfilling their purpose in life. Until some clumsy branch that didn't belong there inserted itself into their midst. A bit of bad luck for everyone involved.

I watched as the guy with the chainsaw cut through the branch to free the wires. Chunk by chunk, the wood came crashing down until just the black lines crossed the gray sky in three parallel tracks. Then one of the lines snapped, leaving only two.

I kept driving.

I sat around in my khakis and polo most of the day, trying to concentrate, trying to write a new song, but the words were all stopped up. My brain was a storm drain filled with garbage. A few words would trickle in and I'd write them down, only to see a moment later that they weren't at all what I wanted to say.

The power came back on around three o'clock in the afternoon, but the phone was still dead. I took a shower and pulled on a pair of jeans I'd left hanging over a chair. There, in the pocket, was Vince Reinhold's card.

Dusty had said obstacles could be useful. But how?

What was my biggest obstacle to success right now? Natalie was leaving, which meant that the band Vince wanted didn't exist. In order to keep his interest, Intersection had to have me and it had to have Natalie. But Natalie was going to New York.

So why not just go with her?

Detroit had a great music scene. It was the testing ground of so many up-and-coming acts. If you could get a Detroit audience to love you, you were well on your way. But New York? New York was the capital of the world. New York was center stage. New York was one giant spotlight. Maybe because it was so big and there were so many acts and so many venues and so many audiences, it would be harder to stand out, but it wasn't impossible. People did it all the time.

We could both go. We could sign with Vince Reinhold's management company. We could cut a record. We could book some gigs. We could make this happen. For real.

Would Natalie have time to be in a band when she was at Juilliard? More importantly, did she actually want me to follow her to New York? She hadn't so much as hinted at such a thing.

I pulled a plain white T over my head and laced up my boots. I hadn't waited to be invited over to the Wheeler house to begin with. I'd stolen someone else's invitation. There was no reason to wait to be invited to New York. I could move to New York anytime I pleased. No one could hold me back. I had feet made of wheels. Natalie had said so herself.

I crossed the street and strode up the driveway with purpose in my steps. That kiss onstage at Saint Andrew's had meant something. I knew it had. I'd felt it in the way she'd responded. Stiff for just a moment—I'd surprised her. Then she'd softened, relaxed, squeezed me back. And if that kiss had meant something, then we meant something.

Maybe when she'd told me about going back to school, she'd wanted me to ask her to stay. But I wouldn't do that. I wouldn't ask her to compromise her goals for me. Deb had said that everything she and Dusty did, the other met with an enthusiastic yes.

Yes, Natalie would go back to Juilliard. Yes, she'd finish what she started. And yes, I would go with her. Yes, I would get the gigs. And yes, I suddenly realized, our whole band would already be there in New York. This would work. This had to work.

I tromped up the porch steps and turned the knob on the front door. Inside, the house was dark except for the soft gray natural light filtering in through the windows. I listened for movement, voices. Nothing. I went downstairs. The family room was dark, the hall darker. The door to the listening room was closed, and the little indicator above the knob read OCCUPIED. That's where I would have been the minute the power came back on too. Was Dusty in there? Or Natalie? Or both?

I checked the studio. Empty. The billiards room. Empty. Then I saw movement through the sliding glass door. Someone was out back. Someone with short brown hair and wearing a black T-shirt.

I watched through the glass as Natalie approached the enormous hole, inching her way forward on the now unfamiliar ground. I slid open the door and stepped out onto the wet flagstone patio.

"Careful," I said. "You don't want to fall into that pit."

She stopped her slow progress and turned my way. "Then give me a hand."

I walked across the patio and onto a soggy strip of grass before reaching the muddy mess the excavation had left behind. What had once been a beautiful backyard now looked like an abandoned construction site. I thought of the drawing of the koi pond plans Natalie had shared with Mike, of her vision of what could be. She knew what it was like to want to make something happen only to be foiled by circumstances beyond your control. At least in this instance. Surely she would understand. Surely she would see the wisdom of my plan.

I took her elbow in my hand. "Where are you headed?"

She nodded at the space in front of her. "To the pond."

"It's more a pit than a pond."

"I'm still headed there."

We took a few more steps. "Here's the edge. Or, what used to be the edge. The rain's washed a lot of the dirt away."

"Help me sit."

"Here? Your pants will get all muddy."

She started lowering herself to the ground. I went with her, slipping a little before my butt hit the ground with a sick kind of squishing sound. "Careful," I said again, more for myself than for her. I pulled Vince's card from my back pocket, smearing it with mud in the process. "Here." I tapped her hand with it.

"What's this?"

"This is the card of a guy who saw us at Saint Andrew's and wants to manage and promote the band."

"Oh?" She took it and ran her thumb around the edges. "You didn't tell me you met any industry folks at the gig."

"I barely remember talking to him, so much else was going on. The card was in my jacket pocket. Dry cleaning lady gave it to me."

"How's it smell?"

"Huh?"

"The jacket."

"Oh. Like dry cleaning. And Camel cigarettes."

Natalie laughed. "I knew it. Can't get rid of Mike that easy." She handed the card back to me. "Did you call the guy?"

"Yeah."

"And?"

"And he's interested. Like I said."

"Mm."

"In both of us."

"Not the whole band?"

"Yeah, the whole band. But I explained to him that they were all in a different city and in school and stuff. He said that didn't matter. Other musicians could be found. But it had to be you and me out front."

"Did you explain to him that I too would be in a different city?"

"Would you?"

"Michael, I told you I'm going back to school. I can't also stay here and front a band with you."

"If you could—if you could do both at the same time—would you?"

"What do you mean?"

"If you could go back to school and do the band—which you started—would you do it?"

"I mean, yeah, I guess so. But—"

"So then ask me to come. Ask me to come with you to New York."

She didn't say anything.

"If you'd really do both," I said, "if the band matters to you . . . if I matter to you, ask me to come."

She twisted a little to face me. "Michael, I—"

Suddenly she was gone, just vanished before my eyes, as she slid into the soupy, muddy mess of rainwater and dirt and silt at the bottom of the pit. I slid in after her, coming down hard in the gray water with a splash that covered us both in splatters of mud. There was a moment of silence. Then we both broke down laughing.

"Oh my gosh, I think I just had a heart attack," she wheezed between laughs.

"You were just gone! I looked and you just weren't there anymore!"

She slipped a little, and I grabbed her to keep her head from going under. She laughed even harder.

"You look like a Jackson Pollock painting," I said, holding on to her shoulders.

"Whatever that looks like."

"A mess, okay? You look like a mess." I smoothed her hair

away from her face, leaving a smudge of dirt across her forehead. "Gosh, you're beautiful."

She stopped laughing.

I stopped laughing.

And time stopped. Just for a moment.

If Uncle Mike hadn't taken me in when Rodney and Slow kicked me out, I wouldn't be here, now. I wouldn't have met Dusty, a man I could look up to and learn from like I should have been able to do with my own father. I wouldn't have met Deb, a woman who dared me to believe in my talent and follow my ambition. A woman who showed me that there is freedom in forgiving others, in forgiving myself.

If Uncle Mike hadn't taken me in when Rodney and Slow kicked me out, I wouldn't be covered in mud and standing in this pit with Natalie Wheeler. This Natalie Wheeler. The one who inspired the best songwriting I'd yet done. The one who is always herself, who never cares what others think of her, who does what she wants to do because she wants to do it.

The one I can't live without.

"Natalie, please. Let me come with you. Give this thing a chance. If it doesn't work out, you lose nothing. But if we don't even try—"

She silences me with a muddy finger against my lips. "I can't answer you if you never shut up."

I stare at her, waiting. She turns her face up to mine, almost meeting my eyes.

"Michael, will you come with me to New York?"

Bonus Track

November 8th and the news is bad. After comparing Saddam Hussein to Adolf Hitler, President Bush is sending 100,000 troops to the Persian Gulf. All the promise of the new year, the new decade, seems to be on the verge of collapsing as we hurtle toward certain conflict. It's about all I hear on the news this morning before I head to the spot where I've eaten lunch almost every day for weeks. But I don't let it bother me. For now, I'm hopeful. For now, I'm untouchable.

The trees are past peak color, and the breeze carries more than a hint of winter as I sit at the edge of the pond, describing what I see between bites of a tuna sandwich.

"The lily pads are turning yellow and brown. There's a lot of scum in the water and leaves floating around."

"What kind of leaves?" Pinky says.

"I don't know. Maple leaves? Oak leaves? Leaves. Yellow ones and some orange and brown."

"You need to learn more about trees."

"I'll put that on my to-do list. Right between 'Fix my car' and 'Find a new place to live.'"

"I told you it's not worth it to fix the car. Just get rid of it. And what's wrong with where you are now?"

I watch a fish swim in the cold water. Deliberate, unhurried, sure. Like life is all laid out for him. Like he knows where he's going. Like he knows what it's all about.

"It's okay, I guess." I pick up a piece of gravel and toss it into the water. The fish darts away.

"That better not have been a penny," Pinky says. "Coins are bad for the fish."

"It wasn't. But hey, if they can survive in this cesspool, they can handle some pocket change."

She whacks my arm. "It's not that bad."

"Your turn," I say.

She takes a sip of Mello Yello. "Okay." She pauses, listening. "Breeze through the trees. Traffic, obviously. The construction crew must be on lunch break." She's quiet a moment. "Horses. Sirens. Oh, and there must be a school group nearby because I hear all sorts of kids."

"Yep. Your four o'clock. All in uniforms."

"Seriously, though, why do you want to find a new place? Are you and Benji not getting along?"

"No, we get along great. It's just, I don't think three of us can fit in that hole in the wall."

She raises her eyebrows. "Three?"

I smile. "Yep. Finally convinced Slow to move out here. Benji's starting with the New York Philharmonic in January, and he won't have time for us anymore. Slow can take his place in the band."

It truly was the beginning of a new era. Maybe not of world peace, but of something just as hard to come by: contentment. Being happy with what you've got. Being happy with who you are and who you're with. Being happy with the work you do, the art you make. Whether or not anyone else likes it. Whether or not anyone cares. Whether or not anyone else shows up.

I crumple up the wax paper from our sandwiches and stuff it into the brown paper bag. "What do you think we should open with tomorrow night?"

"How about that new one you just showed me. The one with that refrain. What was it? 'Don't stop thinking about tomorrow'?"

"Har, har," I said. "It's 'Can't stop thinking about tonight.'"

Pinky smirks. "And why is that?"

I put my arm around her. "Because that's when I get to see you. And seeing you makes every day better."

She lays her head on my shoulder. I tip my head to rest on hers. Like two notes stacked up on one another in perfect harmony.

That, right there. That's what does it. That's what breaks your heart a little. And if it doesn't break your heart a little, why bother?

Experience the Music of

Everything Is

Michael's Mixtape Spotify Playlist

The Listening Room Spotify Playlist

Just Beginning

Find yourself wondering what Intersection's music actually sounds like? Listen to some of Michael and Natalie's original songs, sing karaoke, download lyrics and chord sheets, and even submit your own covers and renditions right here at this secret webpage:

You'll need a password to get in,
but you already know what it is.
Hint: What is Natalie's nickname?

Author's Note

This book was an absolute joy to write. To revisit a simpler time in the not-too-distant past—a time when life for ordinary people included no cell phones, no internet, no streaming television, no twenty-four-hour news—was a pleasant escape from contemporary life with all of its complications. It was also a time of remembering my own personal not-too-distant past.

I don't think I realized just how important music has been and continues to be to me until I was drawing on my own life to fill in all the details of the world of *Everything Is Just Beginning*. As I furnished Dusty's home with turntables and reel-to-reels and high-end speakers, I channeled my dad, for whom listening to music is an art. As I imagined Deb's recordings, I heard my mom's lilting soprano voice. As Michael wrote songs for Natalie, I thought of all the songs my husband wrote for me back when we were in high school and college.

This book would not have been possible without the three people I just mentioned—my parents, Dale and Donna Foote, and my husband, Zachary Bartels.

Dad, thank you for teaching me to actually sit and listen to music rather than thinking of it as mere background noise. Thank you for teaching me how to treat records, reels, cassettes, and CDs, and for trusting me to use your equipment as a child even though I was often flighty, thoughtless, forgetful, and messy with my own things. Thank you for playing your favorite music *LOUD* and showing me how to get lost in it. Thank you for giving me an early appreciation for jazz, big band, classical, folk, blues, and rock 'n' roll.

Mom, thank you for always singing with your whole heart and for being completely unselfconscious about who was listening. Thank you for unwittingly teaching me how to harmonize by listening to you do it. Thank you for singing on stages, at weddings, and at church, thus showing me that the gift of a beautiful voice is something to be shared. Thank you for modeling the joy of performing, whether the audience was just me in the kitchen as we did dishes or a crowd of people at a concert in the park.

Zach, thank you for all the loud, sweaty concerts, and for writing quiet songs that were just for me. Thank you for encouraging me when I thought I'd like to learn how to play guitar and for buying me the guitar I play today. Thank you for helping me grow to love punk and appreciate rap and hip-hop. Thank you for the many mixtapes when we found ourselves living three hours away from each other for a couple years while I finished high school. Thank you for encouraging me to try my hand at songwriting and for making me believe that I could do it without your help.

Special thanks to Kelly Rogers for her insights on the Detroit music scene of the late eighties and early nineties, and to Joy Baade for her insights on living life as a blind person. You have brought a particular authenticity to this story, and I am so grateful to you both for sharing your time and your critiques.

Thank you to Wil Pruitt for being both Natalie's fingers and Michael's voice on the recordings of a few of the original songs I wrote for this story, and for coming up with all the cool fills and solo parts that I would never be able to write (or play). I hope you will continue to find the kind of joy and satisfaction in making music you love that I think Michael and Natalie have found.

As ever, thank you to my agent, Nephele Tempest, and to everyone at Revell—Kelsey Bowen, Jessica English, Michele Misiak, Karen Steele, Anne Van Solkema, Brianne Dekker, Laura Klynstra, and so many others who have played a part getting this book into the hands of readers.

And thank you, God, for giving us, your humble creatures, the desire and capacity to make music.

Craving more from Erin Bartels?

Turn the page for a sneak peek at
The Girl Who Could Breathe Under Water

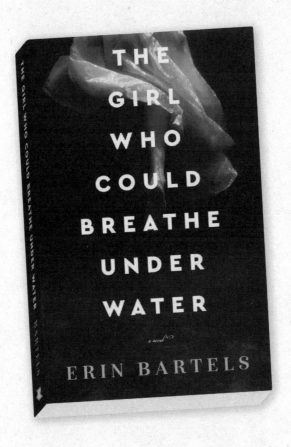

One

The summer you chopped off all your hair, I asked your dad what the point of being a novelist was. He said it was to tell the truth.

Ridiculous.

"Nothing you write is real," I said. "You tell stories about made-up people with made-up problems. You're a professional liar."

"Oh, Kendra," he said. "You know better than that." Then he started typing again, as if that had settled things. As if telling me I already had the answer was any kind of answer at all.

I don't know why he assumed I knew anything. I've been wrong about so much—especially you. But there is one thing about which I am now certain: I was lying to myself about why I decided to finally return to Hidden Lake. Which makes perfect sense in hindsight. After all, novelists are liars.

"It will be a quiet place to work without distraction," I told my agent. "No internet, no cell service. Just me and the lake and a landline for emergencies."

"What about emailing with me and Paula?" Lois said, practicality being one of the reasons I had signed with her three years prior. "I know you need to get down to it if you're going to meet your deadline. But you need to be reachable."

"I can go into town every week and use the Wi-Fi at the coffee shop," I said, sure that this concession would satisfy her.

"And what about the German edition? The translator needs swift responses from you to stay on schedule."

We emailed back and forth a bit, until Lois could see that I was not to be dissuaded, that if I was going to meet my deadline, I needed to see a lake out my window instead of the rusting roof of my apartment building's carport.

Of course, that wasn't the real reason. I see that now.

The email came from your mother in early May, about the time the narcissus were wilting. For her to initiate any kind of communication with me was so bizarre I was sure that something must be wrong even before I read the message.

> Kendra,
>
> I'm sorry we didn't get to your grandfather's funeral. We've been out of state. Anyway, please let me know if you have seen or heard from Cami lately or if she has a new number.
>
> Thanks,
> Beth Rainier

It was apparent she didn't know that you and I hadn't talked in eight years. That you had never told your mother about the fight we'd had, the things we'd said to each other, the ambiguous state in which we'd left our friendship. And now a woman who only talked to me when necessary was reaching out, wondering if I knew how to get in touch with you. That was the day I started planning my return to the intoxicating place where I had spent every half-naked summer of my youth—because I was sure that in order to recover you, I needed to recover us.

The drive north was like slipping back through time. I skirted fields of early corn, half mesmerized by the knit-and-purl pattern that sped past my windows. Smells of diesel fuel and manure mingled with the dense green fragrance of life rushing to reproduce before another long winter. The miles receded beneath my tires, and the markers of my progress became the familiar billboards for sporting goods stores and ferry lines to Mackinac Island. The farm with the black cows. The one with the quilt block painted on the side of the barn, faded now. The one with the old bus out back of the house. Every structure, each more ramshackle than the last, piled up in my chest until I felt a physical ache that was not entirely unpleasant.

In all our enchanted summers together on the lake, there had been more good than bad. Sweet silent mornings. Long languid days. Crisp starry nights. Your brother had thrown it all out of whack, like an invasive species unleashed upon what had been a perfectly balanced ecosystem. But he hadn't destroyed it. The good was still there, in sheltered pockets of memory I could access if I concentrated.

The first step out of the car when I arrived at the cabin was like Grandpa opening the oven door to check on a pan of brownies—a wave of radiant heat carrying an aroma that promised imminent pleasures. The scent of eighteen summers. A past life, yes, but surely not an irretrievable one.

On the outside, the cabin showed evidence of its recent abandonment—shutters latched tight, roof blanketed by dead pine needles, logs studded with the ghostly cocoons of gypsy moths. Inside, time had stopped suddenly and completely, and the grit of empty years had settled on every surface. The same boxy green plaid sofa and mismatched chairs sat on the same defeated braided rug around the same coffee table rubbed raw by decades of sandy feet. That creepy stuffed screech owl still stared down from the shelf with unblinking yellow eyes. On tables, windowsills, and mantelpiece sat all of the rocks, shells, feathers, and driftwood I'd gathered with my young hands, now gathering dust. Grandpa had left them there just as I had arranged them, and the weight of memory kept them firmly in place.

Each dust mote, each dead fly beneath the windows, each cobweb whispered the same pointed accusation: *You should have been here.*

For the next hour I manically erased all evidence of my neglect. Sand blown through invisible cracks, spiderwebs and cicada carapaces, the dried remains of a dead redstart in the fireplace. I gathered it from every forgotten corner in the cabin and dumped it all into the hungry mouth of a black trash bag, leaving the bones of the place bare and beautiful in their simplicity.

Satisfied, I turned on the faucet for a glass of cold water, but nothing happened. Of course. I should have turned on the water main first. I'd never opened the cabin. That was something an adult did before I showed up. And when I went out to the shed to read the instructions Grandpa had written on the bare pine wall decades ago, I found it padlocked.

Desperate to cool down, I pulled on my turquoise bikini and walked barefoot down the hot, sandy trail to the lake. Past Grandpa's old rowboat. Past the stacked sections of the dock I had only ever seen in the water—yet another thing adults did that I never paid any attention to because I could not conceive of being one someday.

At the edge of the woods, I hesitated. Beyond the trees I was exposed, and for all I knew your brother was there across the lake, waiting, watching.

I hurried across the sandy beach and through the shallows into deep water, dipped beneath the surface, and held my breath as long as I could, which seemed like much less than when we were kids. As I came back up and released the stale air from my lungs, I imagined the stress of the past year leaving my body in that long sigh. All of the nervous waiting before interviews, all of the dread I felt before reading reviews, all of the moments spent worrying whether anyone would show up to a bookstore event. What I couldn't quite get rid of was my anxiety about the letter.

Out of all the reviews and emails and social media posts that poured in and around me after I'd published my first novel, one stupid letter had worked its way into my psyche like a splinter under my fingernail. I had been obsessing about it for months, poring over every critical word, justifying myself with logical arguments that couldn't take the sting out of what it said.

Kendra,

Your book, while perhaps thought "brave" in some circles, is anything but. It is the work of a selfish opportunist who was all too ready to monetize the suffering of others. Did you ever consider that antagonists have stories of their own? Or that in someone else's story you're the antagonist?

Your problem is that you paid more attention to the people who had done you wrong than the ones who'd done you right. That, and you are obviously obsessed with yourself.

I hope you're happy with the success you've
found with this book, because the admiration of strangers is all you're likely to
get from here on out. It certainly won't
win you any new friends. And I'm willing to
bet the old ones will steer pretty clear of
you from here on out. In fact, some of them
you'll never see again.

Sincerely,
A Very Disappointed Reader

Maybe it was because the writer hadn't had the courage to sign his name—it had to be a him. Maybe it was because it had been mailed directly to me rather than forwarded on from my publisher, which could only mean that the writer either knew me personally or had done a bit of stalking in order to retrieve my address. It hurt to think of any of my friends calling me a "selfish opportunist." But the thought of a total stranger taking the trouble to track me down in order to upbraid me gave me the absolute creeps.

But really, if I'm honest with myself, it was because deep down I knew it had to be someone from Hidden Lake. Who else could have guessed at the relationship between my book and my real life?

Whoever this Very Disappointed Reader was, he had completely undermined my attempts to write my second book. I knew it was silly to let a bad review have power over me. But this wasn't someone who just didn't like my writing. This was someone who thought I was the bad guy. He had read my novel and taken the antagonist's side—your brother's side.

Now I closed my eyes, lay back, and tried to let the cool, clear water of Hidden Lake wash it all away. But the peaceful moment didn't last. The humming of an outboard motor signaled the approach of a small fishing boat from the opposite shore. Hope straightened my spine and sent shards of some old energy through my limbs and into my fingers and toes. And even though I knew in my heart that it wouldn't be you, I still deflated a bit when I saw your father, though in almost any other context I would have been thrilled.

He cut the motor and slowed to a stop a few yards away. "Kendra, it's good to finally see you again," he said. "I was sorry to hear about your grandpa. We wanted to make it to the funeral, but Beth and I were out of state."

"Yes, she told me."

He looked surprised at that, then seemed to remember something. Perhaps he knew about the strange email.

I swam to the boat—not the one I remembered—and held on to the side with one hand, using the other to shade my eyes as I looked up into his still-handsome face. I didn't ask him where you were that day, and he didn't offer any explanation. More likely than not, he didn't know.

"Beth's in Florida now," he continued. "It's just been me since Memorial Day. I was hoping to catch your mother up here before she put the place up for sale."

"It's not going up for sale."

"No? Figured she would sell it."

"It's mine. Grandpa left it to me."

"That so?" He glanced at my beach. "I can help you put the dock in tonight, around five? I'd help now, but I'm off to talk to Ike."

"Ike's still alive?"

"Far as I know."

I smiled. "That would be great, thanks. Hey, I don't suppose you've heard from Cami? No chance she'll be coming up this summer?"

He looked away. "Nothing yet. But I've seen Scott Masters once or twice this month. And Tyler will be up Friday."

He waved and headed out across the lake to Ike's. I tried to separate the thudding of my heart from the loud chugging of the outboard motor that receded into the distance.

Of course Tyler would be there. Every paradise needed a serpent.

Erin Bartels is the award-winning author of *We Hope for Better Things*, *The Words between Us*, *All That We Carried*, and *The Girl Who Could Breathe Under Water*. A publishing professional for more than twenty years, she lives in Lansing, Michigan, with her husband, Zachary, and their son. Find her online at www.erinbartels.com, on Facebook @ErinBartelsAuthor, and on Instagram @erinbartelswrites.

THE PAST IS NEVER AS PAST AS
We'd Like to Think

In this richly textured debut novel, a disgraced journalist moves
into her great-aunt's secret-laden farmhouse and discovers that
the women in her family were testaments to true love and courage
in the face of war, persecution, and racism.

"A story to savor and share.
I loved every sentence, every word."

—BARBARA CLAYPOLE WHITE, bestselling author of
The Perfect Son and *The Promise between Us*

A reclusive bookstore owner hoped she'd permanently buried
her family's sensational past by taking a new name. But when
the novels she once shared with an old crush begin appearing
in the mail, it's clear her true identity is about to be revealed,
threatening the new life she has painstakingly built.

Revell
a division of Baker Publishing Group
www.RevellBooks.com

Available wherever books and ebooks are sold.

CONNECT
WITH
ERIN

Check out her newsletter, blog, podcast, and more at

ErinBartels.com

 @ErinBartelsAuthor   @ErinLBartels @ErinBartelsWrites

Author photo: © Matthew Mitchell Photography